Around the World Adventure Stories for Boys

Around the World Adventure Stories for Boys

EDITED BY ERIC DUTHIE

ODHAMS BOOKS

The Stories in this Book

The Heidelberg Affair

LIONEL DAVIDSON

IT IS not often a man will face serious physical injury in order to demonstrate a principle. Few people would have thought Hank Engert such a man. He was a big roly-poly of a fellow with round, protuberant eyes and a crew-cut and a rather odd quality of gentle self-mockery. Not a man cast in the heroic mould, one would have thought.

I met him at the American air base. The Americans had got together a fencing team, and our British association had arranged a few fixtures for them. The night I met Engert, they were fighting an RAF team.

I don't think I have ever seen a more preposterous figure for a swordsman than Engert. Some big men are light on their feet, but Engert was not; his every movement was clumsy and elephantine. He was matched with the sabre against a young squadron leader, very slim and very fast, who took the fight by a wide margin. Engert's rueful antics afterwards occasioned a great deal of amusement. He seemed very well liked.

We were drinking in the mess, and I found myself standing next to him. I asked curiously why he had taken up fencing.

He smiled at me amiably: "I want to go to Heidelberg."

It seemed his unit had been stationed in Heidelberg after the war—Engert had not been with them then—and had established friendly connections in the town. The Heidelberg Fencing Association had invited them to a match, and Engert, whose people came from the town, was very keen to go. This was the reason he had taken up fencing.

I smiled when I heard this, because of course the Heidelberg team is very good indeed. I have fought twice against two of their second strings, and lost both times.

"Hell, I know I can't win," he said. "I just want to go there. Three guys from our team went back to the States recently and we're short on numbers. I'd certainly appreciate it if you'd put in a word for me with our captain—Honneger over there."

I didn't think I could conscientiously recommend Engert for any team that had to fight Heidelberg, so I kept quiet. Later, the party got very convivial, and the subject fortunately did not arise again. I drove back to town with the RAF party at three in the morning.

Each event I had refereed at the American air base had ended the same way. I thought now that it was time someone else took a turn. I was getting too old to stay up half the night drinking with these strapping young men.

All the same I was extremely flattered to get an invitation a few weeks later to accompany them to Heidelberg. There was no necessity for them to opt for a British official; it was a very nice gesture, and I accepted.

We flew out together, and I was astonished to see Engert in the party. He noticed my surprise and joined me, grinning.

"Well, I finally made it," he said. "But, by golly, it's been a triumph of mind over matter. I've been practically sleeping with a sword."

We chatted all the way there, and again I found him the most likeable of men—friendly, gentle, civilised, with a little private atmosphere of self-mockery always about him.

The Germans played host with much splendour. They put us up at the best hotel in the place, and after dinner threw a large reception at their club.

"My mother was born in this town," said Hank

I had visited this curious place before. It was called the *Kneip Halle*, and in the old emperor's time it had belonged to one of the quasi-military students' corps. It was a long, low hall with blackened oak walls decked with blood-stained flags and shields. It was quite a large room, but there were only three tiny windows, latticed and deeply recessed. Here, students had kept watch for the police when duels were being fought.

Repellent as it was, the hall was a glittering spectacle that night. The women were beautifully gowned; the men in white ties. Everywhere jewellery flashed and white-jacketed waiters wove in and out.

Amid this scene of sophistication, the party of Americans looked strangely young and innocent. I have never cared very much for the Germans, but now, in the company of the young Americans, I felt an acute distaste for them and their barbarous hall. The airmen did not appear to feel it; they were making themselves very pleasant to their hosts.

Engert indeed had gone further than this. I saw with surprise that he was seated on a sofa with the most attractive girl in the room—a very beautiful brunette—and they were talking with great animation. The girl's male escort, a slim, waspish little fellow with glistening black hair, was standing rather sourly beside them.

The other Americans remained standing, and I noticed Honneger, the team captain, frowning at the sofa once or twice. Peals of laughter were now coming from Engert and the girl.

"Hey, fellas!" Engert cried suddenly. "If this doesn't beat all! You'll never believe it. Hilde here—no, let me work it out myself," he said, putting his hand on the girl's arm as she tried to interrupt him. "My mother was a kitchenmaid in Hilde's grandmother's—"

They sorted it out between them with much amusement, and Honneger, the team captain, seized the opportunity to break for a few minutes. His eyes were on the sofa.

I walked over to the girl's escort, trying to remember his name.

"Herr von Nurigen, isn't it?"

He smiled stiffly. "How courteous of you to remember me. It's a pleasure to have you in Heidelberg again."

I thanked him and we made rather heavy conversation for a few minutes. His eyes were on the sofa.

"Are you fighting tomorrow?" I asked, to distract him.

He said he was.

"What's your weapon?"

"It is immaterial to me. I believe I am matched for the sabre."

"The sabre," I said, and paused. "Who are you fighting?"

"The gentleman sitting next to my fiancée," he said, smiling frostily at the back of Engert's crew-cut.

The party broke up early to allow the visitors a good night's rest. Engert didn't seem to have noticed that he had offended von Nurigen, and I didn't mention it. It looked as if Honneger might have a few words to say; and anyway it was no business of mine.

I had a rather odd feeling about it all the same.

The Americans took it easy next day, and after a light dinner we went to the *Kneip Halle* at eight. There were fewer women this time, but I noticed von Nurigen's fiancée. Neither she nor Engert spoke to each other, and it looked as if a few discreet words had been said on both sides. I was curiously relieved at this. A sabre match, even with both contestants properly masked, is no occasion for personal animosity.

The Americans had improved since I saw them last, and actually managed to take two of the first five bouts. They were very tickled at this, and a good deal of joshing went on as Engert stood up for the sixth bout.

After the usual courtesies, he took up quite a reasonable stance, and waited for his man. Nurigen did the same. For half a minute there was no action at all, and Engert became baffled. Any competent swordsman would have advised him, when facing a man so obviously experienced as Nurigen, to keep his patience and maintain his position. Engert did not do this. In a sudden flurry, he stamped his foot and went in.

Von Nurigen slapped his face twice, quickly and hard

Nurigen stood absolutely firm. I doubt if his body moved an inch. His wrist only moved, fractionally, tying up Engert in the most beautiful demonstration I have ever seen. When Engert, breathing hard, withdrew in disorder, Nurigen went in like a wasp, three, four, five, six magnificent points picked up almost before they could be registered.

He must have repeated this half a dozen times, and after the second it was obvious to all that he was intent only on making a fool of the American. There was no semblance of a contest. It was like some champion boxer inviting a child to hit him, cleverly covering and then opening his guard to dust the child lightly on the nose. He made no attempt to follow up his advantages. It was an extremely insulting and cruel demonstration.

When the result was announced there was an embarrassed silence, and then a little desultory clapping as Engert withdrew his mask, grinning ruefully.

"You certainly had me foxed that time," he said, holding

out his hand to Nurigen. Incredibly, he was the only person in the room not to realise what Nurigen had been doing to him.

Nurigen touched his hand briefly. "Perhaps you will have your revenge another time," he said coldly, and turned away to join his fiancée.

Immediately, everyone was very nice to Engert. Someone handed him a drink and he was soon the centre of a small circle.

The Americans did not win again, and the Germans, victors by six to two, became extremely hospitable. Champagne flowed very freely, and I found myself practising my halting German on the statuesque wife of the club president. I was so involved in this that I did not for a few moments see her eyes had gone wide and glazed, and that a small commotion was going on behind me.

Engert was dabbing with his handkerchief at a wet patch on Nurigen's clothing: he had upset his drink. Every time he tried to apologise, he shook uncontrollably. The effect was to make those standing round have difficulty in controlling their own smiles. Even Nurigen's fiancée seemed to be blowing her nose rather hard.

It was impossible to say exactly what happened next. It seemed that Engert, still apologising, turned to get Nurigen another drink, and as he did so stumbled and trod on his foot. All that I could see was Nurigen trying to withdraw his foot, his arms clutching wildly as he fell backwards. He fell quite heavily, but he was up in an instant, spitting almost, like a cat.

"Gee, I'm most terribly sorry," Engert said. "I'm such a clumsy brute. Won't you please let me—?"

Nurigen said something then in German, very sharply. I couldn't catch what it was, but Engert evidently did.

"Now just a minute," he said slowly. "I said I was sorry. It was an accident."

A number of the Germans closed in round Nurigen to pacify him, but he shook himself, cat-like, and rapped out something else. Engert, flushing darkly, moved heavily forward, and at the same moment, Nurigen slapped his face twice, very quickly and quite hard.

The whole incident was so swift and bizarre that for a few seconds there was a shocked silence with everyone motionless. Then the Americans leapt on Engert, dragging him away, and the Germans surrounded Nurigen. In the space of a couple of minutes there was such pandemonium that the president had to shout his apology at the top of his voice.

"It's nothing at all," Honneger told him. "Just a stupid mix-up. They both lost their tempers. We'll get them to shake hands in a minute."

This seemed very unlikely. Engert, red in the face, was so extraordinarily angry that I couldn't take my eyes off him. It appeared that Nurigen had told him he should have stayed in the kitchen with his mother, and this, more than the slap, had driven him almost berserk.

Nurigen could not be induced to apologise, and presently he went. The president and several of the committee tried hard to smooth things over, but the heart had gone out of the party. Shortly afterwards, it broke up.

We made a sombre journey back to the hotel. The Americans headed straight for the bar, but I was in no mood for further drinking, and went up to my room.

I have never been a very easy sleeper, and after this upset I knew I would not sleep for hours. I put on a dressing-gown and sat up reading in a chair. Quite a long time later I began to nod over the book, and got up drowsily to undress. At the same moment the house phone began to buzz, very loudly in that quiet room. I jumped, and stumbled over to the thing.

It was the night porter, talking rapidly in German. I understood him to say that von Nurigen was below and wanted to see me. I looked at my watch. It was half-past two.

"You are sure you have the right room? He does not ask for Herr Engert, the American?"

No, there was no mistake. Herr Engert was already below with him. Would I come down, or should they come up?

I could not make head or tail of this and stood there blinking owlishly at the wall fixture, more tired than I thought. Half-past two in the morning, Nurigen calling at the hotel. A very unpleasant suspicion came into my mind.

"I'll come down," I said.

I quickly got out of my dressing-gown and into my jacket, and went along the corridor. The porter had brought the lift, and we went down silently.

There were three of them waiting in the hall, Nurigen, Engert and a man I had not seen before. Engert came towards me as I stepped out of the lift. His face was white and moon-like.

"I'm sorry to get you up. Were you asleep?"

"No, no, it's perfectly all right. What is it?"

"This guy has come along to offer me satisfaction." His voice dropped in embarrassment at the word.

"Satisfaction? What do you mean, satisfaction? Has he apologised to you?"

"There is nothing I wish to retract," Nurigen said briskly, stepping forward himself. "I have offered this gentleman the time-honoured remedy if he feels he has suffered insult, and he has accepted. He wishes you to serve him at the *Kneip Halle* in thirty minutes' time."

I gaped at each of them in turn. "You mean you want to fight a duel? Have you gone out of your mind?"

"It's quite all right," Engert said. "I'd like to do it."

His simple, childishly-confident statement rendered me literally speechless. I just took his arm and shook it, trying to find words. "You don't know how—you can't fight a duel with this man. He'll cut you to pieces, don't you understand? He'll put you in hospital. Kick his backside if you want—you're fully entitled to," I said, glaring at little Nurigen, "but, for God's sake . . . Does Honneger know about this?"

"No, he doesn't, and he's not going to," Engert said. "Look, if you don't want to help me, forget it. I've got no right to ask you, but I'm going to fight him anyway."

The situation was nonsensical, and it was difficult to find reasonable words. I suddenly realised how terribly tired I was. I wanted only to push this overgrown boy upstairs, get him safely to bed without argument.

I said, "I shall get in touch with the police immediately."

"That is entirely up to you," Nurigen said. "We have made our offer."

"Let me at least," I said desperately to Engert, "get Honneger. Don't you want an American with you?"

"I've told you already," Engert said, smiling patiently. "You know as well as I do what Honneger would say. And he's my superior officer. Well, thanks, anyway. I'm ready to come with you, gentlemen."

The stranger, a tall, hatchet-faced man, now spoke for the first time, and Engert turned to me. "He says we'll have to change the venue as a precaution, if you don't come. Look, you can't stop this thing. Won't you reconsider? I'd certainly appreciate your help and advice in this fight."

"But you don't have to do it—it's the most senseless thing I ever heard! This man has no right—"

"I know all that," Engert said heavily. "Would you just please accept that I've got a perfectly valid reason for going through with this brawl and come and help me?"

I had never in my life been in such a grotesque situation, and didn't know what was for the best. I thought: if my brain were only clearer, if I could find the words to convince him that this would be no brawl but rather a surgical operation with Nurigen cutting at will... But I knew he would not listen. At least, by being present, I might prevent unnecessary bloodshed.

I went silently with them to the car.

A man was waiting outside the *Kneip Halle.* "This gentleman is a doctor," Nurigen said. "He has experience of these affairs. With your permission he will act as referee."

He unlocked the door and we went in. The hall with its flags and shields was a rather horrible sight at that hour. The hatchet-faced man swiftly placed small boards in the windows to black out the place, and Nurigen locked the door again behind us.

The protective armour and the duelling swords were in a sort of small museum off the changing-room, and the doctor and Nurigen's second brought them out. I helped Engert into his equipment silently, watching the others to see how it went on.

There was a thick jacket of wadded leather to protect body and arms, with a collar up to the chin of some kind of silk whipcord. A pair of barbarous iron goggles that stood out like small teacups protected the eyes and were buckled at the back of the head.

I had never in my life seen such a monstrous sight as these two men creaking in their gross uniforms and prepared to cut each other's heads and faces. Engert's gentle eyes blinked at me from the iron cups. With his crew-cut he looked extraordinarily like some overgrown child dressed as a spaceman.

"Now listen carefully to me," I said softly, "and don't try to think for yourself or argue. This man is out of your class so don't try to attack him. He'll try to mark your face. The answer is to keep your guard up. Never lower it—don't parry

"Listen to me—this man is out of your class; keep your guard up—don't try to attack him."

thrusts to the body or try to fence him. He'll tempt you to do that. Keep the sword in front of your face all the time and let him do the work. Do you understand?"

Engert nodded, rather tensely.

The doctor was carefully wiping the swords with disinfectant, and when he had done, called both parties to the centre of the room. There was some mumbo-jumbo of question and answer, rapped out quickly in German—no doubt a formal statement of insult and a demand for an apology—and then a brief recital of the rules. So far as I could understand it, the fight would last twenty minutes made up of six two-and-a-half-minute rounds, with short breaks between the rounds.

The doctor then motioned to me and Nurigen's second to step back, and when we had done so, stepped back two paces himself.

"*Auf die Mensur bindet die Klingen!*" he said.

The men crossed swords.

"*Los!*"

The duel had begun.

I think I was in more of a panic than Engert. At least he seemed to have remembered my last hurried words. He stood very firmly with his guard well up, and his wrist moving extremely well. Nurigen watched him very carefully, clinically almost, his sword moving very little, testing, feeling, for all the world like some surgeon deciding where to cut.

I felt my own wrist moving to parry the German's flickering blade, and put my hands in my trouser pockets.

The first round was over mercifully without damage. The doctor, who had raised his wrist to look at his watch, cried "*Halt!*" and both swords dropped.

"You're doing very well," I said softly to Engert, supporting his sword wrist to rest it. "Just keep doing that. He'll give you a few openings this time, I expect. Leave them absolutely alone, do you hear?"

Engert nodded, but said nothing. He was breathing rather harder than the exertion demanded, but I could feel no trace of tremor in his wrist.

The doctor looked up and signalled, and I released his wrist.

"Remember, let him do the work. Leave him absolutely alone."

"*Los!*"

Again the two men faced each other, and again Nurigen merely touched, prodded, felt. But imperceptibly he increased the pace until the light, ringing blows were coming two or three to the second, and towards the end he swayed this way and that, opening his guard fractionally, presenting the target. Engert left him alone.

In the last few seconds, without any warning at all, Nurigen stepped lightly to one side—there was a just-discernible interruption in the clatter, almost as if a dumb note had been struck on the piano, and a bright red line four inches long opened on Engert's cheek.

In the same moment, the round ended, and the doctor, crying, "*Halt!*" stepped forward to examine the cheek.

"Superficial," he said to me in English. "I presume you wish to continue?"

My heart was beating so fast that I had difficulty in speaking.

"We continue," Engert said, rather loudly.

I supported his wrist and said nothing at all during this break, for indeed there was nothing I could say. The speed and finesse of that cut was a beautiful, terrifying thing to see. It was plain now that Nurigen had decided just that one stroke from the beginning of the round; his feints and weaves had led directly to it, and there was nothing I could tell Engert that would prevent him taking as many more as the German wished. His only hope was that the slighter man would tire before doing any real damage; his only defence was his strong wrist.

Nurigen's blade was wiped and disinfected before they started again, and in the next two rounds that ghastly dumb note occurred three times more; each one a painful, stinging flip to the scalp. I could feel my knuckles tensing and turning in my pockets to parry the German's lightning thrusts. My heart was thumping very unpleasantly, and I felt sick.

There was no force to any of the blows; it was evident Nurigen did not wish yet to wound seriously enough to stop the fight. He wanted to cut and graze and scar the American to the point of fury; and he wanted to demoralise that fury so that Engert would not dare to face him any longer and would withdraw.

It seemed to me, looking at the American's pitiful face, that it was time he did this. The blood was streaming down his forehead and from his cheek. The whipcord collar was gluey with it, and it had got between the goggles on to his eyebrows.

I said, "For God's sake, man, you've had enough. What do you care if he wins? It proves only that he's a better swordsman, and we knew that before you started. There's nothing fair or decent about this. He's just cutting you about as he wants."

"How many more rounds?" Engert said.

"Two."

His eyes were blinking in the iron cups. His mouth was set very tightly. "How many times has he cut me?"

"Four."

"That's with me just defending myself," he said, with a certain grim humour. "I couldn't do worse if I tried to hit him. You reckon I could hit him?"

It was just possible that he now might. He was hurt, and, the German might think, already demoralised, with only enough spirit left to continue his clumsy, unvarying defence. Nurigen had given up all semblance of guard. He was merely executing fancy thrusts, some to cut, most to frighten. Engert might well surprise him.

I did not tell him this because any fumbling cut he managed to get through might enrage Nurigen to the point of wounding him seriously. But I must have paused too long, or perhaps he reasoned it out for himself, for I felt his wrist tighten.

"Go easy," I said. "Don't take any stupid chances."

"*Los!*"

The moment Nurigen opened, I knew he meant to increase the pressure still further in this round. His sword point moved so fast round Engert's head it looked like a halo. I don't think there can be anything more demoralising than to face a man

Nurigen's sword point played all round his cheek

out of one's class with the sure knowledge that he means to hurt and punish. Engert stood up to this with a certain shocked nobility; bitterly angry, using his wits and his courage, and getting hurt all the same. I had a hot, flooding desire to throw myself on the German and beat him without mercy.

In the first half minute of the hailstorm, he opened up a cut on Engert's other cheek. When the doctor signalled them to continue, his sword point played all round this cheek, never quite touching, always able to, his lips pursed in a smile of concentration.

Towards the end of the round, he executed the nimble side-step that preceded his real cuts, and prodded to the scalp. Engert gave then the finest demonstration of controlled courage I have ever witnessed. Instead of parrying the thrust to his sore head—as almost anyone would automatically have done— he dropped his guard, laying himself quite open to the painful cut. And as Nurigen flashed in, his own sword came round in a tremendous swishing arc.

"*Halt!*" cried referee and second together, almost before the blow landed. But nothing could have stopped that blow; I doubt if Nurigen was even aware of it.

There was a colossal clang, the whir of a broken blade twirling through the air, and Nurigen stumbled. He appeared actually to be leaning against Engert, and when Engert stepped back, he crumpled slowly to the floor.

I think all of us exclaimed in shock and horror as we hurried to the fallen man. He was on his face, and we turned him over. The doctor carefully lifted his head and examined it slowly, and then he stared at us in astonishment. There was not a mark on Nurigen.

"His goggles," Engert said. He was still standing, panting heavily. "I think I hit his goggles."

The doctor carefully lifted the goggles and grunted. Nurigen had the fanciest-looking black eye I have ever seen. The release of strain at this somewhat comical and humiliating injury for a swordsman was so great that I sat back on my heels and felt a vacuous smile spread over my face. There was presently a very odd sound from the two Germans. They were chuckling. In half a minute the three of us were rocking back on our heels helpless with laughter.

Nurigen must have been out for two or three minutes, and when he came to he was in a vicious temper.

"No more fighting, I am afraid," the doctor said, smiling broadly. "You are slightly concussed."

Nurigen stood up and stamped his foot. His face was chalk white and his lips in a thin line. "I congratulate you," he said, holding out his hand to Engert.

Engert looked at the hand and knocked it roughly aside. "Congratulate me!" he cried. "What in hell have you got to congratulate me for? Why, you impossible little fool, can't you learn anything?"

I noticed for the first time that he was still in a towering rage. He had been mopping his head with a towel during the somewhat hysterical hilarity, and he now bunched his huge fist in front of Nurigen's face.

"You see this?" he said. "If I'd lost this brawl I'd have beaten your ears off with it. I'm bigger than you and I can always do that. But it doesn't give me any *right* to do it. You don't have to congratulate me—don't you see that? The only reason I fought you was to demonstrate that; because one way or the other you'd have got yourself beat up, brother. And you know what that proves?"

He was literally shaking with rage, and the doctor, busily sponging Nurigen's eye, motioned me to stop him. I put my hand on his arm, but he brushed it off.

"It proves that a big ape can always hurt a little one!" he shouted. "That's all it proves. It doesn't mean he's got a better case, or he's got any right to hurt him. Any mean guy with some fancy way of hurting people has got to learn that little thing, and I just hope you've learned it."

This seemed to me doubtful; Nurigen's sour little face was creased in a most venomous scowl.

When the doctor had finished with him, he patched up Engert. His wounds looked a great deal worse than they were; the cuts were all minor and unlikely to leave much trace. All the same, he smelled like a casualty ward. When we left, without the others, he was still tensed up. There were no taxis at that hour, however, and on the walk back he gradually became silent.

In the hotel, he shook my hand. "I'm sorry to have dragged you into this thing."

"So am I." I was tired, and very short with him. "The whole thing was absurd and unnecessary."

"You think that?" he said seriously. "You don't think he's learned a lesson?"

"Only to be more cautious and strike harder next time."

"And the doctor and that other guy?"

"I didn't lose a night's sleep to show a small group of Germans that violence doesn't pay. It's getting very late."

"Yeah. Well," he said, stepping clumsily from one foot to the other, "you've got to fight that kind of thing wherever you find it. Peaceable people have got to."

There was a certain unapologetic, invincible freshness of spirit here that, despite the irritations, one could not but admire. Perhaps, after all, it was true that one had to go on restating the obvious; that every generation had to go on restating it with whatever courage it could muster. And certainly Engert had shown high courage in his maladroit tilt at the enemy. There was something very American about this; and perhaps it had not been so absurd and unnecessary after all.

So, thinking this, I held out my hand to him. "Goodnight, Don Quixote," I said, unable to repress a smile; and went up to bed a good deal more cheerful than anyone has a right to be in that bloodthirsty town.

The Mystery of the Mascaret

ROGER PILKINGTON

IT WAS late in the afternoon when the lock-gates opened at the end of the canal from Le Havre. The two boats ran out into the River Seine, with the *Dabchick* leading. The *Marigold* always let the other boat lead, because Ronald, skipper of the *Marigold*, had never steered in France before, whereas Peter of the *Dabchick* was an old hand. Old in navigating, that is, rather than an old salt. He was sixteen, the same age as the other skipper.

The crews of the two cruisers were much the same too. Each had a mate and a ship's boy. Mate of the *Marigold* was Caroline, the captain's younger sister, and the junior of the family was William, who really preferred to be called bosun, and not ship's boy. And in just the same way Peter Branxome, skipper of the *Dabchick*, had Jill and Michael as crew. And Jill was a better cook than Caroline, who never got much further than corned beef hot and corned beef cold.

Peter led out to cut across the muddy water towards the opposite shore, but the sight of a big cargo vessel sweeping down river on the falling tide made him wisely decide to keep to the near side until she had passed. Then, with the *Marigold* only fifty yards behind him, he crossed the stream and turned to head for Paris.

Just beyond the suspension bridge at Tancarville the river course turned a bend to the right, and Peter hugged the bend as close as he dared in order to take the water where the tide ran less strongly. But even there the pace of the ebb was so great that neither of the yachts was making up river at more than a couple of knots. Peter eased down and beckoned the *Marigold* to draw up on the beam.

"There's no point in punching up against this stream," he called across. "I think we'll do best to anchor round beyond the bend and wait till we have the tide behind us tomorrow. What do you say?"

"Good idea," Ronald shouted back.

Scanning the shoreline, Peter noticed some heavy piles a short way off shore and he nosed up to the second one, so that Jill could drop the noose of the bow-rope over it. Then he dropped back towards the pile astern, and Michael managed to fling a great loop of a heaving-line over it in order to haul the stern rope round the post and back on board again.

The *Marigold* drew alongside, and with fenders between them the two craft lay snugly together on the *Dabchick's* bowline. Peter turned off the engine and he had just stepped aboard the other craft to help Caroline make fast at the stern when one of the French barges which had left the lock behind them began to draw level. The skipper was holding the big wheel with one hand and waving his other to and fro.

"*Pas là, pas là*," he shouted.

"What's the matter with him?" muttered Ronald.

"*Pas là!*" called the Frenchman. "*Le Mascaret arrivera pendant la nuit. Boom!*" He made a gesture of an explosion.

"I didn't catch what he was shouting about," Peter said in a puzzled voice.

Jill rather prided herself on her French. "He said that the *Maskeray* is coming here during the night—boom! Or it might have been the *Masquerade*."

"Pas la! Pas la!" called the Frenchman

"Masquerade? You mean a sort of pageant thing?" Caroline asked.

"No," said Michael. "They don't have pantomimes on the river. It's the name of a ship, of course. He was trying to tell us that these are its moorings."

"Well, why can't it push off and go somewhere else? We got here first," William said.

"H'm. That's true. All the same, we don't want to be smashed up in the night," Peter pointed out. "If the ship is coming in here then I suppose we must move. Better be on the safe side. We can pull in somewhere else just a short way ahead, I imagine."

Reluctantly the two boats cast off again and moved upstream. Half a mile further on Peter on the *Dabchick* noticed a pair of oil jetties on the opposite shore. There were no ships lying alongside, so after waiting to let a big tanker come down the centre of the river he moved across and drew gently up against the first of the piers. Once more the *Marigold* came up on the outer side and tied up.

Twice whilst supper was being cooked aboard the *Dabchick* a barge punching upstream hooted long and loud. On the first occasion the barge-master shouted something which nobody heard and then passed on his way with a deliberate shrug as though he had done his best but to no avail. The second time, however, one of the deck hands on a smartly painted tanker-craft stood on the bows and signalled with his arms in semaphore.

"Quick," Michael, Peter called. "There's a chap signalling."

Michael was a scout at school, and he specialised in signals. He could do morse, and semaphore too. He stuck his head out of the hatch, then scrambled on deck. "MASCARET," he spelled out. "Mascaret."

Peter waved to show that he had understood. "They seem to have the thing pretty well on their minds," he said. "I wonder why there's all the fuss."

"Oh, just because they're French," Michael said. "French people can never go on without a lot of fuss and bother. I suppose it's the way they're made."

Peter laughed. "Still, this must be a gigantic ship if they're all so excited about her."

"Are you sure it's a ship?" William asked. "I thought mascaret was that stuff Caroline puts all round her eyes when nobody's looking."

"I don't," Caroline objected. "And anyway, that's mascara."

"You don't, but it's mascara. How do you know, if you don't?" William giggled. "Ow!" He jumped as his sister kicked him under the table.

"It's all very strange," Ronald said. "It's a mystery. The mystery of the *Mascaret*."

"It's not a mystery at all," Michael said. "The *Mascaret* is a ship. Anyone can see that. But however big she may be there's still plenty of room on this side of the river. We shan't be in her way."

"We can always move up if necessary," said Peter.

Neither Ronald nor Caroline nor Jill were anxious to stay

up and watch for the arrival of the *Mascaret*. Nor was Peter. They were all too sleepy after a day which had consisted for the most part in cruising under a hot sun, and then exploring Le Havre while waiting for the tide. Michael and William were equally sleepy but they had enough curiosity to insist upon staying on deck until midnight. So after the washing-up was finished and the two skippers and their sisters had one by one turned in for the night young Michael and William got out the fishing lines and baited-up hopefully with fresh pieces of bacon fat.

The last of the ebb-tide traffic had ceased by this time, and everything on the river was quiet. The two craft, moored side by side, rocked ever so gently in the curious rhythmic ripples caused by the turn of the tide. William sat on top of the *Marigold*'s after cabin, a line in each hand, whilst Michael lay beside him stretched out flat, each of his middle fingers having a turn of line around it. He gazed up into the blackness of the sky overhead and saw the thin crescent of moon low down over the hills.

"New moon," he said. "It's only a couple of days old. That means spring tides, so we ought to have a real good flow to push us up to Rouen tomorrow. Then in another couple of days we might make Paris."

"That's great," William said. "When we get there I'm going up the Eiffel Tower."

"I'm going to go out and eat snails before I do anything else," Michael said, after he had thought for a bit. "Yes, snails—definitely. We have a French master at school, and he's always raving about how wonderful Paris is, and all the museums and the places connected with history. You know— Versailles, and the prison of the French Revolution and all that kind of thing. 'It makes history live if you know the background,' he always says. But I hate trailing round museums and buildings and things. I want to have an exciting time. After all, you can't get snails in England."

He pulled at his lines to make sure that neither of them had managed to pick up a fish.

"That's true," William agreed. "But the Eiffel Tower is

where I'm going first."

There was silence for a while. Michael was thinking about the snails and wondering how many he would eat at a sitting, when William interrupted his dreams. "Are we tied up good and tight, Michael? The tide's running up fast, and we're hanging out on the stern rope instead of the bow."

Michael sat up and looked. The sterns of both craft were projecting into the river at an angle as the water pressed between them and the timbering of the jetty front. The rope from the *Dabchick*'s stern bollard to the top of the jetty looked unpleasantly straight and taut, and although the rope itself was a strong one Michael agreed that the mooring should be made safer. Instead of the two boats being held independently, the single stern line of the *Dabchick* was having to hold the weight of both and withstand the force of the tide too, because the push of the tide itself made the bow rope drop slack.

"I'll go up on the jetty," he said. "I'd better take another line over, just to make sure."

"Looks to me as though we should slack off at the bow," William said.

"Yes, that would help. But another stern line would be a good thing anyway. It's at the stern that the tide is working on us."

"We've got a good rope on deck. I'll get it."

"That's fine," Michael said. "Give me the noose end, and I'll take it up on to the top of the piles."

"Still no sign of the big ship *Mascaret*," William remarked as he put down his fishing lines and started to disentangle a heap of rope on the deck. "I hope she comes before we turn in. I'm getting sleepy."

"Of course she might have gone in by those piles round the corner," Michael pointed out. "Or she may not be coming at all."

At last William had the rope sorted out and he handed the noose to Michael. "Hadn't we better tie another on the end? It's not very long," he said.

"We've got a spare one down below," Michael replied. "I'll fetch it, and we can knot them end to end."

He stood up, crossed to the *Dabchick* and disappeared down the companion ladder, stepping softly so as not to awaken Peter and Jill. Creeping very quietly through into the after cabin he opened a locker under his bunk and began to feel about in the dark for the spare rope which he knew was stowed there. He soon found the coil and drew it out silently. He was just closing the locker when he heard a thud on the forward end of the boat and William's voice calling urgently from the top of the ladder.

"Michael. Michael. Quick!"

"Sh! You'll wake everybody up," whispered Michael loudly as he scrambled through with the rope.

But William hardly dropped his voice. "Quick! Come up! There's something happening."

Michael knew from his voice that something was wrong and

"Michael. Michael. Quick! Come up! There's something happening."

he raced up on to the deck, heaving the coil of rope up with him.

"Listen!" William pointed downstream.

A distant noise, swelling louder second by second, came towards them. It was a queer but frightening rumble like that of the thundering of a great waterfall or the torrent running over a dam. It was not a mechanical sound but something ominous, breaking the stillness of the night with a dull relentless roar. The two boys stood motionless, staring out over the dark surface of the water down river as the rushing sound grew continually louder and louder.

Suddenly Michael saw something which made his hair tingle and sent a chill running down between his shoulder blades. He tried to speak, but couldn't. There, only a mere hundred yards away from them, was a great wall of water ploughing up the river, its crest curling white and steep and its edge sweeping the bank.

In the same moment William saw it too. Leaping on the *Marigold* he snatched the noose of the spare rope, stumbled back on to the inner boat and across the deck towards the jetty steps.

"Take the other end," he panted desperately. "Tie it on anywhere. I'll get the noose on."

Michael grabbed the rope, hauling it over quickly to find the loose end. The roaring surge of the tidal bore was rushing down upon them but he did not panic. "Go on, William, quick! You'll make it!"

At last Michael had the end, but there was no time to run to the *Marigold*'s stern to tie it on the outer boat. Instead he twisted it twice around the base of one of the *Dabchick*'s stanchions amidships, put the end over, round, and through the loop. There was no time to start making complicated knots.

"I've made it fast, William," he shouted. "Get to the top and drop it over a bollard. Hurry up!"

William was already at the top of the iron ladder, and as he scrambled over the edge on to the jetty Michael put his head through the hatch of the *Dabchick* and shouted for all he was worth.

"Hold on!"

In the next second he flung himself aboard the *Marigold*, opened the hatch and repeated the warning. "Hold on tight. Look out!"

But there was no time for those aboard either boat to be more than aware that somebody had awoken them with a shout. The crest of the first wave of the tidal bore was curling above the sterns, and its upward slope pushed them out even more obliquely from the jetty. Michael flung himself flat on the *Marigold*'s fore-deck beside the hatch and gripped the base of the deck-rail tightly with both hands just as the great wall of water struck.

Up on the jetty William was desperately looking around for anything to which he could secure the extra rope. There was no bollard within reach, nothing but the bare planked top of the landing stage. He heard Michael shout "Hold on tight!" and as a last resort he threw himself on the planking, pressing the rope as hard as he could over the jetty edge.

William did not see what happened next, for the two little ships were hidden from his view below the edge of the tall jetty. First he heard a splitting crunch, then the fearful sound of smashing crockery as the two craft were rolled nearly on their beam-ends. Finally amid the curious rush of the water came the singing snap as the stern line parted.

It all happened so quickly he had no time even to let go. In a wrench that tore at his wrists and shoulders the line he was still holding was pulled irresistibly over the edge. With a frightened cry William shot over the edge of the quay and struck the water thirty feet below, just behind the first main wave.

Still holding the rope and smarting painfully where his face had hit the water, William kicked out furiously for the surface. He was just afloat when the second wave lifted him high in the air and dropped him down again behind it. Once more above the roar of the water he heard a horrible clatter as everything inside the boats was rolled from side to side. Three more lesser waves followed, and then the swell began to even out. More conscious of the fact that he was still alive than of

*The stricken craft swung wide and William was dragged
irresistibly off the quay*

anything else William now saw that the jetty lay some way behind him and was receding. Desperately he hung on to the noose in the turmoil of the bore.

On board the boats Michael was the only one not taken completely by surprise. Jill had heard his call, but she had done no more than to open her eyes and stare sleepily at the ceiling when something tipped her bunk on its side and flung her violently on to the floor in a mass of bedding. She struggled to her knees just in time for the second wave to throw her across the cabin, and she pitched head first into the mattress of the empty bunk opposite her own.

Peter had sensed danger more quickly. Feeling the curious surge which ran ahead of the wall of the bore he had just swung his legs over the side of his bunk to run on deck and see what was the matter when the boat heeled over and he half threw himself, half fell on the floor, and the tipping slid him from one side to the other.

The *Marigold* had even less warning. Caroline did not hear Michael's shout at all, and her rude awakening was when the water poured in through the open porthole just above her pillow. Choking and spluttering, she was shot heavily out of bed to be buried in an avalanche of blankets, water, and her own clothes from the rack above, to which were added her suitcase and four drawers from the cupboard as the ship heeled back again.

Ronald was sleeping soundly on the starboard side of the ship, up forward, and the first roll forced him against the cabin wall. Quickly he grabbed the outer side of his bunk and succeeded in holding his place. Michael was on deck, but he survived the onslaught of the rushing water through sheer determination not to let go. He buried his head between his outstretched arms and felt the thud as the two boats pounded together, then the wrenching as the light lines which held them side by side snapped like cotton when the craft heeled right over.

But he did not lose his head. The moment he felt the swell subsiding he scrambled to his knees and sprawled towards the bows, soaked to the skin. The *Marigold* was still lunging heavily in the aftermath of the bore, but Michael knew what had to be done. It was vital that the ship should not be carried on to the rocky shore and smashed.

Steadying himself with legs splayed out sideways he fumbled hastily for the anchor, then suddenly remembered that the *Marigold* did not carry one. If only Peter would appear on the *Dabchick*'s deck, Michael could fling a line over to hold her.

Ronald staggered on deck in his pyjamas. "Where's William?" he asked.

"He's on the jetty," said Michael. "He had just run up with

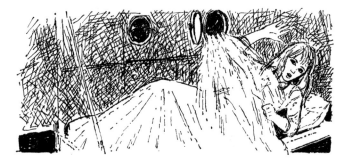

Caroline got a rude awakening

another rope. He's safe enough. Is Caroline all right?" he asked.

"I hope so. At least she's still there."

Only a few yards away the *Dabchick* was drifting up the river on the heaving water. The lights came on in her cabins and Michael saw Peter scramble quickly through the hatch.

"It's all right, Peter," he called. "We're all safe. Throw over the anchor and heave me the end of a rope. You'll find the spare one on deck."

Peter quickly threw down the kedge, but the new line was nowhere to be seen. It had been tipped overboard. He was just about to go below for another when he heard a cry from somewhere between the boats. Michael heard it too, a wet, gasping splutter more than anything else.

Quickly Michael seized the remains of one of the light lines which had held the boats together.

"It's William," he gasped. "Quick, Peter. William's somewhere between the boats. Keep them apart. He might be crushed between them." He called reassuringly towards where he could now make out a splashing close to the *Dabchick*'s side.

"All right, William. I see you. I'll throw the lifebuoy."

"Don't worry," William spluttered. "I've still got the rope."

"Haul him in, Peter," Michael shouted. "It's that rope tied on amidships, below the rail."

Hurriedly Peter took up the line and drew William in alongside. Then lying right down on the catwalk he held on with one arm and reached for the boy's hand with the other. At last he had hold of him safely, and when Jill too found her way up on deck over the wreckage strewn about inside the boat, she helped her brother to haul William aboard.

"Take him below, Jill. I'll see that we're tied up to the others again." Peter went back to the bows to recover what was left of the bow rope, and heaved the end across to Ronald. The *Marigold* swung, and began to straighten up a short way astern.

Jill, pale with the shock of what had happened, took William down below. He was shivering in his wet clothes and she picked up a blanket from among the debris. "Here, take this, and get your wet things off," she said, trying to sound calm.

"I'm sorry," he spluttered. "I tried to hold them, but I couldn't."

"I shouldn't think anything could have held us in that," said Jill. "What on earth happened?"

"I think I know," he said with a shiver. He struggled to undo his tie, but his fingers were numb with the strain of holding the rope.

"Here," said Jill. "I'll do it." She worked at the knot, and suddenly William laughed.

"You wouldn't have a French dictionary aboard?" he asked.

His fingers were too numb to undo his tie

"I know we haven't one on our boat."

"I think there's one in the drawer under my bunk," Jill said as she managed at last to free the knot in his tie. "I'm sure there is. But why on earth do you want a dictionary just now?"

"Can't you guess? You go and look for it. I can manage my clothes," William said.

Still puzzled, Jill rummaged in a drawer and brought out the book. William drew off his dripping shirt and dumped it on the floor.

"Have a look and see what it says under 'mascaret'," he repeated as he pulled the blanket over his shoulders. "Go on, I want to know."

Jill turned the pages until she found the place.

"Mascaret, noun, masculine," she read out slowly, peering

at the small print in the dim light. "Tidal wave. Especially the great bore of the River Seine which reaches a height of several feet."

William laughed. "That's what I thought. And I'll tell you something else."

"What's that?" It was Michael who put his head in at the door.

"Only that if you're abroad and people try to tell you something—as the barge-men did—then perhaps it's a good idea to find out before it's too late!"

Charley's Tiger

JACK FINNEY

IEXPECT Johnson will be re-elected President of the United States, or maybe it'll be Rockefeller or Nixon, next time. But it might, it just *might*, be Charley. There's a one-in-ten chance, I'd say, and we could probably do worse. Oh, they say he's a charlatan, a confidence man—and, off the record, they're right. For hard-bitten practicality and gouging in the clinches, he could give odds to a loan shark. But—and I'm not making a speech—he's a dreamer, too, an artist warmed by the fires of genius, a shrewd and shifty poet at heart, and when it comes to pulling rabbits out of the hat I promise you he'll produce them by litters.

If Charley gets in the running at all you'll certainly read about his boyhood and see his early photographs till you're sick of them—that thin, composed, alert little face behind tortoiseshell glasses. And you'll see the old newspaper clippings reproduced once more; the stories and several dozen photographs that ran for a week, thirty-odd years ago, in the

Galesburg, Illinois, *Register-Mail;* the follow-up interviews in the big Chicago papers next day; and the page-three wire story from the files of the *New York Times.* You might, if you can remember Calvin Coolidge, even recall the story yourself. Charley was the boy who hypnotised the tiger.

Yes, he did; don't think I'm remembering through a golden haze. In the things that counted with boys Charley was unquestionably a genius. One summer vacation Charley bought for two dollars—every cent he had—an immense dusty carton of unsold Easter-egg dyes from the grocery store at eight o'clock one Tuesday morning. By eight-thirty, using the upstairs telephone at his house, he had instructed five of us to meet in his basement and to bring along the big metal clothes boilers our mothers all used on washdays. By nine, when we met, Charley's mother had gone to the Tuesday morning sewing group at the church. Ten minutes later the five of us dispersed at Charley's direction, each to an assigned territory Within forty minutes we were back, each with at least one and some with two and three white or semi-white neighbourhood dogs of all sizes and breeds, two white Angoras, and one mottled-white alley cat.

Charley was ready. The two stationary laundry tubs were filled with warm, sudsy water for the preliminary baths; the clothes boilers were each half full of dye; a section of the basement—the drying area—was neatly paved with newspapers; and Charley, seated above us on the basement stairs, was ready to direct and oversee the fast, efficient, assembly-line operation he had planned.

We were finished on schedule by noon when the neighbourhood was briefly busy with husbands coming home for lunch. Then Charley gave the signal and—dry and combed now— fourteen excited red, green, violet, vivid yellow, sky-blue, and purple dogs, two sullen scarlet cats, and a final experimental red-white-and-blue one were simultaneously released on a flabbergasted neighbourhood.

This accomplishment had the clean-cut touch of genius, and we knew it. It was a conception so far above the routine traditional mischief of the rest of us that it was beyond envy and only to be admired and accepted with gratitude. Even then, as you can see—call it pump-priming, if you like—Charley never hesitated to spend what was necessary to the largeness of his purposes; he was broke for a week after the episode of the dogs but it was obviously necessary and worth it. Then, as today, he understood that accomplishment carries its price.

But there was more to Charley than flash. In between his larger spectacular achievements ran a steady workaday stream of minor though always talented activity. He devised a simple effective method of dipping the entire supply of school blackboard chalk, stick by stick, into a thinned solution of shellac, coating each with a hard, invisible shell which eliminated blackboard instruction for a day and a half. Charley found the pet cock at the back of an untended pipe down at the pop-bottling plant, which, when turned, released a warm, uncarbonated delicious stream of grape pop, and we used it at intervals for a week till Ed Krueger got careless and was caught.

And it was Charley, at the tattooing booth of a travelling carnival, who had a red-and-blue rose-wreathed heart labelled "Mother" worked on to his chest in genuine tattoo ink—though without the use of the needle—to the awe-struck envy of us all, till it began to wear off and he admitted the hoax.

He made things work. The essence of success ran in his veins—there was the key to Charley's character. And when he showed up, that memorable morning, after breakfast and the mail delivery, with a paper-bound volume of instructions on hypnotism, we all felt in our bones that Charley would become—perhaps already had become—a skilled practicing mesmerist.

There were five of us—four boys and Agnes, the tomboy sister of one—and we had gathered, as we did often that summer, in Mrs. Councilman's back yard. I remember that day and all those long ago, deep-summer days in Galesburg, Illinois, with a terrible nostalgia. Already the sky was a hard hot blue, the air shimmering with sun. The grass under our bare feet was faded and dry and the tree locusts were sawing their wings for yards and blocks and miles around us.

Today, I suppose, we would have known about the tiger hours earlier and been safe behind doors; radios would have been issuing urgent warnings and sound trucks would have been touring the streets. But in those days—on that day— news spread slowly and haphazardly, by word of mouth. And at the moment when Charley sat down on the grass to show us the book, only a handful of circus men knew that a young and thoroughly dangerous tiger was out of his cage and on the prowl.

We discussed Charley's book for a time; then Ken Garver ran up the tree, and we all followed. The tree was the reason we so often gathered in Mrs. Councilman's yard. It was thick-boled and squat, the trunk slanting out from the ground at a forty-five-degree angle, so that with a short running start, a barefooted boy could run right up the trunk to the lowest branches. We sat roosting in the tree and talked desultorily about the circus out at the fairgrounds. I don't remember that we were ever especially excited over a circus, and none of us ever carried water for the elephants. We were taken to the circus every year by our parents, or given money to buy tickets, and we were reasonably interested and talked about it a little.

But mostly, that morning, as at the beginning of every day, we were waiting for something to happen, for some activity, set off by a stimulus from outside or inside our minds, to begin. And the day, filled with promise, stretched far ahead, each hour infinitely longer and richer than any have ever been since.

Mrs. Councilman came out of her house and greeted us pleasantly, and Agnes, lowering her voice sympathetically, said, "How's Mr. Councilman?" Mrs. Councilman nodded sadly and said, "Fine." One or the other of us inquired each day about her husband's health as though he were an invalid, and Mrs. Councilman responded as though he were. Actually, the man—slight, pale, and half his wife's buxom size—went to work every day in a machine shop. But he suffered, whiningly, from a perpetual plague of vague ailments.

Once when Charley and I were in the bathroom of their house—we had the run of the place—the door of a large wooden cabinet on the floor was ajar and we stood astounded, staring at shelf after shelf crammed with prescriptions and pills, great bottles of tonic and liniment, Nerve-Aid and sleeping tablets, most of them with Mr. Councilman's name on the labels, and for a moment we had a dim awareness of the kind of half-life that poor man lived.

Smiling benignly, Mrs. Councilman stood by our tree, enjoying the sun. Then Agnes, her voice surprised, said, "There's a tiger." She shrieked, and sat staring across the yard. There are, or were, no fences or alleys in Galesburg; all the back yards of a block blend into one and it is possible to walk, as we often did, for block after block through the gardens and back yards of the town. We all turned to look, and there, impossibly, ambling towards us from the next yard, his tail erect and switching slightly, was an enormous tiger.

It was outside of all experience, past belief, yet there, indisputably, *was* a tiger; and we saw the muscles slide and the white hairs of his chest, just under the shoulders, spread apart and come together with each silent step.

He could have reached Mrs. Councilman in a single leap, killing or maiming her with a swipe of his paw. But instead, just within our yard now, he sat down, a colossal cat with foot-long white whiskers, and returned our stare, gazing at us through the slitted pupils of his immense yellow eyes. For a moment frozen in time, we all simply stared, he at us, we at him. Then the animal's small ears flicked, one at a time, and flattened on his skull. Soundlessly, he opened his mouth, and we saw the great shiny-wet fangs.

In a sudden hoarse whisper, Charley said, "Up in the tree!" and reached down and grabbed Mrs. Councilman's hair. Then Charley, and in a moment Ed Krueger, Ken Garver and I, clutching the branches with our legs, tugging at Mrs. Councilman's hair and the collar of her dress, tried to drag her up the slanting trunk of the tree. She came to life then, and grasping the trunk, scrambling awkwardly, managed to catch hold of the lowest limb and drag herself, moaning softly all the time, up into the branches with us.

For perhaps a full half minute longer, the tiger sat in the

*Clutching to the branches, we tried to drag Mrs. Councilman
up the slanting trunk of the tree*

sun, staring up at us with a lively and terrible interest. Agnes began to cry softly, and Mrs. Councilman, climbing higher, managed to reach up and get an arm around her waist to comfort her. Then the tiger's hind end raised, and he trotted to the house, and sat, his back towards us now, staring up at the partly opened first-floor window of Mrs. Councilman's pantry.

Each of us, I'm sure, was certain that in only a moment this impossible situation must end; that, as always in any predicament beyond a child's ability, adult help would be quickly forthcoming. But time passed and the summer sound of the locusts droned on. Then, incredibly, in the street around at the front of the house, a car door slammed, and we heard a woman's voice call out, "Hello, Mrs. Garver. Hot, isn't it?" We heard Ken's mother reply cheerily. A screen door banged shut. The car started up; then the sound of its motor diminished, and once again there was no sound but the steady drone of the locusts. It came to us then that the world was going on about its business in blank ignorance of us, and no help was on its way.

Now the tiger stood up, placed his forepaws up on the wood side of the house, straining his neck towards the window, and growled in his throat; and the prickling fright came washing over us.

It was Charley who understood first. "The window reminds him of the place he's fed at," he said. At the sound of the voice, the tiger's head turned, and he stared at us over his shoulder for a moment. Then, once more, he strained up towards the window and growled, a deep terrible sound, and we heard his claws clinking and scratching on the painted clapboards, and knew this was a savage and dangerous beast.

Carefully, Charley planted both feet in the main crotch of the tree, slid off his branch, and crouched, out of reach of Mrs. Councilman's free arm. "I think," he announced to us then, "that I can hypnotise that tiger."

"Charley!" Mrs. Councilman shrieked. "Don't you move!" And again the tiger turned to stare.

Charley didn't answer. From his back pocket he pulled a bandanna and handed it up to me. "If he comes running, throw this in his face; it'll confuse him," he told me. He pulled his book out of his pocket, opened it to the first page, and ran a finger down the table of contents. Then, looking up at us, smiling reassuringly, Charley nodded. "Yep," he said, "there's a chapter on animal hypnotism." He shoved the book in his pocket and dropped from the tree, landing on his feet beside it.

For seconds Charley stood poised, ready to leap for the tree again, but the animal across the yard continued to stare up at the half-open window. Then—not calmly, I'm certain, but coolly—Charley began slowly walking towards the back steps and screen door which led into the kitchen of Mrs. Councilman's house. At the third step, the tiger's head swung towards Charley, and Charley—helpless now, far from safety by several seconds and steps—could only walk on, an undersized ten-year-old boy staring at a four-hundred-pound tiger a dozen yards away. It sounds like incredible bravery, yet I doubt that courage had anything to do with it. It is simply that, for a mind like Charley's, some opportunities are just too big to lose.

My faith in him wavered and died. This, I knew, was too big, beyond any boy, even Charley. I knew he'd over reached himself, that in the next seconds he might actually be killed before my eyes. But he went up the fourth step, the fifth, and the sixth; then his bare foot touched the porch and suddenly he bolted, stumbling and crashing in through the screen door. Then the kitchen door slammed shut, and we heard the sliding bolt on the inside shoot home. The tiger trotted to the stairs, gazed up them, then returned to his position under the window.

Then it occurred to me—I knew that Charley was a showman, a lover of the hoax, but no fool—that he had no intention of trying any such nonsense as hypnotising this tiger, and that he was simply going to telephone the police. When he did not appear at the pantry window, I was certain of it, and waited for the sound of the receiver being removed from the wall phone in the kitchen. But seconds passed, and I heard nothing. Then, presently, we heard Mrs. Councilman's icebox open, heard the clink of a milk bottle and the rattle of paper. Then the icebox door slammed shut, and a moment later

Charley's composed face appeared at the window.

He glanced down at the sitting tiger, who licked his chops. Then Charley spoke, raising one arm to show us the open book in his hand. "It says here"—he studied the text, apparently reading as he talked—"that in hypnotising animals it is necessary first to obtain their attention and confidence with food." He laid the book down on the open working shelf just below the level of the window.

Then he held up a large, shallow, thin wood dish, the kind butchers used in those days to pack ground meat in; it was heaped, we saw, with blood-red hamburgers, Charley set the dish down at one side of the window. His hands were busy for a moment; then he held them up and we could see that he was packing a handful of ground meat into a baseball-sized sphere. Taking careful aim, he tossed the ball, underhanded.

The animal growled, and Charley quickly tossed the meat

It struck the tiger squarely on the nose, and he recoiled, a blur of tan and black, snarling. But he had smelled the meat. His tongue swiped his nose, and he scooped the ball from the grass with his front teeth, swallowed it instantly, then stretched his neck towards the window, yearning up for more.

Charley had a second meatball ready, poised in his left hand; now the fingers of his right hand began rhythmically extending and drawing back, his arm moving slowly back and forth, making passes in the air at the tiger's staring eyes. "Your eyes are getting heavy," he murmured to the tiger. "You are getting sleepier and sleepier." The animal growled, and Charley quickly tossed the meat. This time the tiger caught it in mid-air and swallowed it in a gulp, instantly staring up for more.

Charley made another meatball, holding it up for the tiger to see, and the animal reared up, his forepaws scratching the side of the house, his face no more than four feet from Charley's unwavering eyes, his attention complete. Charley prudently lowered the window a bit more; then his fingers again undulated gracefully, his arm swaying like a charmed snake, and it would not have surprised me at all to see miniature lightning lines dart from his fingertips to the tiger's fascinated eyes. "You want to *sle-e-ep*," he droned. "Your eyes are *so-o-o* heavy." He tossed the meatball, and again the tiger snapped it up in mid-air.

The Councilmans' dinner made seven or eight meatballs; and, after each, Charley murmured steadily of sleep, *sle-e-ep*, his arm making graceful passes. Then the meat was gone, and the beast sat there growling, wide awake as ever, his appetite only tantalised, obviously. Charley left the window, the icebox door opened and slammed shut, and Charley reappeared with half a dozen pork chops lying on the butcher's paper they'd been wrapped in.

Again Charley murmured to the tiger, while his arm swayed, the fingers curling. Then he tossed out a chop. The tiger caught it, chewed just once, and we heard the bone crunch to splinters. Then he gulped, the chop was gone, and still he yearned up for more, his tail switching, his ears steadily flattening and rising.

In the tree, we sat silent and motionless—all but Mrs. Councilman. From time to time she would moan softly, and say, "Oh, my God," in utter anguish and despair. Charley must have seemed insane to her, tossing her pork chops to the tiger at regular intervals and murmuring unceasingly. "Your eyes are so *heavy,*" he droned. "You want to *relax.* Relax and rest. Rest every weary muscle, and sleep, sleep, sle-e-ep." From time to time, he would glance down at his book, and once he raised it, and we all stared at the cover while Charley turned back a page and studied the text.

He must have seemed mad to Mrs. Councilman and even we had doubts that Charley really knew what he was doing. But we watched intently for any signs of success, and were not actually surprised when presently they appeared.

"You can't keep your eyes open," Charley was saying, his fingers waving like ribbons in a breeze. "And now they are closing, *closing.*" And they did. The tiger dropped to his belly, his forelegs extended, and yawned tremendously. Then he turned his head to look back at us, and his eyes blinked lazily, and actually closed for a moment.

But he growled immediately, opened his eyes, and stood up once again, and Charley tossed him another chop. The tiger caught it, but this time he lay on his belly to chew, lazily, the bone crunching again and again. He swallowed, dropped his chin to his paws, and gazed dreamily up at Charley.

"Sleep," said Charley. He glanced at his book, then nodded to us vigorously, smiling. "Sleep," he said, "you are so very tired." And the tiger yawned, and rolled on his side, blinking repeatedly. "Rest." Charley's voice dropped to a whisper. "Rest and sleep. You are, oh, so weary."

He stood for a moment, looking down at the tiger, then tossed the last chop, which fell on the grass not an inch from the tiger's nose. The animal sniffed it without stirring, his nose twitching, and seemed to debate whether to bother taking it or not. Then he did, raising his head just far enough to pull the chop into his mouth with his teeth. He lay back then, chewing slowly, his eyes heavy and blinking.

"Sleep," said Charley, "sl-e-e-p, your are so very tired."

"Yes," said Charley, more softly than ever, "you are going to sleep." In a soft soprano, he began to sing, leaning far out of the window, "Sweet and low, sweet and low; wind of the west-ern sea-ee. Sweet and low, sweet and low..." He paused, humming softly, studied the motionless tiger, then turned from the window.

A moment later we heard the telephone receiver being lifted from the hook and I waited to hear Charley ask for the police. "Give me the *Register-Mail* office," he said briskly. "Emergency." There was a pause; then Charley said, "Send someone down here, quick," and he gave the address. "There's a tiger in the back yard. We captured it. *Yes,* the one from the circus. He's *here,* right now, hypnotised, but I don't know how long the trance will last, so get down here fast. And be sure you bring a cameraman!" Then he hung up.

The screen door opened slowly, and Charley cautiously

"Okay," said Charley, and the man snapped the pict

appeared on the top step and looked down at the tiger who was lying with his head on his forepaws, his huge tongue occasionally flicking out to lick his whiskers, his eyes closed.

"Sleep," said Charley, slowly coming down the stairs. Both hands now—one a little behind the other—were at work, the fingers curling and uncurling at the tiger's head. "Rest," said Charley, "every muscle relaxed." The tiger sighed, his striped side and white belly swelling tremendously; then the breath hissed through his nostrils and he lay there in the grass breathing quietly, fast asleep.

I suppose it must have taken several minutes but it seemed to me that almost instantly we heard car brakes squeal, then the sound of running feet approaching. The *Register-Mail* reporter came charging around the corner of the house into the yard, his camera in his hand, then stopped, his heels digging into the grass, as he saw the tiger on the ground. A split second later the chief and another policeman came

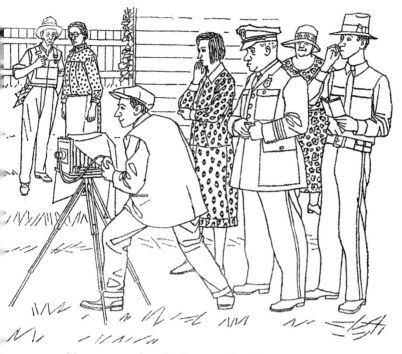

t appeared in over one hundred papers in nine states

plunging into him, almost knocking him over. Then they all stood gaping, staring down at the tiger, then up at Charley.

Casually, Charley stepped forward, his thumbs hooked in his belt, to the tiger's side. "Don't worry," he said. "He's scientifically mesmerised."

The newspaperman recovered first, and raised his camera.

"Wait," said Charley. He took his book from a back pocket, opened it and held it at chest level, as though he were reading, the cover facing the camera. He spread the fingers of his other hand, aimed at the tiger's nose, lifted one foot and planted it gently on the tiger's ribs. "Okay," he said then, and the man snapped the picture that appeared in over one hundred papers in nine different states.

We were climbing down from the tree and the yard was suddenly filling with people, the newspaperman snapping photographs of the house, the open window, us, the tiger, Charley, and everything else in sight. I am sure, in spite of the evidence lying on the ground before them, that the newspaperman and the police would never quite have believed what had happened, but an adult, Mrs. Councilman, had been there too, and she confirmed in excited almost hysterical detail the fact that Charley had indisputably hypnotised the tiger.

It seems strange, now, to recall this omen of the future. I still had Charley's bandanna in my hand and I wanted to return it. But even as I approached him I was dimly aware that he had passed irrevocably into a sphere beyond and above me, and I stopped beside him in awe. He was talking easily to the adults crowded around him, and I'd no more have interrupted than I'd interrupt the President of the United States. So I simply tucked the bandanna part way into his hip pocket, opening the pocket gently and cautiously so as not to disturb him. I caught a glimpse of, and for an instant touched, an object in his pocket. Then Charley turned, smiling graciously, and pushed his handkerchief deep into his pocket. The circus men arrived at that moment with a huge net, and then—all at once and all together—the frantic mothers came and we were all, including Charley, whisked from the scene.

The event was a screaming sensation. A full third of the *Register-Mail*'s front page that night was occupied by the picture of Charley, book in hand, his foot on the tiger's chest; and the headline was set in the type that had been last used to announce the Armistice after World War I.

Three Chicago newspapermen came in on the afternoon train. Charley held his first press conference on his front porch, serving coffee and explaining modestly that any boy could have done it. And that night, from the main ring of the circus, Charley was introduced as a hero. The caged tiger sat beside him, and as the band played "Columbia, the Gem of the Ocean," Charley, his book in his hand, made graceful passes at the beast who simply sat there this time, glaring crossly at Charley as though his head ached. At Charley's request, the rest of us were with him standing on the sawdust in the spotlight sharing his glory. He always took care of his friends.

Actually, I only mentioned the episode once to Charley and that was the day it happened just before the Chicago reporters arrived. "That empty bottle I saw in your pocket this morning," I said casually as we waited on his front porch. "The only other bottle I've seen just like it was on a shelf in the Councilmans' bathroom—and it was full then. Full of Mr. Councilman's sleeping tablets."

Charley considered this comment, staring thoughtfully out at the street. Then he said quietly, "I had a phone call from the company that printed my hypnotism book. They've heard the news and they want to print my picture in their ads with a signed testimonial, and they're paying me for it—a nice piece of money. Enough," he added delicately, "for everyone. You helped me," he said, and clapped me on the back. "You held the bandanna in case it was needed. I want to split the profits with you; I want you for my partner from now on." He put his arm affectionately around my shoulders. "I think you've got the right qualifications," he said, and we shook hands on it.

Just then the Chicago reporters drove up in a rented car, and while they interviewed Charley I hung around in case he needed me to back up his story.

I guess you can see that I think Charley's a great man. I don't say his methods would always stand the full light of day, but for that matter neither did those of any great President we've had. His aims, though—and this is what counts—are right, and he usually achieves them, one way or another. Don't get me wrong; I'm not announcing Charley's candidacy. In fact "Charley" isn't his first name at all and I haven't even hinted at his last because I don't want to seem to be speaking for him. But frankly, I'd love to see him nominated and elected, not only because I think he'll make a fine President, but because I'll make a pretty good Secretary of State myself. As Charley himself has said, with an arm around my shoulders, I've got the right qualifications.

Call Him Hero

STEPHEN ANDREWS

THE Viscount airliner thundered through the night sky, then banked into an impatient orbit. Inside the noisy cabin, Mr. B. S. Crone peered through his spectacles at his pocket watch.

"Tut, tut! We should have been over Cairo an hour ago. I just fail to see why the airlines cannot fly to their time-tables. I suppose the heavy tourist traffic at this time of year is responsible for the delay, but if it is, the airline should have anticipated the fact and made adequate allowances. How on earth anyone can organise their own personal programmes in the midst of such chaos is utterly beyond me." Mr. Crone returned his watch to his waistcoat pocket. "Nevertheless we must not be dejected. Now as I was saying, Rawlinson, in Egypt we shall visit the ancient temple at Luxor. The temple is one of the most impressive relics of ancient Egypt. It is in a superb state of preservation. Each of its fourteen pillars is fifty-two feet high..."

Steve Rawlinson, the eighteen-year-old school captain, slid down in his seat as his unpopular history master droned on and on. Steve was in a party of thirty schoolboys on a trip to Egypt. The rest of the party were singing their favourite camping songs at the tops of their voices. Steve would have loved to join in the choruses. He had led the singing from London to Malta, but it was unfortunate that on the final stage of their flight, he found he was sitting next to Mr. Crone, who went on and on and on.

"Rameses II reigned sixty-seven years and filled all Egypt with his own monuments, some of them beautiful. The rock temple of Abu Simbel, to my mind was his greatest achievement..."

Steve sank lower and lower into his seat. Suddenly the cabin loudspeaker brought the school party to order.

"Attention, please, attention, please. This is your captain speaking. Unfortunately I regret to say that we will be making an emergency landing within the next few minutes. There is no need for alarm. Would you all fasten your safety belts, please?"

Mr. Crone peered out of the window. "Strange," he said. "I detect no mechanical failure." He sat back in his seat, fastened his seat straps, took off his glasses and slipped them into his breast pocket. "This is a confounded nuisance."

The airliner's nose dipped and the aircraft gently descended. The aircraft engines, by their sound, were functioning satisfactorily. Lower and lower they sank towards the black void which was earth. Suddenly the aircraft rumbled as if it was about to fall to pieces, but Steve knew the cause of this was the undercarriage being lowered. Provided the landing lights were switched on, there was no reason why the airliner should not make a satisfactory landing, wherever they were. Although where they were, Steve could not imagine. Certainly through the windows, he saw no sign of any airfield approach, or city lights.

For a while the aircraft levelled off with the engines roaring to hold her, then it happened. The aircraft bumped the ground and shot up in the air again. It bumped again, spun round in a giddy ground loop, and skidded to a halt.

Steve fumbled with his seat harness, freed himself and kicked open the emergency exit. His legs felt like jelly as he jumped out into the sand, but he was relieved to see, by the light of the moon, that the aircraft was down in one piece, although to judge by the buckled propellers, it would never fly again. Steve helped the other survivors, including Mr. Crone, out of the rear exit. In spite of the disaster, no one had been killed though few had escaped cuts or bruises and the navigator had a broken arm. All were in fairly good spirits. The survivors sorted themselves out. The captain, with a bandage around his forehead, stood on a small rising of sand to address the passengers.

"Can I have your attention, please? First of all I want to apologise to you all for the inconvenience caused because of this mishap. I can promise you that provision will be made for you to continue your journey as soon as possible."

"What happened?" snapped Mr. Crone from the back of the crowd. "Did you run out of fuel?"

The captain gulped. "No. We lost our way due to a navigational error. Our compass repeaters were sixty degrees out of true. However we did manage to send out an SOS message, so rescue aircraft will be searching for us at present. Until they find us, I want you all to keep out of the sun, when it rises. Our main problem will be to conserve what little water we have. As you can see, the sun will soon rise, so I suggest you find yourselves some cover under the wings."

As the boys moved away, Mr. Crone walked up to the captain. "When do you expect the rescue aircraft to find us?" Steve heard his master ask.

"Quite frankly, I don't know. I'm afraid..." The captain took Mr. Crone by the elbow and led him away out of earshot.

Steve shrugged his shoulders and turned away. He looked around the desert. The full moon made the night almost as light as day. The sand itself was silver and gold. The desert was clean, beautiful and fascinating. Whatever the danger,

All were in fairly good spirits

Steve sensed no fear.

"Rawlinson," called Mr. Crone, taking Steve aside. "We're in trouble. I understand from the captain that there is a possibility that our distress signal was not picked up. It was certainly not acknowledged. Although aircraft will undoubtedly be looking for us, we are so far off track that they won't be looking in this area. Probably our only chance of survival is for someone to go out and bring help. The coastal road is believed to be about forty miles to the north, and there, presumably, will be a certain amount of motor transport, even in this under-developed part of the world. Since I was in the Welsh Guards in this desert during the war, and know a little of its problems, I volunteered to bring help. The captain can't go—it is his duty to stay with the survivors—and you know the rest of his crew were more knocked about than we were."

"Can I come with you, sir?" asked Steve, not caring to wait in the heat, but when he realised he had asked to be alone in the company of his crusty old history master for a day at least, he wished he had not volunteered.

"As a matter of fact, the captain suggested I should take someone with me, and as you are senior boy, naturally I thought of you first. But I must warn you that the going will be tough. It is not at all like a hike in Wales. This desert is a killer, and there's no guarantee that we'll survive."

Steve shrugged his shoulders. Once on the march he guessed Mr. Crone would be too tired to yap. He knew it would be agony just waiting in the desert to be rescued.

"I'd still like to come, sir," he said.

"Steve was given a tube of anti-sunburn lotion to rub on his skin, a rubber bottle of water, a large sun hat and a pocket compass. Suitably attired, he waved to his cheering school pals, and with Mr. Crone, set off northwards across the moonlit desert, determined to make the most of the coolness before sunrise. The sand was soft, not at all suitable for fast walking, but Steve did not mind. He had young legs to forge him on his way. What irritated him from the start was that Mr. Crone dropped ten yards behind.

"There's no need to walk so fast, Rawlinson," said his master. "We have a long way to go yet."

"But the sooner we reach the road, the sooner we will be able to send help."

"And save your breath for walking."

Steve smiled to himself. He wished Mr. Crone would save his breath.

Soon the crashed aircraft and the survivors were left far behind in the sand dunes. On and on Steve walked, with Mr. Crone trailing behind, across the empty desert. Steve felt he was making good time, although without the master behind him, he could have covered twice the distance. After two hours, Mr. Crone sat on the sand.

"We've been marching for two hours now. Take off your shoes and socks and wiggle your toes."

Steve walked back to his master. "We've only just started. The boys are relying on us to bring help as soon as we can. We can't let them down by wasting time like this."

Mr. Crone pulled off his socks and lay flat on his back. "Do as I say, boy."

Steve was furious. He ignored the old man's command. For a moment he was tempted to walk off and leave him, but he knew there would be plenty of opportunities later. It wouldn't be long before Mr. Crone could walk no farther. Steve stood over his master, despising him.

After about ten minutes, Mr. Crone shook the sand out of his socks, put them on his feet inside out, then replaced his shoes.

"Dear, dear, time flies. I hate to say this, but we must be getting on."

Steve turned his back on his master and walked away in disgust. He glanced back once, and saw Mr. Crone trailing fifty yards behind. Steve faced the front and walked stolidly on.

The sun rose overhead into a clear blue sky. Its brilliance was dazzling, in fact it was quite impossible to look into the sky. The sand too, was no longer a rich golden yellow, but dazzling white, and painful to the eyes, so it was only possible to see through half-closed eyes. The ground beneath their feet was soon like a hot-plate, the air around them like the inside of an oven. The slight breeze swirled up a few fine grains of sand, which when they struck the bare skin, felt like red-hot needles. The fierce sun beat down upon their heads like a battery of electric fires. Steve felt discomfort in every step. He knew the tortures of the desert were about to begin, and he was impatient to reach his destination, to put his agonies at rest.

"Rawlinson, Rawlinson," cried Mr. Crone. Steve turned slowly to face his master staggering up behind him. "We've been travelling four hours now. It's time for another ten minute break."

Steve collapsed on the sand. His feet were swollen, and his tight shoes hurt. He pulled off his shoes.

"Good boy," said Mr. Crone. "Take off your socks. It's uncomfortable if your socks stick to your feet. Take them off."

Steve pulled off his tight shoes, lay in the sun and closed his eyes. So far, he thought, they had travelled well. Of course it was tiring walking through loose sand, but it was possible, by walking on the ridges of the sand dunes, to avoid the worst patches. After the four hour march, Steve's bones began to ache, but that was only to be expected. He would cheerfully bear this discomfort for the sake of finding help for his stranded school pals. He felt thirsty of course, so he unscrewed the cap of his rubber bottle and raised the bottle to his lips.

"Don't drink any of that yet," said Mr. Crone, snatching away the bottle and replacing the cap.

"But, but . . ."

"The first rule of the desert is to preserve your water," said Mr. Crone, throwing him the sealed bottle.

Steve caught the bottle. "You have a rule for everything, don't you?"

"This water is to keep you alive, not to satisfy your thirst

"Don't drink that yet," said Mr. Crone

whenever you want it. We don't know where the next drop
will come from."

Steve clipped the bottle back on to his belt. He was thirsty
all right, but he knew he could last out as long as his master.
He licked his lips and tried to forget his thirst.

"Time to move on," said Mr. Crone, putting on his shoes and
socks.

"But we've just stopped!"

"We've had our ten minute rest."

Steve put on his shoes, and tightened the laces as far as his
swollen feet would allow. He gritted his teeth. He was
determined to show his master no sign of weakness.

Again they set off across the desert. With every step, the
agonies of the scorching sun became more painful. Steve tried
to lick his lips, but he found the tongue in his mouth was like
a dry lizard, and his throat like leather. With the utmost
difficulty, he led the way across the desert. He longed, not to
reach the coastal road, but only for the next rest.

After another two hours, Mr. Crone called a halt. Steve
collapsed on the sand, but found it so unbearably hot, that he
could not lie there. He rolled over, then pushed himself to his
feet. His hands were red raw.

"When do we drink?" he croaked.

"Tomorrow," answered Mr. Crone with difficulty. He
changed his socks around, replaced his shoes, stood up and
pointed out the way. Steve nodded, and again took the lead.

Apart from the brief ten minute stops every two hours, when
Mr. Crone changed around his socks, they staggered across the
desert. Steve watched the sun move over to the west. He longed
for the sunset. Then at last it would be cool enough to lie down.
Then at last he could sleep.

The sun was a brilliant red orb above the horizon, but the
scarlet skies of the sunset held no romantic notions for Steve
now. Fortunately the twilight in these latitudes was short. The
sun descended quickly below the horizon, and the night drew
across the sky like a diamond studded curtain. Mr. Crone called
a halt, and Steve collapsed on his knees, and then on his face.
At last he could let his aches and pains disappear in sleep.

"Rawlinson, Rawlinson, wake up!"

Steve raised his heavy eyelids. His head ached. "What's wrong?"

"You've had your ten minute rest."

"Ten minutes? I want to sleep."

"How far do you think we've travelled?"

Steve knew they had walked steadily for ten hours. "Oh, about twenty miles. We're half way there."

"We've travelled less than a mile an hour. We've travelled nine miles. That makes thirty-one miles to go!"

"Thirty-one?" echoed Steve weakly. He knew now that he would never complete the journey.

"Come on, Rawlinson. Night is the best time to travel. You can miss a night's sleep for once."

Mr. Crone helped Steve to his feet. Steve was completely shocked. At this rate, it would take four or five days to reach the coastal road. Steve knew he could not last more than another day in the sun. He staggered after his master, who had now taken the lead.

The terrain changed to a rocky plateau, which made it possible to walk faster, but the night grew colder. Steve shivered. His muscles stiffened and were difficult to move. Although the night chased away the burning pains of the day, it brought agonies of its own. Mr. Crone led the march throughout the night, only stopping for ten minute breaks every two hours. With mixed feelings, Steve welcomed the burning sunrise.

The cruel sun repeated its tortures of the previous day. Steve's mind drifted aimlessly. He no longer knew, nor cared of the time and place. The hot air burnt the inside of his lungs with every breath he took. He tore open his shirt front, but this did not ease the pains in his chest. His head, too, throbbed with the heat. He swept his hand across his brow and was dimly aware that his hat was gone. For a moment he hesitated, looked vaguely round, then staggered on, automatically following the stooping figure before him.

Steve's aimless thoughts were roughly broken by someone shaking him.

"Where is your hat?" said Mr. Crone in a voice no stronger than a whisper. They both stared back through reddened eyes, seeing nothing but endless empty sand. "Don't lose this one," whispered Mr. Crone, as he removed the sun hat from his bald head and placed it on Steve's.

"No, sir, I can't take yours," but no sooner had Steve said this than his legs buckled and he collapsed on the sand.

Mr. Crone had whipped out a large handkerchief and was knotting its four corners. This he placed on his own head.

For a moment he grinned down at Steve. "You're still just a boy," he said, and looked almost genial. Then he pulled Steve to his feet. Steve felt his own arm being placed around his master's neck and found himself forced to go on.

More than once he urged Mr. Crone to leave him. "Go on yourself. You have a chance. I can't make it, sir."

But all Mr. Crone would say was: "We've got to keep going."

Steve completely lost all sense of time. He was half-dragged and half-carried on his way, yet even in his state of semi-consciousness, he still felt the aches in his body.

Suddenly Steve was dropped and left undisturbed on the sand. He heard a shout. Summoning all his remaining strength, he raised his head and looked out over the desert. About forty yards away, he saw Mr. Crone staggering across the desert waving his arms. Beyond him trekked a nomadic caravan of about thirty camels loaded with bundles of merchandise. The sight revived him. He struggled to his feet, feeling a need to shout with joy but was only able to utter hoarse, low cries. His cruel march was over. His suffering school companions would be saved. Two Arabs came running to his assistance and supported him back to the caravan. A leather bottle was pushed between his lips, now swollen like bicycle inner tubes, and he heard the water sizzle down his throat.

The young have a remarkable power of recovery. After he had moistened his parched mouth, Steve found he could talk again.

"Thank you," he said to the Arabs who had given him the water. However, Mr. Crone was not so fortunate. He collapsed on the sand and made no attempt to drink the water which was spilt into his mouth.

"Sunstroke!" said a little fat Arab, sprinkling water over Mr. Crone's face, shoulders and arms.

"Will he be all right?" asked Steve anxiously. The little fat Arab nodded. "We will keep him out of the sun."

There was a sheikh in the party. He was tall and black-bearded, and had a noble bearing. He was dressed in white, flowing robes, and had a gold-hilted dagger in his belt. He glared at Steve with his black penetrating eyes, and boomed in a deep voice in some strange language. The little fat Arab interpreted.

"Who are you?"

"I'm from a British civil aircraft which crashed in the desert. There are thirty survivors waiting to be rescued. Can you help?"

"You lie. Civil aircraft do not fly over this desert."

"But it's true, I tell you."

"We know there are Europeans in the desert arming rebel tribesmen. Our troops are searching for them."

Fear blent with amazement in Steve as he stared at the sheikh and his interpreter. That the Arabs might be unfriendly, had never crossed his mind, and to be accused of gun-running was too ridiculous. Yet now he felt something like panic as he thought of all those awaiting rescue and depending upon him.

"Do I look like a gun-runner?" said Steve desperately. "I am a schoolboy!"

The sheikh smiled cynically, his eyes approving the athletic and well-built form of the school captain. "You are a very big schoolboy!" he said. The interpreter langhed and nodded. It was a good joke.

"You must believe me," cried Steve. "The crashed aircraft is back there in the desert. There are thirty boys trying to shelter under its wings. They have little water. Go and look for yourself."

The sheikh gazed across the desert. "It would take a month to find an aircraft in the desert," he was translated. "You will be taken to the army for interrogation. They will get the truth

"You are a very big schoolboy," said the sheikh

out of you." He struck his boot with his riding whip, turned on
his heel and marched away.

Steve tried to follow, but was held back by the Arabs.

"They will die in this sun," he shouted. "They will *die* ..."

"Be calm," said the little interpreter, and added: "They are
indeed dead, if ever they existed outside your imagination."

"Dead? They were alive when we left them. What do you
mean?"

"As our noble sheikh says, we could not find a crashed aircraft in the desert so far off our caravan routes. But we know

you lie. We were warned by the army to watch out for the gun-runners."

"But can't you speak to Cairo airfield? They'll confirm that an aircraft is missing."

The little Arab laughed. "You lie so convincingly. Don't you know Cairo is a thousand kilometres away?"

"Well, what are you going to do? You can't mean to do nothing?"

"We camp here tonight, then we proceed to market at Sebha. There you will be handed over to the army for interrogation. If you are telling the truth, you will be released. If you are a gun-runner, you will be shot."

"And how long will it take to reach Sebha?"

"We will reach Sebha in fourteen days."

"Fourteen days? Then my friends are certainly dead. And your lack of action will have killed them!"

For a moment the little Arab looked shaken. Then he shrugged his shoulders again: "It is the sheikh's orders," he said, and nothing Steve could say after that had any effect. "In the desert, the sheikh's command is the law."

However, Steve was treated hospitably. He and Mr. Crone were given food, drink and a tent in which to sleep. Mr. Crone was in a bad way, and he moaned and groaned in a semicoma. Steve, in spite of his problems, found his eyelids were heavy, and as soon as he put down his head, he fell asleep.

He awoke with a start, as if from a bad dream. It was night, and the camp was silent, apart from Mr. Crone's moans and groans.

Steve found he could sleep no more. He felt responsible for Mr. Crone's sunstroke, because he had used his master's sun hat. He also felt guilty because he was resting in a comfortable tent, whilst his school pals were waiting to die. But he was told by the Arabs that the coastal road was thirty kilometres to the north. It was a long way.

Yet the ground was hard, and he felt it might be possible to cover the distance in two days. On a sudden impulse, he decided that it was his duty to make the attempt. He scribbled a note explaining his intentions, and pinned it to his pillow. He

Noise filled the sky but Steve's mind could scarce grasp its significance

filled his pockets with food, and the two rubber bottles with water from a pitcher. He said a brief prayer, and slid under the bottom of the tent. The guards, sitting around the camp fire, did not see him. He slipped away into the dark.

With his heart thumping inside his body, he walked as fast as he could, using the pole star to check his compass reading. After two hours, he stopped for a ten minute rest to change his socks around as he had seen Mr. Crone do, then he carried on as before. Steve had got clean away from the camp, but he knew that he had his own life in his hands. He knew that should his strength fail, there would be no one to urge and drive him on.

He made good going through the night, and when day came, suffered once more all the agonies of the desert, the blistered feet, the raw red skin, the red-hot sand grains, the pains with every step and with every breath. It was the return to a nightmare. Yet this time there were long stretches of hard sand where the going was less arduous, and he must have made about half the distance to the coast before his strength began to fail.

"I must go on... I must go on..." he kept telling himself, but by late afternoon, he was staggering like a drunken sailor and every time he fell, the effort to rise left him weaker than before. His mind, too, began to stray and he kept forgetting to consider the direction in which he moved. To remind himself, he kept the little compass tight-clutched in his hand. Its safety became an obsession with him. His rests grew longer and he lost count of time.

A buzzing filled his ears. It grew steadily louder, but many moments passed before he grasped its significance. Then the sky was filled with noise—the noise of a powerful petrol engine.

He stood upright, swaying, staring at the sky, his blood-shot eyes seeing nothing but its brilliance. Like a man surrendering, he raised both his arms, waved them feebly, turned himself around so that he faced every direction, and then fell flat on his face.

When Steve came to, he found he was being lifted. A

helicopter stood on the sand, its open door ready to receive him. He tried to speak, but his mouth, throat and lungs were so dry that he could make no sound. His face was sponged down and he was given a drink. His rescuers were Libyan airmen, their craft a rescue helicopter reconnoitring the coastal area.

As soon as he could speak, he told them what had happened. "Our aircraft crashed about forty miles inside the desert," he said. "They will be in bad shape now, and need help quickly." He told them too, about Mr. Crone in the hands of the desert tribesmen.

"He is being taken to Sebha."

"Take it easy," said a Libyan airman. "We'll find them. Don't you worry now."

News travels fast. When the re-united school party arrived back at Rhondda, Steve found a reception party waiting to welcome him. The colliery band played, and the crowds cheered. Steve tried to explain that it was Mr. Crone who deserved the credit, and indeed Mr. Crone shared his triumph, but his protests were put down as modesty on the part of the school captain. Steve was a hero, Steve was the toast of the town; but he had his own hero. A few days ago, Steve thought his master miserable and narrow-minded, an elderly bore. But he had seen him face almost certain death with coolness, courage and determination, and now saw him for what he was — a person of quality. By his example, his master had taught Steve his greatest lesson, and what he had taught, Steve would never forget.

Smith versus Lichtensteiger

WESTON MARTYR

SMITH stood 5 feet 5 inches in his boots, weighed nearly 10 stone in his winter clothes and an overcoat, and he had a flat chest and a round stomach. Smith was a clerk in a small branch bank in East Anglia; he was not an athlete or a fighting man, although he followed the fortunes of a professional football team with great interest, and he had fought for a year in France without ever seeing his enemy or achieving a closer proximity to him than one hundred and twenty yards. When a piece of shrapnel reduced his fighting efficiency by abolishing the biceps of one arm, Smith departed from the field of battle and returned to his branch bank.

For forty-nine weeks each year Smith laboured faithfully at his desk. But every year in early April, Smith suddenly came to life. For he was a yachtsman, and he owned a tiny yacht which he called the *Kate* and loved with a great love. The spring evenings he spent fitting out, painting, and fussing over his boat. Thereafter, as early as possible every Saturday afternoon, he set sail and cruised alone amongst the tides and sand-banks of the Thames Estuary, returning again as late as possible on Sunday night. And every summer, when his three weeks' holiday came round, Smith and his *Kate* would sail away from East Anglia together and voyage afar. One year Smith cruised to Falmouth in the West Country, and he likes to boast about that cruise still. Once he set out for Cherbourg, which is a port in foreign parts; but that time, thanks to a westerly gale, he got no further than Dover. The year Smith encountered Lichtensteiger he had sailed as far east as Flushing, and he was on his way back when a spell of bad weather and head winds drove him into Ostend and detained him there three days.

Lichtensteiger was also detained at Ostend; but not by the weather. Lichtensteiger had come from Alexandria, with a rubber tube stuffed full of heroine wound round his waist next his skin, and he was anxious to get to London as quickly as he could. He had already been as far as Dover, but there a Customs official (who had suspicions but no proof) whispered to a friend in the Immigration Department, and Lichtensteiger found himself debarred as an "undesirable alien" from entering the United Kingdom. He had therefore returned to Ostend in the steamer in which he had left that place.

Lichtensteiger stood 6 feet 1 inch in his socks, weighed 14 stone stripped, and he had a round chest and a flat stomach. He was as strong as a gorilla, as quick in action as a mongoose, and he had never done an honest day's work in his life. There is reason to believe that Lichtensteiger was a Swiss, as he spoke Switzer-Deutsch, which is something only a German-Swiss can do. His nationality, however, is by no means certain, for he spoke French like a Marseillais, German like a Würtemberger, and English like a native of the lower West-side of New York.

When Smith and Lichtensteiger first set eyes on each other, Smith was sitting in the *Kate*'s tiny cockpit, smoking his pipe and worrying about the weather. For Smith's holiday was nearly over; he was due at his bank again in three days, and he knew he could not hope to sail back while the strong north-westerly wind continued to blow straight from East Anglia towards Belgium. Said Smith to himself, "Hang it! I've got to sail tomorrow or get into a nasty fix. And if only I had two sound arms I *would* sail tomorrow and chance it; but a hundred-mile beat to wind'ard all by myself is going to be no joke. What I need is another man to help me; but there isn't an earthly hope of getting hold of anyone in this filthy hole."

Lichtensteiger was walking along the quay. He glanced at the *Kate* and her owner with a disdainful eye and passed on, because neither the boat nor the man held any interest for him. But in Lichtensteiger's card-index-like mind, in which he filed without conscious effort most of the things he heard and saw, there were registered three impressions and one deduction: "A yacht. The British flag. An Englishman. A fool." Having filed these particulars, Lichtensteiger's mind was about to pass on to the problem of how to get Lichtensteiger to London, when an idea flashed like a blaze of light into his consciousness.

Said Lichtensteiger to himself, "Thunder and lightning! If I had a little boat I guess I wouldn't worry myself about smuggling my dope through no Dovers and suchlike places. With a boat of my own then I would be a smuggler classical and complete. But what's the use? I ain't got no boat and I ain't no sailor. But hold! Attention! The English yacht. That fool Englishman. There are possibilities there. Yes. I guess I go back and take another look at that guy."

Lichtensteiger's second survey of Smith was detailed and thorough, and it confirmed his previous judgment. "Easy meat," said Lichtensteiger to himself, and then, aloud, "Evening, stranger. Pardon me, but I see you're British, and I guess it'll sound good to me to hear someone talk like a Christian for a change. I'm from Noo York, and Otis T. Merritt's my name. I'm over this side on vacation; but I'll tell you the truth, I don't cotton to these darned Dagoes and Squareheads here, not at all. So I reckon to catch the next boat across to your good country, mister, and spend the balance of my trip there with white men. That's a peach of a little yacht you got. I guess you have a first-class time sailing around in her. It's just the kind of game I've always had in mind to try for myself. I'd sure like to look her over. Where are you sailing to next after here?"

"Harwich," answered Smith. "Come aboard and look round if you like by all means; but I'm afraid you won't find very much to see here."

"That's a peach of a little yacht you got."

"Why, she's the finest little ship I ever set eyes on," cried Lichtensteiger a few minutes later, settling himself on the cabin settee. "And to think you run her all alone. My gracious! Have a cigar?"

"Thanks," said Smith. "I do sail her by myself usually, but this time I'm afraid I've bitten off more than I can chew. You see, I've got to get back to Harwich within three days. If I had another man to help me I'd do it easily, but with this wind blowing it's a bit more than I care to tackle alone."

After that, of course, it was easy for Lichtensteiger. He did not ask Smith if he could sail with him; he led Smith on to make that suggestion himself. Then he hesitated awhile at the unexpectedness of the proposal, and when he finally yielded to persuasion, he left Smith with the impression that he was doing him a favour. It was very beautifully done.

That night Lichtensteiger transferred himself and two suitcases from his hotel and slept aboard the *Kate*. At daybreak next morning they sailed. Once outside the harbour entrance Smith found the wind had fallen to a moderate breeze, but it still blew out of the north-west, making the shaping of a direct course to Harwich impossible. Smith, therefore, did the best he could. He put the *Kate* on the starboard tack and sailed her to the westward along the Belgian coast.

It did not take Smith long to discover that Lichtensteiger was no sailor. He could not steer or even make fast a rope securely. His passenger, instead of helping him, was going to be a hindrance and an infernal nuisance as well. Lichtensteiger did all those things which must on no account be done if life is to be made livable in the confined space aboard a small boat. He grumbled at the motion, and the lack of head-room in the cabin. He left his clothes scattered all over the yacht, and he sprawled at ease in the cockpit, so that every time Smith had to move in a hurry he tripped over Lichtensteiger's legs. By mid-day Smith had had as much of Lichtensteiger's company as he felt he could stand. Now that the weather was fine and looked like remaining so, he knew he could easily sail the *Kate* home by himself. He said, "Look here, Merritt; I'm afraid you don't find yachting in such a small boat is as much fun as you thought it was going to be. See those buildings sticking up on the shore there? Well, that's Dunkirk, and I'll sail in and land you, and then you can catch the night boat over to Tilbury nice and comfortably. I'll run you in there in half-an-hour."

Smith's suggestion astounded Lichtensteiger, and produced in him so profound an alarm that he forgot for a moment that he was Merritt. His eyes blazed, the colour vanished from his face, and tiny beads of sweat hopped out upon it. Then Lichtensteiger emitted some Switzer-Deutsch curses of a horrid and disgusting kind, coupled with an emphatic assertion that nothing, not even ten thousand flaming blue devils, could force him to set foot upon the suppurating soil of France. In fairness to Lichtensteiger it must be stated that he very rarely forgot himself, or any part he might happen to be playing. But the toughest ruffian shrinks from venturing into a country which he has betrayed in time of war. And this is what Lichtensteiger had done to France. More precisely, he had twice double-crossed the French Army Intelligence Department. And the penalty for doing this, as Lichtensteiger well knew, was death.

Since Lichtensteiger succeeded in escaping from that country by the skin of his teeth, France was a place which he had taken the most sedulous pains to avoid, and at the sudden prospect of being landed there he lost his grip of himself for fifteen seconds. Then he pulled himself together and grinned at Smith and said, "Dunkirk nix! Nothing doing. I guess not. And don't you make any mistake, brother; I think this yachting stuff's just great. I'm getting a whale of a kick out of it. So we'll keep on a-going for Harwich. Sure, we will. You bet. And no Dunkirk. No, sir. No Dunkirk for mine. Forget it."

Smith said, "Oh! All right," and that was all he said. But he was thinking hard. He thought, "By heavens! That was queer. That—was—*damned* queer. The fellow was scared to death: He turned absolutely green. And he sweated. He was terrified. And he yammered, in German, too, by the sound of it. By Gosh! I wonder who he is? *And what it is he's been up to?* Whatever it was, he did it in Dunkirk—or in France, anyway. That's plain. To look like that at the mere thought of landing in France! Heavens, he might be a murderer, or anything. Cleared out into Belgium and hanging about, waiting his chance to get away probably. And here I am, helping him to escape. Oh Lord, what a fool I was to let him come. I actually *asked* him to come. Or did I? Yes, I did; but it seems to me now that he meant to come all the time. He led me on to ask him. He's a clever crafty devil—and he's twice my size! Oh, hang it all. This is *nasty.*"

Smith was so absorbed by his thoughts that he did not notice the change of wind coming. The *Kate* heeled suddenly to the puff, her sheets strained and creaked, and she began to string a wake of bubbles and foam behind her. "Hullo," said Smith, "wind's shifted and come more out of the north. We'll be able to lay our course a little better now; she's heading up as high as nor'-west. I'll just see where that course takes us to if you'll bring up the chart."

Lichtensteiger brought the chart from the cabin table, and Smith spread it out upon the deck. "Not so good," said he, after gazing at it for a while. "We can't fetch within forty miles of Harwich on this tack. A nor'-west course only just clears the Goodwins and the North Foreland. Look."

"Then why don't you point the boat straight for Harwich," said Lichtensteiger, "instead of going 'way off to the left like that?"

"Because this isn't a steamer, and we can't sail against the wind. But we'll get to Harwich all right, although if this wind holds we won't be there before tomorrow night."

"Tomorrow night," said Lichtensteiger. "Well, that suits me. What sort of a place is this Harwich, anyway? Walk ashore there, I suppose, as soon as we get in, without any messing about?"

"Oh yes. But we'll have to wait till the morning probably, for the Customs to come off and pass us."

"Customs!" said Lichtensteiger. "Customs! You don't mean to tell me the Customs'll worry about a little bit of a boat like this?"

"Oh yes, they will," Smith answered. "Harwich isn't the hole you seem to think it is. It's a big port. We're arriving from foreign parts, and if we went ashore before the Customs and harbour-master and so on passed us there'd be the very devil of a row."

"For crying out loud!" said Lichtensteiger. "What a hell of a country."

Before Lichtensteiger finished his thinking the sun had set, and when he came on deck again, with his plan of action decided upon, it was night. Said he, "Gee! It's black. Where the hell are we now, anyway?"

"A mile or so nor'-west of the Sandettie Bank."

"That don't mean nothing to me. Where is this Sandettie place?"

"It's about twenty miles from Ramsgate one way and eighteen from Calais the other."

"Twenty miles from Ramsgate?" said Lichtensteiger. "Well, listen here, brother. I guess I've kind of weakened on this Harwich idea. It's too far, and it's going to take too long getting there. And I find this yachting game ain't all it's cracked up to be by a long sight. I reckon Ramsgate, or anywhere around that way, will do me fine. Get me? Now you point her for Ramsgate right away and let's get a move on."

"But, I say—look here!" protested Smith. "I don't want to go to Ramsgate. I mean, I've got to get back to Harwich by tomorrow night, and is we put into Ramsgate I'll lose hours and hours. We can't get there till after midnight, and you won't be able to land before daylight at the very earliest, because the Customs won't pass us till then. And—"

"Oh hell!" broke in Lichtensteiger. "Customs at Ramsgate, too, are there? Well, say, that's all right. I'll tell you what we'll do. We won't trouble no flaming Customs—and save time that way. You land me on the beach, somewheres outside the town, where it's quiet and there's no one likely to be around. I'll be all right then. I'll hump my suit-cases into this Ramsgate place and catch the first train to London in the morning. That'll suit me down to the ground."

"But, look here! I can't do that," said Smith.

"What d'you mean, you can't? You can. What's stopping you?"

"Well, if you will have it, Merritt," answered Smith, "I'll tell you straight, I don't like being a party to landing a man—any man—in the way you want me to. It's illegal. I might get into trouble over it, and I can't afford to get into trouble. If they heard in the bank I'd lose my job. I'd be ruined. I'm sorry, but I can't risk it. Why, if we got caught they might put us in prison!"

"Caught! You poor fish," said Lichtensteiger. "How can you get caught? All you've got to do is to put me ashore in the dark in that little boat we're pulling behind us, and then you vamoose and go to Harwich—or Hell if you like. I'll be damned if I care. And you can take it from me, now, brother, you've got to put me ashore whether you like it or not. And if you don't like it, I'm going to turn to right here and make you. See? All this darned shinanyking makes me tired. I'm through with it and it's time you tumbled to who's boss here. You steer this boat for Ramsgate, *now,* pronto, and land me like I said, or by God, I'll scrape that fool face off the front of your silly head and smear the rest of you all over the boat. So—jump to it! Let's see some action, quick!"

Smith doubled up and dropped on the cockpit floor

Smith had never encountered a really *bad* and utterly unscrupulous human being in all his life before. It is even doubtful if Smith had ever envisaged himself as being involved in a fight which was not more or less governed by the Marquis of Queensberry's rules. He would never have dreamed of kicking a man when he was down or of hitting anyone below the belt, and he made the mistake of believing that Lichtensteiger must, after all, be more or less like himself. Smith believed that Lichtensteiger's threats, though alarming, were not to be taken seriously. He therefore said, "Here! I say! You can't say things like that, you know. This is my boat and I won't..."

But Smith did not get any further. Lichtensteiger interrupted him. He drove his heel with all his might into Smith's stomach, and Smith doubled up with a grunt and dropped on the cockpit floor. Lichtensteiger then kicked him in the back and the mouth, spat in his face and stamped on him. When Smith came to he heard Lichtensteiger saying, "You'll be wise, my buck, to get on to the fact that I took pains, that time, not to hurt you. Next time, though, I reckon to beat you up good. So—cut out the grunting and all that sob-stuff and let's hear if you're going to do what I say. Let's hear from you. Or do you want another little dose?"

Smith vomited. When he could speak, he said, "I can't... Ah, God! Don't kick me again. I'll do it. I'll do what you want. But—I can't—get up. Wait—and I'll do it—if I can. I think my back's—broken."

Smith lay still and gasped, until his breath and his wits returned to him. He explored his hurts with his fingers gingerly, and then he sat up and nursed his battered face in his hands. He was thinking. He was shocked and amazed at Lichtensteiger's strength and brutal ferocity, and he knew that, for the moment, he dare do nothing which might tempt Lichtensteiger to attack him again. Smith was sorely hurt and frightened, but he was not daunted. And deep down in the soul of that under-sized bank clerk there smouldered a resolute and desperate determination to have his revenge. Presently he said, "Better now. But it hurts me to move. Bring up the chart from the cabin. I'll find out a quiet place to land you and see what course to steer."

Lichtensteiger laughed. "That's right, my son," said he. "Pity you didn't see the light a bit sooner, and you'd have saved yourself a whole heap of grief." He brought the chart and Smith studied it carefully for some minutes. Then he put his finger on the coast-line between Deal and Ramsgate and said, "There, that looks the best place. It's a stretch of open beach, with no houses shown anywhere near. It looks quiet and deserted enough on the chart. Look for yourself. Will that spot suit you?"

Lichtensteiger looked and grunted. He was no sailor, and that small scale chart of the southern half of the North Sea did not convey very much to him. He said, "Huh! Guess that'll do. Nothing much doing around that way by the look of it. What's this black line running along here?"

"That's a road. I'll put you on the beach here, and you walk inland till you get to the road and then turn left. It's only two miles to Deal that way."

"Let her go then," said Lichtensteiger. "The sooner you get me ashore the sooner you'll get quit of me, which ought to please you some, I guess. And watch your step! I reckon you know enough now not to try and put anything over on me; but, if you feel like playing any tricks—*look out*. If I have to start in on you again, my bucko, I'll tear you up in little bits."

"I'll play no tricks," replied Smith. "How can I? For my own sake, I can't risk you being caught. You're making me do this against my will, but nobody will believe that if they catch me doing it. I promise to do my best to land you where no one will see you. It shouldn't be hard. In four or five hours we'll be close to the land, and you'll see the lights of Ramsgate on one side and Deal on the other. In between there oughtn't to be many lights showing, and we'll run close inshore where it's darkest and anchor. Then I'll row you ashore in the dinghy, and after that it'll be up to you."

"Get on with it, then," said Lichtensteiger, and Smith trimmed the *Kate*'s sails to the northerly wind and settled down to steer the compass course he had decided on. The yacht slipped through the darkness with scarcely a sound. Smith steered and said nothing, while Lichtensteiger looked at the scattered lights of the shipping which dotted the blackness around him and was silent too.

At the end of an hour Lichtensteiger yawned and stretched himself. "Beats me," he said, "how in hell you can tell where you're going to." And Smith said, "It's easy enough, when you know how."

At the end of the second hour Lichtensteiger said, "Gee, this is slow. Deader 'n mud. How long now before we get there?" And Smith replied, "About three hours. Why don't you sleep? I'll wake you in time."

Lichtensteiger said, "Nothing doing. Don't you kid yourself. I'm keeping both eyes wide open, constant and regular. I've got 'em on you. Don't forget it either!"

Another hour went by before Lichtensteiger spoke again. He said, "What's that light in front there? The bright one that keeps on going in and out."

"Lighthouse," said Smith. "That's the South Foreland light. I'm steering for it. The lights of Deal will show up to the right of it presently, and then we'll pick out a dark patch of coast somewhere to the right of that again and I'll steer in for it."

By two a.m. the land was close ahead, a low black line looming against the lesser blackness of the sky. "Looks quiet enough here," said Lichtensteiger. "Just about right for our little job, I reckon. How about it?"

"Right," said Smith, sounding overside with the leadline. "Four fathoms. We'll anchor here." He ran the *Kate* into the wind, lowered the jib and let go his anchor with a rattle and a splash.

"Cut out that flaming racket," hissed Lichtensteiger. "Trying to give the show away, are you, or what? You watch your step, damn you."

"You watch yours," said Smith, drawing the dinghy alongside. "Get in carefully or you'll upset it."

"You get in first," replied Lichtensteiger. "Take hold of my two bags and then I'll get in after. And you want to take pains we don't upset. If we do, there'll be a nasty accident—to your neck! I guess I can wring it for you as quick under water as I can here. You watch out now and go slow. You haven't done with me yet, don't you kid yourself."

"No, not yet," said Smith. "I'll put you on shore all right. I'll promise that. It's all I can do under the circumstances; but, considering everything, I think it ought to be enough. I hope so, anyhow. Get in now and we'll go."

Smith rowed the dinghy towards the shore. Presently the boat grounded on the sand and Lichtensteiger jumped out. He looked around him for a while and listened intently; but, except for the sound of the little waves breaking and the distant lights of the town, there was nothing to be heard or seen. Then, "All right," said Lichtensteiger. And Smith said nothing. He pushed off from the beach and rowed away silently into the darkness.

Lichtensteiger laughed. He turned and walked inland with a suitcase in each hand. He felt the sand under his feet give way to shingle, the shingle to turf, and the turf to a hard road surface. Lichtensteiger laughed again. It amused him to think that the business of getting himself unnoticed into England should prove, after all, to be so ridiculously easy. He turned to the left and walked rapidly for half a mile before he came to a fork in the road and a signpost. It was too dark for him to see the sign; but he stacked his suitcases against the post and climbing on them struck a match. He read: "Calais—1½."

The Bonnie Fighter

DAVID PEDDIE COWAN

MY NAME is Alan Breck Stuart, but let me tell you right away that I am no bonnie fighter. In fact, the sound of a shot fired in anger turns my inside to water and my knees to jelly.

What's in a name, they say? Behind mine, there was a constant fear; a fear of being unmasked as a very young sheep in wolf's clothing. For at the time of my tale I was a boy—a boy fighting in a man's army.

We were in Burma, harried by the Jap invaders; and my job was to take rations on a pack-mule from our base camp to the troops in outposts some miles away.

My talent as a muleteer was meagre. You could have guessed this had you seen me staggering through the jungle with my mule's pack saddle on my aching shoulders, the sweat dribbling from the end of my long nose and spattering moon craters on the dust of the path. But where was my mule? This was the second time it had happened—the second time Molly, my mule, had given me the slip. I swore it would be the last. I wouldn't carry that pack saddle back again for all the tea in China.

But the worst was over.

I looked down the grass-covered hillside to where the thin

rope of blue smoke snaked up the trunk of a tree. Hidden there was the camp. My eye followed the line of the long winding pathway and my mind rejected it. I stumbled off the path and struggled through the waist-high grass in a bee-line for "home".

Sergeant Craigie and the cook, Dim Jim, were the only ones in camp. Craigie was splitting a log. He pointedly ignored my bedraggled arrival, for already he knew all. There was Molly, arrived back ahead of me without her pack saddle. I could see her under the trees tossing her nose bag contentedly.

I placed my rifle against a tree and shrugged myself free from my equipment. I looked across at Molly. At the sight of her I felt my anger bristle anew. "I'm havin' no more to do wi' that one, Sergeant," I said.

Craigie looked up. His expression was one of mild surprise. "Did you get the rations to the Vomul Post?" he asked quietly.

"I did that," I said. "I ran nearly all the way there tryin' to keep up wi' her."

The Sergeant smiled: "I'll see that your commendable speed is mentioned in the right quarter," he said. He took another whack at the log and straightened up slowly. "What's the matter, Jock? Can't you handle her?"

"Handle her?" I said. I could feel my anger flaring. "I'd like fine to handle a pick shaft on her hide for five minutes."

Craigie stood leaning on his axe handle with an air of great patience. "All right, Jock," he said. "Tell me all about it."

"On the way there," I began, "she hit a tree in her hurry. So when I got the rations off at Vomul, I took the saddle off to put the blanket straight. Man, as soon as I had it off, she headed for home. I didn't even have time for a cup o' tea."

Craigie's eyes twinkled. "One o' the hazards o' warfare," he said.

"I caught up with her at the watering point but just as I was about to slap the saddle on her, she slips from under it and heads for home in earnest."

"You didn't carry that saddle all the way from Vomul?"

"Aye, I did that, every foot o' the way," I said with a catch in my voice. The enormity of my humiliation came flooding over me, and I felt myself on the verge of tears. I seized up my towel and rubbed my face and neck. I nodded towards the mule. "Man, she could show the Japs a thing or two when it comes to low cunning." I looked at Craigie. "Can I not hand her over to someone else? I swear it—she'll be the death o' me yet."

Craigie was thoughtful. "I just can't understand it," he said. "She was in the Pack Artillery for three years. She's been very well trained you know."

"Man, they knew fine what they were doing when they got rid o' her," I said.

"Oh, I don't know," said Craigie. "They did say something about her being burned by a hot gun barrel." He waved a hand at her. "That scar on her rump. They said she would start to lash out if she got the smell of a gun again, but she should be all right for carrying rations."

Cook and Sergeant howled like a couple of hyenas

"She would be all right if she carried her own saddle back every time," I said. "That's the second time, too. Ach, ye'd think that I was the mule and no' her."

That twinkle was in Craigie's eye again. "Now that ye know what it feels like to be a pack mule, Jock, you ought to be able to bring a lot more understanding to the job." He started to laugh.

I could see Dim Jim sniggering away in the background as he tended his dixies. Suddenly, the cook and Craigie howled like a couple of hyenas. Molly looked round at them. With her nose bag hanging down, she had the droll look of an old lady looking at them over her specs. She seemed to think it was very funny too.

My pained look set off fresh bursts of mirth.

"Aye, ye can laugh!" I said bitterly.

Craigie regained his composure. "Look, Jock," he said, putting his axe down, "have a word with Murphy when he comes in off patrol today. Maybe he'll take her off your hands. He seems to understand animals."

"Aye," I said. "He ought to at that," I said. "Irishmen and mules have a lot in common."

The Sergeant's smile was without humour. The sort of small toothy grin of a tinker's dog before it bites your hand off. He put on his "On Parade" look. "We'll have to change camp again. That Jap gun opened up after you left this morning. They pulled out again before our artillery could get on to it. Come on—we'll have to get moving."

"There's more than one Jap gun there," I said.

"Not according to Intelligence," said Craigie.

"What do Intelligence know about it? They don't come out here."

Craigie put on his patient look again. "The Gurkhas have found their empties at different places. The Intelligence blokes say it's the same gun. They can tell by the mark of the striking pin."

It did not take long to move camp to a dense clump of evergreens and bamboo where the telltale wisp of camp fire smoke would be less visible from the hills.

About five o'clock, the dusty, sweat-streaked, six man patrol, returned to camp and reported all clear in the hills. I waited patiently until they had all washed and fed, before I approached Murphy with my proposal to hand over Molly.

Murphy looked Molly over as if he was a prospective buyer. "Ach, the trouble wi' that one is her feet," he said wisely.

"She has no trouble with her feet when she wants to be off," I said.

"Sure an' ye must be blind as a bat, Jock," said Murphy. "She's got a sore off-hind on her."

The terms "Off" and "Near" confused me. I did not wish to appear to be entirely ignorant. I approached Molly with caution. I stroked her nearside rump tentatively. She seemed placid, so I stooped and picked up her nearside hind foot. Suddenly, Molly moved convulsively and lashed out with both hind feet. I was no acrobat, but I did a sort of cart-wheel handspring and landed in a heap at the foot of a clump of bamboo. I got up from the dust. A red madness seized me. "I'll beat ye're bloomin' lugs off," I snarled and caught up a pick shaft.

Murphy stepped in and restrained me. He went over to Molly, soothing her with soft Irish endearments. He stroked her and without any difficulty, picked up the other hind foot. He took out his jack knife and removed a piece of flint wedged in the frog. Molly looked round at him softly. There was understanding between them.

Murphy gave me a pitying look. "That stone's been there since O'Riley's mother died. She couldn't put any weight on that foot at all."

I stood shuffling uneasily.

"Ach, I'll take her off your hands for a week or so. Sure, I can't stand to see a beast ill-used like that at all," said Murphy.

I was inwardly rejoicing at my good luck, when there was a hissing rush overhead and the crash of an explosion as a shell landed fifty yards beyond the camp. There was another. It landed short. The men scattered to take cover.

Murphy went back to Molly and untethered her. He was

Scarce had Murphy untethered her when the third shell landed

driving her before him out of the line of fire, when the third shell landed enveloping him in a cloud of dust and smoke. The mule trotted on leaving Murphy lying on the litter of dead leaves. I caught hold of Murphy and managed to drag him clear as three more shells exploded in the camp.

Murphy sat up. "Glory be!" he gasped. "Did that blasted beast kick me head off?" Gingerly, he fingered a three-inch scalp wound on the back of his head.

"How do ye feel?" asked Craigie.

"Och, me head's full o' thistledown," mourned Murphy. "All me brains have run out av the back o' me head."

"Hold still, man," said Craigie as he examined the wound. "If ye ever had any, they're still in there. But ye have a nasty scalp wound; it'll have to be stitched." The Sergeant turned to me. "Take him down to the Field Dressing Station. He'll have to go back to Imphal."

Murphy had a splinter of metal embedded in his skull. The prospects were that when he got back to Imphal, he would be flown back to India.

On the way back to camp, I was absorbed in gloom. The thought of taking over the mule again just when I had got rid of her, depressed me no end. I found myself envying Murphy his wound.

I cursed myself as a sentimental fool for having volunteered to take over the mule in the first place. Truth was I had never seen a mule in my life until I came into the army. I was moved by the patience and endurance of the ugly, innocent-looking animals. The treatment meted out to them by some of the Indian muleteers distressed me no end. So I took over Molly, imbued with the resolve that I would change the order of things in the world of mules and men.

But my mule was a realist. She was quick to sense my inexperience and she took shameless advantage of it. My high resolve had gradually become tainted with the desire to get rid of my charge at the first reasonable opportunity.

With Murphy *hors de combat* my opportunity was gone; and there stood Molly under the trees like the shadow of doom in the growing dusk.

I wrapped myself in my blanket beneath the open sky, knowing that tomorrow would be another day of battling with Molly on the long trek to the post at Monglang. I breathed deeply of the cool mountain air and turned my back on the dark shadow of the mule. The jewels of Orion swam in the clear sky as I sank to sleep.

The following morning dawned bright and cool. I felt strong and cheerful in the new day. I sang as I busied myself with the preparation for the trek with the rations to the Monglang Post. Molly looked meek and obedient under her heavy load.

"Can't give you an escort today either, Stuart," said Craigie "But you can take Murphy's sten gun. It's lighter than your rifle and it'll be more effective if you do meet anything."

I put on my phoney fighting look. "Ach, it'll be nae bother at all, Sergeant. If I meet the Jap army, I'll just liquidate it wi' a squirt from my sten gun an' then we can all gae hame."

Once Molly got warmed up, she moved along at a smooth mile-devouring pace. I was able to keep a sharp lookout ahead as the path dipped and climbed through the jungle-covered hills.

The arrival of rations and mail at a post is always a happy event and I found myself enjoying the banter as I came into camp. "Halt! Who goes there?" came the challenge.

Before I could reply, a voice from the underbush replied: "Haggis on the hoof."

I took the precaution of tethering Molly this time before I unloaded. The midday meal was ready and I was able to enjoy a carefree lunch. After the meal, I collected the empty ration sacks which I rolled in a bundle and strapped to the pack saddle. It was just two o'clock when I took the long downward trail to the ford over the Tweesin Lui on the way home.

As always, on the homeward journey, I let Molly go ahead. She had an annoying habit of treading on my heels or nudging me off the path if I walked in front of her.

I felt relaxed and happy. I knew that the Japs would be unlikely to be patrolling during the heat of the day. I enjoyed the gentle down-hill gradient as I let my eyes wander over the lush tropical growth of plantain, bamboos and evergreens. The beauty of the jungle grasses powdered with dust along the edge of the trail caught at my fancy. Dust had a beauty all of its own. Dust was my destiny.

I came to a deserted Chin village. Molly stopped to graze on the new grass of the cleared area. I filled my haversack with small limes from one of the trees. There was a big bunch of bananas that took my eye. I was thinking about cutting it down, when I saw that Molly had gone on. I picked up my sten gun and ran after her and caught sight of her about a hundred yards ahead as she went round the bend on the final descent to the river. I was not worried. She would stop for a drink.

As I came round the bend, I saw Molly standing in the

shallow water. Five Jap soldiers were standing round her jabbering and gesticulating. A squat authoritative figure gave a curt order and my mule was led away. The remaining Japs concealed themselves in the jungle. They were laying an ambush—an ambush for me, the muleteer.

I looked down at my sten gun and pushed the magazine home. I was shaking like a frightened horse. I put my hand on my hip pocket seeking the assurance of the two loaded magazines I carried there. They were gone.

A great surge of fear hit me. I stood there, my mouth agape in shock. I had always known that I was no soldier, but the stark realisation that I had no guts at all, struck me like a blow. I had a momentary vision of my corpse lying by the trail, powdered with dust and buzzing with flies. Panic flashed its lightning in my mind. I turned and ran blindly back along the trail.

I had covered about fifty yards, when I saw the two sten magazines lying on the path. They must have dropped out as I ran after Molly. At the sight of them, my panic vanished and a measure of confidence began to seep back into me. I picked up the magazines and went off the path to make a wide and stealthy detour through the jungle. I came out on a rocky bluff overlooking the ford. I knew that the Japs were still down there. There was a stillness of fear about the place.

After about half an hour, their patience exhausted, six Japanese soldiers came out of the underbush. There was a curt command and they moved off leading the captured mule.

"They're welcome to her," I said under my breath. She had been the source of all my troubles. Let the Japs have her for a change, I thought. Mentally, I listed her sins against me and drew some comfort from the formidable list, but, after a little, the truth kept nudging at me and I grew sick of kidding myself.

If I had been up with the mule at the ford, I would be dead now, I thought. As it was, by my slackness, I had allowed the Japs to capture my mule without even a protest.

A great disquiet began to grow in me. I once got seven days for losing my water bottle. What would I get for losing a

There she was, surrounded by jabbering Japs,

mule? Ye gods, I wondered. Next to commissioned officers, mules were about the most sacred things in the whole army. You almost had to salute them. I reflected mournfully on my probable fate and decided that maybe it would have been better if I had been shot at the ford over the Tweesin Lui.

I waited in hiding for another half hour. Then I ventured fearfully across the ford. I hurried up the trail away from the river. It was a long hard climb and by the time I reached the ridge, I was gasping and soaked with sweat. I was completely sold out.

As I paused to regain my breath, I could hear my pulse thundering in my ears. I fancied that it sounded just like a galloping horse. I looked along the trail in sudden fear and saw Molly coming up the path from the river at a canter. On the pack saddle was a long ungainly object that bobbed up and down. Every now and again, the mule gave a bucking kick but she was unable to rid herself of the load.

She came past me at speed swerving to avoid my hands. I saw that the load was a gun barrel. It was the gun that had been shelling us! The gun they moved around so that we could

...elf agape and shaking like a frightened horse

never guess its whereabouts—the only weapon of its kind within many miles of jungle. Molly was dark with sweat and flecked with foam. There was no stopping her. She was running wild.

My relief at seeing her again vanished in a dark thought. The Japs would be coming up after her. They wouldn't let their gun go like that and there was at least six of them.

I went off the trail and hid myself in the grass. I had a horror of being shot in the back as I ran along the trail after the mule. My fear was a terrible debilitating thing. It infected everything around me. The very grasses trembled and whispered in terror at my touch.

After a little, I looked up and saw two stocky figures trotting up the trail towards me. A tall slight man followed about sixty yards behind. I crouched down again. The two Japs were abreast of me. They stopped. I knelt up slowly. My sten was on single shot, but when I tried to take aim, I couldn't keep it still. They were bound to spot me and the sten was waving about like a wand. In desperation, I switched to automatic. The leading Jap heard the click. He looked full at me. His eyes were cold and deadly. I grasped the sten in fright and it went off like a two-stroke motor bike.

The leading Jap was caught in the deadly stream as he turned and fell over his comrade who was already down and coughing in the dust.

I swung the sten round on the slim man still standing on the path. I was pressing the trigger and wondering why it wouldn't fire. Suddenly, I realised that the magazine was empty.

The slim man had the lean build and dark skin of an Indian. He threw up his hands. "Nay, sahib," he shouted urgently. "Um nay Japan. Indian soldier, prisoner of war."

The sten went off like a two-stroke motor bike

"Who are you?" I demanded.

"Abdul Sardur Khan, sahib, Frontier Force Rifles, captured at the Sittang River."

"What are you doing fighting for the Japs, then?"

The Indian shrugged. "Want carriers to go to India. Carry guns and stores." He spread out his hands in delicate appeal. "Just coolie work, sahib."

I looked at this ragged ghost of a once proud soldier and was moved by his dignity. "Man, I'm pleased that ye're no Jap. But I'll have to take ye back with me."

"Bote atcha, sahib." His salaam was a stately acceptance.

"What about the others, Abdul?" I asked. "Will they be coming after us?"

The Indian shook his head. "Nay, sahib. Japan sergeant's leg broken when mule get loaded with gun. Kick sergeant on leg. Bote bad wallah." He shook his head. "Other soldiers carry sergeant back. No come."

About half a mile from home, we came upon Molly. She was down on her side. The gun barrel had swung round and was jammed under the roots of a tree. There was foam on the mule's neck and under her belly and a deep groove across her rump that oozed blood. She looked a sorry effigy of the impish Molly that I had come to know.

We unsaddled her and got her up and on to the path again. I replaced the saddle. She just stood there in the dust, head down and trembling. I felt a stirring of compassion for the poor dumb brute. I spoke to her and stroked her fears away. She turned her dark eyes on me with a look so soft and pathetic that a strange feeling that was akin to love flooded over me and I felt tears sting my eyelids.

"All right, lassie," I said. "We'll do the donkey work." I turned to Abdul. "We can carry the gun barrel between us. We haven't far to go."

"Atcha, sahib," said Abdul eagerly. He drew a kukeri which he carried and went to a clump of bamboo. He cut a stout pole about ten feet long. He looked up smiling: "Japan carry gun like this." He pushed the pole through the bore and secured it expertly with strips of green bamboo. We hoisted the load to our shoulders and got under way. Molly ambled ahead of us slightly lame.

As we came down towards the camp, I could see Sergeant Craigie talking to a tall British Officer of the Gurkhas. A section of the Gurkhas were scattered around the camp, alert and watchful as well-trained dogs.

For the first time, I noticed that the back of my right hand was grazed and was bleeding freely. Slyly, I smeared some of the blood on my cheek. I was ready to make my triumphal entry with the captured gun.

As we came into camp, I was aware of a sudden hush. It was exciting and wonderful. We dumped the gun barrel on the ground. I straightened up and gave the officer a quivering salute.

"Private Stuart reporting, sir," I said firmly. "One Jap gun captured, one prisoner taken and two Jap soldiers killed."

"What?" said the officer. "Did you do all that on your own?"

"Aye, sir, I did that." I flicked a drip of blood from my hand. "Just me and my mule."

I looked at Molly. She was standing there on three legs, utterly weary and dejected; dumbly making her report, and I was suddenly sick of pretence. I wiped the blood from my face. "Well, sir," I said. "The mule really did most of it." Then I told the officer what had really happened, for I couldn't take the glory—not after what we had been through together.

"Man, but she's a bonnie fighter," I said.

Skin of the Crocodile

NORAH BURKE

DID I tell you the time I dived into this river to fetch up a crocodile I'd shot, and the son of a devil was not dead, only stunned?

Ah! Well, listen—

Of course, as I am the only man in our village with a rifle, I have had much experience over the years protecting our poor crops against the pig and porcupine and deer which visit us from the jungle, and the leopards which sometimes come for our goats. Even tigers still trouble our cattle, though there are fewer than there used to be when I was a boy.

My rifle is a good one, look. See how well that wire is put on to mend it. I was able to get copper wire, too, that does not rust. I oil this rifle and look after it, for it has much to do.

"Hey, you, Buldeo," Debi Singh will call out to me. "Come and sit in my field tonight and get the old porker—that son of a pig—who is rooting out my potatoes."

I have to be careful of my ammunition, which is expensive—though I save the cartridge cases, of course, and refill them myself—but I can see that Debi Singh is tired from sitting out

99

with tins and clappers all night to keep some of his crops to feed his children, who seldom have enough to eat.

But then that is so for many of us. Most of the year we have to be careful, and we cannot feed wild animals as well as ourselves. Many of us are weak from malaria, especially those who sit out to protect the crops, for the chill wet mists reach up as high as the platforms on which we sit.

"Buldeo!" I hear my name called. "If you want the biggest panther in the whole of India; why, he killed one of my goats last night, and I can show you the kill, too, covered up with thorns, so he means to be back—"

Well, I have looked after us all for years; and in good years I see the children with full bellies. They laugh in the sun, they run with strong legs, and I think of that year when the monsoon failed; we ate the bark of trees, and men had no strength to protect what little food we could grow. So I walk along and look about sharply everywhere with my splendid eyes to see what else I can do to keep us all safe against the jungle. I listen with my fine ears to hear what the leaves and birds are saying.

The first time I saw this crocodile I was watching some duck in a shallow backwater of the river. They were those little ones with bits of green on the head—I do not know the name— and as the sun was behind me I could see every speckle, and those bits reflecting like peacock feather. I was just thinking, *Why, it shines like a rajah's turban ornament,* when there was a surge—a ripple and what I thought was a little crocodile rose among the ducks.

Next moment I realised that what I was looking at was not a whole, small, mugger crocodile, as I thought, but the head of a huge one.

Ohé! What a sight! I have never seen such a creature. The ducks took no notice of him, for crocodiles do not usually bother them much. But this time—one snap of those great jaws and he swallowed a duck whole, like a crumb, and sank again at once while all the other ducks bounced up off the water in a storm of wings and noise.

I really do not know why such a monster—he was longer

than two buffaloes—should bother with a morsel like a duck, and a little one at that, when a whole goat at least would be needed to satisfy him. But perhaps he was just annoyed at them for swimming about over him.

Of course, mugger crocodiles prefer their meat old. When they seize some animal come to drink they drown it and then store it somewhere in holes they dig in the banks, or in underwater caves, until it has rotted. But a little thing like a duck they swallow as it is.

Now I knew well that though we always have muggers in our river, we had not till now had this giant. I know most of the animals in our forest, and this was a stranger. I warned everyone that there was this crocodile in the river and that care must be taken when the women went for water, or if the boys took the cattle across the ford for grazing.

I myself kept a keen look-out for him, to shoot him if I got the chance. This is never easy, as you know. Bullets from the heaviest rifles have been known to glance off big crocodiles, which are made of stone. It is best to aim at the eye or the soft skin behind the foreleg.

But we saw no more of the big mugger for a time, though he took up his abode in our piece of river and seemed likely to stay.

Everything he wanted was to hand. There were deep pools in which to sink himself during the hot weather or if danger threatened. Plenty of fat fish to eat—I have seen shoals of *kalabanse* shimmering in the pools like a shawl under the water. He could fill himself on those, as well as on other things. He could catch monkeys easily when they were drinking, and deer. Then there were long clay banks upon which he could bask in the hot sun. In places this clay is soft, but in others dried to rock, cracked by the sun and drilled by old floods. I always studied these clay banks to see if I could discover his favourite lying-out place.

In fact I was there the day I heard them shouting for me from the village, and I could tell by their voices that something bad was happening.

I raced back as fast as I could. The crocodile had seized

one of the cows at the ford and was trying to pull it into deep water.

Racing up, I recognised the cow. It belonged to the orphan Harkwar and was a great pet, besides being his only animal. The crocodile had hold of this poor cow by the nose. Men and boys were beating the water with sticks, branches, anything that lay to hand, and they were throwing stones. Two of them had hold of the cow's tail to try and save her. Others were holding the boy Harkwar to stop him from dashing into the water to beat at the crocodile with his bare hands.

The noise! Everyone shouting and splashing—I dared not fire for fear of hitting someone. But as I came pounding up I

I dared not fire for

shouted to them all to get out of the way, and when I could I let fly.

Bapri bap! I did no good. It was impossible to take proper aim, even at close range, because the mugger was lashing about in the water and I still panting after running.

I may have hit him, but he took no notice. The cow gave way and with one gigantic curl the crocodile dragged backwards into deeper water and sank at once with his prey.

It was a terrible moment, and as I looked about at everyone in the absolute silence that fell I thought, *Next time it will be one of us.*

Harkwar began to sob . . .

. . . itting someone

Well, we recovered, as one has to, from these experiences—little Harkwar, too—and now the fear was that people would forget, as they do when a danger is out of sight, that it is still there. They would be careful for a few days, and then not.

I determined to get that crocodile.

Often I watched for him at the ford and in other likely places, and several times I saw him and he saw me. We got to know each other. We became old enemies.

What a reptile! Why, it may have been in my great grand-father's lifetime when the heat of the sun hatched the egg containing this crocodile and the little devil scurried like a scorpion for the river—I have seen kites gobbling up those small ones as if they were a hatch of lizards. He may have grown fast or slowly: if there is food they develop, but if not then they wait and grow later. Another thing, if the teeth are torn out in some struggle, new ones appear—a terrible creature.

Once I nearly had him. He was lying with only nose and eyes out of water, as they do, and there was driftwood round about so I did not immediately pick him out. His eyes were on me before mine were on him. He must have been waiting to see if I would notice him, because the moment the lines of driftwood focused themselves for me into crocodile he saw recognition dawn in my face and sank without a sound into the gloom of deep water before I could raise my rifle.

I waded a little way into the sunny shallows to see if I could attract him out of the deeps—oh, you can see everything in plenty of time in the clear, stony water just there—but he was too wise to give me another chance.

That crocodile recognises me, I thought. *Perhaps he even knows that I am the one who fired at him at the ford. I daresay he means to get me ...*

But then I, for my part, meant to get him. There was war between us and only death would settle it. He meant to catch me off my guard one day and drag me down as he had dragged the cow. As for me, I intended to stretch his skin at the earliest possible moment.

What a trophy that would be! To show my grandchildren!

I neglected my other work in order to learn more about this crocodile and his habits. I searched the river up and down, from the place where it leaves its rocky valley and gabbles out wide and shallow over white stones. Even in the sun the water there is yet cold from the mountains, and no muggers go up beyond that place because they do not like the cold.

And I went downriver, too, until I was many *kos* from home. I went past the pool where I had seen a small python swimming that morning and down as far as the cliffs where the fishing eagles nest each year in that very tall tree. Once I went up to get the eggs, you know, but never again! They attacked me! I got only one egg too. The shell is just dirty grey, but if you hold it up to the light it is quite dark emerald.

Well, anyway, I came to decide that the best place to wait for this crocodile was by the clay banks. Wherever the clay was still soft I could see his drag marks; and also there was a persistent rotting smell in that part of the river. I used to wonder what it was until one day I found a place where hyenas had been digging in the clay of the river banks, which was hard there, and cracked, and a smell coming out. This must be the crocodile's larder. Underwater there would be the entrance to some chamber scoured out in the clay by the whirl-pools you can see there during flood. Here he stored his kills.

If I lay in wait here every day, I thought, the time must come when I would get a cool, unhurried shot at him.

Of course I saw him several times before that day came, but either he was too far to fire at or else I could not get a clear line at eye or armpit. But at last the moment came when this monster climbed out on to a clay bank just below me, and I could aim precisely at his right eye.

Bang! The shot went ringing through the valley, sending up the birds. The mugger was thrown into spasms, each contortion taking him towards the water.

I could see I was going to lose him, for a dead crocodile sinks. This was the biggest thing I had ever shot and every man wants a trophy to show for his hunting. I began tumbling down the hillside in order somehow, to stop him reaching the deep water, though what I could do I did not quite know.

Down on the shore I dared not approach the brute, for they can kill you with the tail, of course, and though this one was dead or in his death throes, as I thought, he was still twisting about as a snake does long after it is dead. They say no reptile dies till sunset of the day it is killed.

He reached the water and, while his struggles grew less and less, the current took him out. He ceased to move. He lay there, dead it seemed, and then he sank, leaving behind a twist of bloody slime. I was going to lose him. I was desperate. I snatched off my *dhoti* and waded out, for I thought that if I could get something round his tail perhaps I could drag him back to land.

Of course I could not possibly have lifted such a monster alone—why, it takes sixteen men to pick up a body like that—but this was in the water, remember, so I thought I could manage.

The crocodile had turned upside down, as they do when they die, like fish, and he was sinking into the mist of green water below us. I dived after him. We reached the bottom, where I began at once to get a loop round his tail. At my touch his muscles thrilled, but you know how any reptile will move even after its head is flat, and I thought that was all it was.

Half a minute later I rose for air and went down again. This time, when I touched the crocodile, he jerked and then suddenly righted himself. With the most terrible shock I realised he was not dead—that he was recovering.

Of course, I dropped everything and made for the surface as fast as I could. But he was faster. He threw himself round to see what had touched him, and he came for me at once. Half-conscious though he was, he was faster than I. With two swimming strokes of that powerful tail he reached me and seized a leg. I had time to gulp only one breath, and then he was dragging me down. Of course I struggled, but there was no chance for me. Soon I breathed water and lost consciousness.

If the crocodile had been fully conscious himself that would have been the end of me, I suppose, but he was still stunned from the effect of the bullet. Evidently he did not hold me down in the water as long as muggers usually do with their

*At my touch he jerked around—with the most terrible shock I
realised the beast was not dead*

prey, but pushed me up through an underwater entrance into one of his store chambers while I was still alive, because when I regained consciousness I was lying on a steep slope, head down, in darkness, among filth. A ray of light was falling on me through a crack above and a strong current of fresh air blowing over me.

I was in severe pain and sick, too, but the water must have run out of my lungs as I lay like that, nearly upside down, and then the air revived me.

Below my face there was an opening into the river—an underwater opening. Through it I could see the bottom of the river, lit by green sunlight, and what I first took to be ripple marks in the sand down there, but then saw was a part of the back of the crocodile.

He was resting outside this dreadful den where he had put me and presently he would crawl up into the ghastly chamber to take his feast. I could see remains round me from other things which he had stored and eaten here. I recognised the horns of the poor cow.

When I recovered consciousness I was very sick, almost too ill to care what happened to me. But when that was over I became possessed of terror and also a determination to live. My leg was not broken, although deeply torn. The pain was getting worse and I was covered with blood, but still alive.

This was clay, through which the hyenas had tried to dig down to get at the crocodile's larder. Could I dig myself out?

There was a shoulder blade lying there, of some big animal, and I began to work as quickly and silently as I could. The clay here inside was soft and I scooped my way upwards, throwing the stuff behind me as I went, to make some kind of barrier to delay the crocodile if he took a look into his den.

I was doing well. Behind me the tunnel down to the water was nearly blocked with clay and bones. Above, only a thin layer still held me in.

But this layer had been dried by the sun and was baked almost to rock. As I began to jab at it the noise must have woken up the crocodile for I heard him enter the tunnel behind me. There was an ugly squelch, a slush, a wheezing and a yet more fearful smell. I dug like a madman. I could see trees and sunlight... breathe the sweet air... almost I could get my head through...

Behind me there was a minute's silence as the crocodile's slow brain began to understand what was happening. Then I heard the most terrible clawing sounds, a suck of clay and the drag of a heavy body in the evil darkness as he pushed into the pile.

I don't know if I cried out in my terror. I hope not...

He was at my very heels as I burst out of my prison. How I pushed myself through the small hole I had made I cannot imagine, but somehow in my frenzy I did. Covered with clay and blood I crawled up the hillside, to collapse higher up among the trees, in safety. After that somehow I got home, where my wife treated my wounds at once with the juice of the *brahm buti* plant. I went away to wash and purify myself.

The crocodile? I came back for him later. I set a wire noose in his den and finished him off. That night the children danced on his carcass and stabbed at him with sticks. Here is the skin for which I nearly lost my life, see! It is so long I had to lengthen my house to take it in.

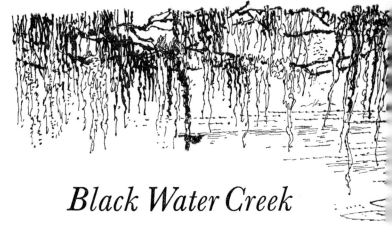

Black Water Creek

ROBERT CRAIG

THE forest towered around him, greyed with the lacework of
Spanish moss, and the creek lay among the trees like a
twisted ribbon; a glistening ribbon the colour of strong tea.

His father, sitting directly behind him in the stern of the
little dinghy, leaned forward until he could whisper in Jeff's
ear.

"Look!" he said. "There! On the bank."

Looking where his father pointed, Jeff saw the curling movement of a deadly snake leaving the water.

"Water moccasin," his father told him as if he didn't know.

The snake disappeared among the cypress trees of the shoreline and Jeff's breath sucked in through his teeth with the
natural excitement a boy has for everything in the woods. He
was stirred by even the sight of the shafts of golden light the
late sun javelined through the tree-pillared world. He was
fascinated too by the butterflies that, like flying flowers, danced
in and out of the purple shadows and the rich light.

His father had taught him how the vines and trees fought
one another for sunlight, each trying slowly to strangle or
suffocate the other. He knew too how the animals lived on
each other's flesh and blood; frogs on insects, 'coons on frogs,

alligators on 'coons. Yet it was only in this Florida wilderness where the massive silence was just nicked at by the song of a bird and the fussing of the dinghy's outboard motor, that he found escape from his own troubles, his own fears, and his own sense of failure.

"Jeff," his father said from right behind him, "watch that tree ahead. It's a fresh windfall. It's big. It could be dangerous."

Ahead of them a great maple had its roots undercut by the current and the wind had toppled it across the creek from bank to bank. Its main column had snagged high in tall ash on the far shore, but its still-leafy crown hung almost to the water.

"I don't like the look of it," his father said, "but we can skim under it. Just don't touch it. Duck low."

The dinghy began moving under it and the tree, beautiful even in its dying, loomed above them.

"Watch your fly rod," Mr. Pitkin called sharply. "Get that tip inside the boat."

Jeff had forgotten his rod. He'd left it propped beside him; its tip, angling upward, was already tangling in the tree. If he broke the tip of his rod now! He yanked it backwards. The butt caught on the stern and as the dinghy pushed in under the tree the rod bent until he knew it was going to snap.

His father cut the motor dead, but it was too late. Right there the current wasn't strong enough to break the momentum of the boat fast enough, and Jeff began fighting the branches of the maple to save his rod. He felt the jarring blow against his wrist of a heavy branch that had been screened by leaves, and instinctively he grabbed at it to stop the boat. For a second he would always remember he was looking at the sky above the creek, and he saw it rolling in on him. And then he knew it wasn't the sky falling on him; it was the tree.

The heavy branch lunged at him viciously and he barely slid out from under it, passing it over his shoulder. His shout of warning was cut in half as the dinghy swamped and he was plunged deep under the dark water. His lungs, only half-full of air, sucked convulsively at his closed throat, and in his moment of utter fear he realised he was pinned to the muddy creek bottom by the many-fingered hand of the tree. On his back he could see the light of the day through the amber water. He struggled furiously but his feet weren't under him and he had no leverage.

There was an instant when he knew he was going to drown, but even in that tick of time he saw his father swimming deep beside him, pulling frantically at the pinioning branches. His father yanked and heaved for what seemed an endless time, although it couldn't have been more than seconds until Jeff felt the weight of the branch on his chest lighten. He wasn't out from under it by any means but he squirmed, mad with fear, and felt it tear his shirt and skin. The sense of floating was like being reborn. He rose; the water broke from his face, and all his life he would remember the sugar-sweet taste of that first breath of air.

He found his father floundering along beside him and he saw that already the current had carried them downstream of the tree. Ahead and to their left where a long-dead log tipped gently into the water, the bank seemed firm enough for a landing, and they struck out for it. The running water slewed them into the mossy edge where they lay on their stomachs in the shallows panting and staring at each other. His father's eyes were only a foot away from his own and his face seemed oddly pale.

"Okay now?" he asked Jeff.

"Yeah. And you?"

"I've hurt my leg," his father said, his teeth making a grating noise. "I—I think—it must be broken."

This seemed immediately impossible to Jeff. His father had been always so stalwart, but the spreading whiteness round his father's mouth, the deepening lines of pain in his face, and the little moans of breath ended Jeff's disbelief.

"Take my hands," his father said. "Pull me all the way in."

Jeff stood up still dazed with surprise, and his father held up his hands to him like a child. Jeff took his father's hands in his

He pulled him up the land as if beaching a boat

113

own and pulled him through the water and as far up the land as he dared, as if he were beaching a boat.

"I can pull you to that sand mound," he said. "It's dry there."

"Let me try it myself."

The sand mound was only ten feet away and his father started pulling himself towards it with his arms and pushing with his right leg, his left leg trailing along strangely useless. Jeff helped him by lifting and pulling him gently by his belt, but he was appalled by the flopping, crippled body of his father. When his father had travelled the terrible ten feet and rolled over on his back to gasp, Jeff knelt beside him, and his tears filled his eyes and ran down his cheeks.

Of all the troubles he had caused—of all the wretched things he had done this was the worst, and he almost couldn't stand the accumulated mass of his anguish. Voices echoed in his mind. His mother shouting at him and crying, "That table has survived for over three hundred years and you have to snap the legs off it!" His sister: "I'll tell Mother you almost set the house on fire!" His maths teacher: "I'm giving you an A in carelessness, an F in algebra." His English teacher reading out the marks: "Jeffrey Pitkin, D minus." His principal: "If I catch you fighting in this school once more I'll expel you." Josephine Wilcox: "If you kiss me again I'll tell my mother." The city magistrate: "I'm releasing you into the custody of your father, but if you're ever caught driving even a motor scooter in this town before you're eighteen I'll remand you to the juvenile court."

And his father? "Make your bed." "Mow the lawn." "Stay away from Josephine Wilcox." "Get to work." "Calm down." "Grow up." "Think."

His father did something even more annoying to Jeff. He was constantly apologising for him as if Jeff were feeble-minded. "He hasn't any judgment yet." "He's growing too fast." "He's only fourteen." "He's at a clumsy age." "He has one foot in boyhood, the other in manhood, and he's stuck on the threshold." "Yes, dear, I'll talk to him again."

And those man-to-man talks! Jeff had thought he was going

to be subjected to another one last night. His father, however, had just sat there on the edge of the bed, rubbing his eyes and drawing one long breath after another for what had seemed a long time.

"We'd better go fishing over the weekend," he'd said finally. "We could leave tomorrow after lunch. How about the St. Johns? We could leave the cruiser on the river, take the dinghy up some sidestream, fish for bass, get back aboard for some sleep, loaf Sunday morning, get home in the afternoon. How would you like that?"

That's all his father had said, and here they were miles up the Black Water and he'd broken his father's leg.

"I'm sorry, Dad." His voice trembled so badly he could hardly control it. "It was my fault. I can't do *anything* right."

"It wasn't your fault." The hand he reached out to Jeff squeezed his arm hard. "I saw how dangerous the tree was. I handled the boat poorly." He let go of Jeff's arm and lay there gasping, trying to gather his strength. "See if you can straighten my leg out," he asked finally, "but easy, boy, easy!"

Jeff saw that although his father had rolled his body on to his left side, his left leg hadn't turned over at all, and Jeff's stomach tightened. He didn't want to touch that leg, but it had to be done, and holding it by the shoe he turned it as slowly and gently as he could. His father's fists were so tight they turned white. He cried out only once, however, and then it was a muffled groan.

"That's better," he said at last. "Now scoop the sand round it and over it. I don't want it to move."

Jeff worked intently, covering his father's denim trouser leg with sand from foot to thigh, and when he finished his father seemed to rest a little more easily.

"Now take a look at the dinghy," he told Jeff, "and find the vacuum kit. It has hot coffee in it."

Jeff worked his way along the shore back to the fallen maple and found that it was entirely prone now, its heavy branches embedded in the creek bottom. Still weak with worry and dismay, he walked out along its thick body until he could see the dinghy. Its white inner decking was showing lemon-yellow through the dark water, and he could see that the ugly muscled branch—undoubtedly the one that had barely missed him and broken his father's leg—had speared through the hull just aft of the thwart on which he'd been sitting. In a dreadful imagining he saw himself still down there pinned on his back—drowned. He shuddered violently and looked round for the vacuum kit. He found it half floating alongside his broken rod and caught in the dead fingers of the maple.

It was only while his father was sipping his second cup of coffee that he looked any better at all.

"We're in a jam," he said. "Do you know how bad it is?"

"How bad?"

"We didn't tell anybody where we were going. We didn't know ourselves. Nobody comes up this creek except crazy fishermen like us. It could be a long time before anybody came up this far."

"Somebody will see the cruiser."

"Remember we anchored it where it would be hard to see."

"But sooner or later somebody will see it."

"Yes, finally," his father admitted, "but there are lots of cruisers anchored in streams off the St. Johns. Even if they saw it, the chances are nobody'd think anything of it, unless they were looking for it." He took another sip of coffee. "My guess is," he went on, his voice a little more ragged with each word, "that your mother won't even get worried until Monday. If they start looking Monday, they might find us in a week."

They'd gone north on the St. Johns River to where the Wekiva flowed in from its forested land. They'd turned west into the Wekiva and followed its narrow, winding channel to its confluence with Black Water Creek. They had anchored the cruiser in the last deep water, and gone on up the twisting Black Water in the dinghy. The Wekiva and the Black Water made a long squiggly Y, and they were at the top of the right branch of that Y. Directly across from them—on the Wekiva—there was an isolated fishing camp on the top left branch of the Y. Jeff was thinking of that fishing camp, and it was as if has father could read his mind.

"It's four miles straight through the woods to that fishing camp on the Wekiva," he said.

"I could walk that," Jeff told him.

"Not that four miles." In spite of his weakness, his father's voice took on that old tone of command for a moment. "You could get lost in those four miles and *never* be found. Even if you could cut your way through it, even if you had a compass, there are swamps to get through and hummocks crawling with more and bigger rattlesnakes than you've ever seen. Don't try it."

The sun was beginning to set and the three-quarter moon was sliding up into the sky behind the lacework of trees.

"It can't be far back to cruiser," Jeff said.

"It's six miles."

"If I just floated and followed the current I'd make it."

"No." His father's voice had dropped to a whisper. "Not tonight. We'll get through tonight somehow."

He seemed to nod, and closing his eyes he dropped off into what looked like sleep.

"Dad?"

There was no answer. The distorted shadows of the forest climbed in round Jeff and the great silence was accentuated by the hum of mosquitoes that were swarming awake with the setting of the sun. They bit his ankles, hands, neck, and face. They even slipped their tiny blood-sucking snouts through his shirt. There was no escape from them and he trembled under the insane touch of fear. To think at all he had to make himself breathe rhythmically.

It was the sudden but subtle torturing by the mosquitoes that interrupted his fear of the growing darkness and drove him to action. He zipped open the bulging side-pocket of the vacuum kit and took out the items one by one, realising for the first time the marvellous survival value of each one: a spoon, plastic container of salt, a snake-bite kit, the steel cylinder that held their dry matches, and the bottle of insect repellent three-quarters full.

Frantically twisting off the top of the bottle of repellent, he slopped the oily fluid into the palm of one hand and started to rub it over his face and neck, but he stopped. His father lay in front of him, helpless with shock. It was too dark now to see them, but he knew the mosquitoes must be already covering his father's body. He remembered that even with a broken leg his father had found the courage to rip him free from the river bottom, and starting at his one exposed ankle he began smearing him with the repellent. He unbuttoned his father's shirt and smeared his stomach and wide chest. He covered his arms, throat, and face. He even remembered to smear some on his father's thinning hair.

In spite of the dark, the loneliness, and his own tortured skin this service to his father gave him a sense of strength he had never before had. It had always been his father who had protected him, and now *he* was protecting his father. *He* had made this decision, and he knew it was the right one, but when he had finished there was no repellent left for himself.

He had heard that mosquitoes could kill a man, and by the time he had made a fire of dried palm shards and dead logs he knew *how* they could do it; bite by bite ... a thousand bites ... ten thousand! He had made his first decision, however, and now he knew what his second would be.

"Dad!" he said, kneeling beside him.

For an answer his father made only a sound in his throat, but Jeff was desperate and he took his arm and shook him.

"Dad! Wake up! Coffee!"

His father came slowly awake. Jeff helped him to lean on one elbow.

"I'm going back to the cruiser," Jeff told him, helping him to sip the last cup of coffee. "Tonight."

"Yes," his father said slowly and thickly, "I guess you'll have to try it. Keep with the current. Never get out of it. Feel for it. Watch for it. Keep—keep your head. Don't let yourself panic." He took a deep breath to steady his shallow breathing. "When you get down to the Wekiva the river widens into a kind of lake. Remember?"

"Yes."

His father took another sip of coffee.

"It's deep," he went on, labouring over his words. "You'll

have to swim for the cruiser. Swim hard... kick hard... splash... lots of noise."

"Why?"

"Just do it. Don't ask."

"Alligators?"

"They'll stay away," he said, admitting Jeff was right. "They don't like too much noise."

He wrestled his fingers into a pocket and took out a key.

"Ignition key for the cruiser," he said, giving it to Jeff. "Whatever you do, don't lose it."

The key was a talisman. It meant he had to go; it meant he had to make it, and with a suffocating sense of foreboding he put it in the tight watch-pocket of his blue jeans.

When he looked back at his father he saw him staring at the grease on his fingers. He rubbed a little more off his chest and studied it in the dancing red light of the fire.

"Repellent?" he asked. "What about you?"

"I'll be under water."

His father managed a tight smile.

"Thanks, Jeff," he said, and put out his hand. "It's going to be rough," he went on as Jeff took his hand. "It'll take guts—but you'll be all right if you don't panic."

Jeff wanted to take his father's hand briefly and let go of it, but he didn't. His father was what little security he had, and the river trip was ahead and he was frightened of it. It lay ahead of him in much the same way that his life did—demanding and ominous—and he wasn't ready for it. A night heron croaked in the darkness. The mosquitoes were biting every inch of his exposed skin. He had to go. He couldn't get away from that trip. He had to make it.

"You'll be all right?" he asked.

"Yes. Good luck, boy."

Jeff took his hand away rom his father's, and knowing that this was the easiest part of his odyssey, he stood up and walked towards the water, trying to look unafraid and resolute. At the touch of water he lunged forward and the cold current embraced him and soothed his insect-bitten skin; but he was instantly engulfed in a swirling dark world that was silvered

The woods around him broke into a riot of noise

only on the top with moonlight.

Breast-stroking to keep his balance, he let the current carry him. He watched the tree-lined banks go by and judged that he was moving about as fast as a man walking. Six miles. Could he make it in two hours? As if for an answer the current slammed him into a jagged, submerged log. It hit him full in the stomach and he was jarred as if he'd walked into a wall. But the creek water didn't let it go at that. It threw him off balance, crowded him on over the log, gashing the soft skin of his side and ripping his shirt. It flipped him upside down and washed him along relentlessly. He came up coughing, choking, and treading water.

"All right," he said when he could, "keep your hands in front of you. Dog paddle, stupid."

Within twenty feet he found out how right he was. His hands hit the next submerged log a split second before his body did and he managed to squirm round it with only a scrape on one leg. After that it was the sharp, broken stubs of old branches protruding from the logs that bothered him. They were like underwater knives waiting to tear at his skin and clothes.

Sometimes the creek was so shallow his bare feet raked through the ooze on the bottom, touching all kinds of dead, moss-covered debris from the forest. Sometimes the water pooled into holes so deep he could go completely under into its darkness without touching anything. It was his master and yet his only hope. It pummelled him, rolled him as if still trying to drown him, and yet it carried him and guided him through the otherwise pathless forest.

Once he found himself beached on a mid-stream sand bar. The width of the pool there and the lilting breeze kept the mosquitoes away and he lay down to rest, his body crying for sleep. He'd wait until sunrise and go on, but even as his eyes closed he thought of his father. He pushed himself to his feet, walked along the sand bar to its end and splashed back into the water.

And then there were the animals of night. He floated within a foot of an egret before it squawked like a startled witch and flapped away, turning into a silver kite on its way to the moon.

At a bend in the creek where he missed the channel and stood up unexpectedly to look for it, the woods round him broke into a riot of noise—squeals, grunts, the pounding of running hoofs and the crash of bodies in the brush. The wild hogs startled him so that he could only stand there in the moonlight and try not to sob, until the mosquitoes drove him back into the water. He saw a doe and two fawns dance away among the trees as if they were ballerinas, and often he came too close to the clownish shapes of 'coon, 'possum and armadillo. And then there was the stuffy-looking bird with the recurved bill. If he hadn't seen it fly before it called, he might have collapsed with shock. It yelled like a man being throttled, its scream echoing through the naves of the forest.

He saw so many animals so close because he was floating in absolute silence with only his head above water. All along the wild river he surprised them at their hunting and drinking, and little by little he became accustomed to looking for them without fright.

It was the unseen and unknown things that lived and died in the black water around him that seemed far more threatening. Time and again he saw the silvered water ahead of him break and splash, and occasionally he saw the silhouette of a powerful back lift above the surface and glide back into the water around him.

Bruised and ripped as he was, Jeff was beginning to think he'd make it to the cruiser when he hit the log jam. There was a channel through it, but when he remembered where it was, it was too late. Completely water-soaked the logs were piled from the mucky bottom to within three inches of the surface, and they lay beneath him like criss-crossed fingers slippery with moss. When he went over the first one and banged into the second one, he found he could neither float nor crawl over them. When he tried to crawl, a knee would slip off and down he'd go between logs, his feet entangled in strange undergrowths.

On his third lunge his right leg wedged in among three or four logs and he fell over backwards, sure that he too would break his leg, but the bone held. He was on his back, however, held by one leg like a 'coon in a muskrat trap while the current flowed over him. Every time he tried to sit up he dammed the running water with his body and was pushed back, and every time he relaxed the water ran over his face and up his nose.

The bone, sinews, and skin of his leg were fired with pain, and his lungs were choked with water. Every time in his life he'd ever been in trouble there'd been someone—his father—to help. Even now, knowing what had happened to his father, he found himself expecting that he would appear and help him. Once he even managed to shout for help because the image of his father was in his mind. There was no answer, of course, and the image faded, and a voice within him said, "You're alone. There is no help."

The next time he came to a partially sitting position he grabbed the thigh of his trapped leg, and in spite of the extra agony he pulled himself still farther forward until he could reach up into the current far enough to grab another log. From there he pulled himself far enough forward to release his wedged leg. After that, what if the logs did tear at the sides of his stomach? He pulled himself across them, and by the time he slid off the last one into deep water he was so exhausted he could hardly swim to the shore although it was only ten yards away.

During his fight to make the shore he noticed that the creek was much wider and markedly warmer. Even the bottom was sandy to the touch of his feet. Clothed now in only the remnants of his jeans, he stood up quietly and stepped towards the shore and into the sharpest terror of the night.

The moon disappeared out of a clear sky and he was instantly imprisoned in a furious, flailing blackness. There were great wings of death beating him and stroking him, and he yelled in horror. He heard his own yell again and again, and as quickly as the moon had disappeared it reappeared and the wings were gone. He was utterly incapable of thought, but his eyes saw the great blue heron pounding off into the moonlight on its eight-foot wing span.

He fell back into the water, crawled to the bank, and lay down until his mind began to explain what had happened. The

Jeff yelled—great wings of death were beating him

heron must have been gliding in for a landing to hunt in the
shallow water. Coming in that way, edge-on in the moonlight,
he wouldn't have seen it, and he'd stood up right in front of
the gliding bird.

Finally the mosquitoes reminded him that he was alive, and
he thought of where he was and of his father, and the need to
care for his father rose uncontrollably. His own muscles and
lungs were beyond weariness, but he crawled back into the
water where the current was so slow he had to start swimming.

He thought perhaps he had a mile to go, but at the next bend
the channel broke sharp right and widened quite suddenly into
an oval looking-glass of water and there was the cruiser. He
scrambled once again for the shore and let the mosquitoes bite

unheeded while he avidly studied the lake, iridescent under the moon.

The cruiser lay back on its anchor-rope, and a patch of mist on the water made it seem far away. From somewhere in the trees an owl to-hooed at him derisively, but nothing moved on the surface of the lake. He was not fooled by the exquisite sublimity of the night. The reptiles were there. He knew too that distance over water is easily misjudged, but he decided that it couldn't be more than three hundred feet away. Only a hundred yards to the end of fear. But could he make it? No. He couldn't. He had neither the strength nor the courage left. But he knew he was going to try to get to the cruiser whether he made it or not.

With sudden decision he sprinted down the narrow sandy beach, diving into the water with a stinging slap and a splash of silver.

Thrashing at the water with every stroke and kicking up a white plume behind him, he swam until his arms ached and his lungs hurt, and when he stopped the cruiser seemed as far away as it had before.

He looked behind and saw that the shore seemed to be almost as distant as the boat, and he turned towards the boat and went on again with his furious swimming.

The next time he looked ahead the anchor-rope was only a stroke away. With the nylon line in his hand he found that the deck was far too high above him and he clung to the rope, feeling like bait, and gasped. The propeller! Sloshing his way to the stern, he reached for the gunwale, stepped up on the propeller, and hauled himself aboard to fall on the decking of the cockpit like something wounded, but his hand was already groping in his watch-pocket for the key to the ignition.

When the engine was going and the anchor up, he turned the cruiser and headed down the Wekiva for the St. Johns River. He followed the drifting paths of the moonlight-tinted water hyacinths, and the wake of the cruiser boiled out to wash the shores with motor-made waves. He thought it would take half an hour to the St. Johns and maybe an hour to Sanford, but misfortune isn't a steady flow of trouble.

He rounded a sharp bend in the Wekiva, and as the moon seemed to move to one side there came the sound of shouted curses from the darkness of a cypress stand. The channel was wide, and he cut the engines and spun the cruiser back in its own wake.

"Who do you think you are?" a hoarse voice yelled at him. "Come ovah hea and I'll break yo damn neck!"

He could see them now, two fishermen in a small flat-bottomed boat that plunged and reared like a frightened horse in the cruiser's wash.

Jeff pulled the cruiser in beside them, completely unafraid, and sure of his ability to meet even an angry man.

"Come ovah here and I'll break yo' damn neck!"

"There's been an accident," he said, and the strength of his voice surprised him. "My father's up the Black Water with a broken leg."

"How far up is he?" the man asked, anger suddenly gone from his voice.

"About six miles."

The man turned to his companion.

"Make fast, son," he said, "and git aboard. We're going up the Black Water."

The fire he had left burning so brightly was only a glowing ember when he came back to it, and the moon was low in the west.

As the fishermen's boat skidded up the bank he jumped clear, ran to where his father lay so quietly, and dropped down beside him.

"Dad! I'm back. A Mr. Wilson and his son are here. We've got a boat to take you out."

His father opened his eyes, looked at Jeff for a long moment, and slowly reached out and put his hand on his shoulder.

"You're a good man, Jeff," he said quietly.

Sir Galahad and the Bad Man

HARWOOD STEELE

BLUE-STREAK Joe", the "bad man", rode into Mustang at full gallop.

Mustang (population 300) lay dozing on a hot midsummer afternoon and on a branch of the Canadian Pacific Railways a few miles north of the State of Montana. Up till now, nothing could have been quieter. But now Joe proved that this peace had been no more than the calm before the cyclone.

As he dashed past Ping Ling's Laundry, the first place he came to on Main (the only) Street, he raised his hands and began to utter war-whoops, while from his guns blazed a deafening fusillade.

Mustang snoozed on. It had heard the shots and the yells, but waking up Mustang took time. Arriving at the far end of the street, Joe halted. Disappointment, born of the town's seeming indifference, sat heavily on his face, while his lanky, powerful figure, in the conventional panoply of the cowboy, drooped sadly. But, not to be beaten, he reloaded and, putting spurs to his horse, rode back along Main full blast, as if less than one jump ahead of the entire Blackfoot Nation.

So now Mustang yawned, sat up and took notice. Men, women and, inevitably, swarms of children ran out to gape at this strange being, and curious heads appeared at many windows. They did not stay there long. As soon, in fact, as their owners realised that the being was a bad man, firing real bullets from real revolvers, they ducked back into cover. Joe, delighted with results, hastened the disappearance of the staring faces at the windows by firing at them.

Opposite the Lone Wolf saloon, he dismounted. Terrified outposts spread the news: "Sacred rattlesnakes, boys, he's comin' in here!" There followed a wild dash for safety. Chick, the bartender, deliberately ignoring the common emergency, protested strenuously against an invasion of the bar, vowing, when the invaders howled down his assertion that they had no business there, that there was only room for himself. As he was a large, fat man, who took up a great deal of space, this was very nearly true.

The announcement of Joe's approach had barely been made when all hands except the gentlemen under the tables had disappeared. These were not cowards. None of them had a weapon. Canadian cowboys did not carry guns on social occasions.

Joe came in. His first procedure was to root everybody out of cover. The bartender, stuck almost immovably in a sort of cupboard, refused to emerge. Joe fired a bullet into the bar above his head and, with quite exceptional agility, Chick, yelping pitifully, bounced out of his hiding-place like a rubber ball from a box.

"Drinks for the house!" commanded Joe, revolvers pointed.

"Ah, say, d'you want to land me in the breadline?" asked Chick, who was also the proprietor.

"Make it slippy," Joe insisted.

The drinks were produced. The house sheepishly, yet not ungratefully, drank "Blue-streak's" health. But the kick in the liquor evaporated somewhat when the visitor made a team of Mustang's leading citizens, long past such capers, dance a

Highland reel to "Turkey in the Straw", shakily strummed out by Mozart Schmidt on the Lone Wolf piano while Joe's revolver shots kept time. Worse followed. "Forty-Rod" Milligan, perpetual mayor, who chanced to be present, was ordered to stand against the wall, holding out his hat, which the bad man riddled, poor Chick punctuating the silences between with wails of anguish as ricochets smashed mirrors and went through pictures.

Some murmured a word about sending for a Mounted Policeman.

"Mounted Policeman, huh?" Joe sneered. "One of them red-coated luridly adjectival very improper nouns? Why, there's no such guy in Mustang! But you shorthorns can tell the Mounted Police, from me, that this galoot will fight 'em all at once, free-for-all or go-as-you-please, any time they dare—yep, dare—to poke their snoots into my hog-wash. So long! I'll call again. An' Mr. Blue-streak Joe, from Antelope, is my name."

With that he left, wisely headed, in spite of all his big talk, for the boundary line.

He was almost clear of Mustang when he saw Betsy, draped over her home fence and watching him coolly. His spectacular arrival Betsy had greeted with delight, as something to break the town's utter monotony. And her scorn for the timidity of its people—"a hundred able-bodied men bulldogged by one lone cowboy"—had held her at the fence for the past ten minutes, in the hope of just a squint at him. After all, wasn't he like one of Tennyson's Knights of the Round Table? Wasn't he? No, he wasn't. But at least he bore a mighty close resemblance to his false knaves, churls and caitiffs, which was something.

At sight of her, Joe halted—Betsy, a strapping, handsome girl, could halt a locomotive. Clumsily he took off his hat, grinned from ear to cauliflower ear, and said, "Lady, how do!"

Her reply surprised him, "Put an egg in your boot and beat it!" Then she flounced back into the house. Joe's grin widened. He liked 'em lively. "I'll be back!" he yelled, as he pressed on leaving yet another heart tied to Betsy's saddlehorn.

Superintendent Praed commanded the district concerned with these nice goings on but, at the time, knew nothing about them. The catch was that the Mounted Police, totalling only a few hundred men to safeguard an area bigger than most European countries, let alone Texas, could not afford to post a constable permanently in Mustang. And before Forty-Rod Milligan could lay a complaint against Joe in the lap of the nearest detachment, the bad man was safely in Montana.

Praed rasped, "They want me to send out a man whenever a duck quacks!" Still, he promised to post a single constable, temporarily and as a special case, in Mustang, with orders to gather Joe very quietly in, should he reappear. He did not believe that Joe would reappear. But even a single constable would stop Mustang shying at its own shadow. And, if the bad man actually did come back, that constable could deal with him.

Better send "Flaming Andy" (Constable Andrew Clint). Andy's hair was the colour of vermilion war-paint, clashing horribly with the scarlet of his serge jacket and, being big, broad-shouldered, fearless and impulsive, he was the spittin' image of a buffalo bull. His day-to-day record suggested an ambition to raise as much merry hell as he could within the limits of the North-West Mounted Police Act (36 Victoria, Chap. 35). This made him what his sergeant-major called "the thorn in my tortured flesh." But he did everything important well, and could and would bring in Old Man Coyote and every other devil known to priest or medicine man if the Commissioner so ordered it. Besides, Andy was getting restless.

So Praed told him, with a grizzly growl: "Go to Mustang! Stay there till Blue-streak Joe shows up again! Arrest him! If he resists, you know the drill—"

"Yes, sir," said Andy, looking as if saddle-soap wouldn't melt in his mouth. "I can use just enough force to overpower him but no more—see *The Constable's Manual*, Sec. 6, Para. 4, footnote!"

"Exactly!" snapped Praed, while Andy made himself scarce with his best salute.

Meanwhile, Betsy made Mustang feel small. Blue-streak Joe,

she said, had branded the townsmen for what they really were; and what *that* was she detailed through a vocabulary astounding in a nice young girl who had never even been to Saskatoon.

Now Andy rode into Mustang, not war-whooping on the dead jump but slowly, with dignity and in full dress, to restore confidence. Sitting as straight in the saddle as the lance he bore through the Musical Ride, he looked as if his entry should be heralded by a great flourish of trumpets. Mustang shouted its welcome. And even Betsy, back at the home fence, said "My!" But that was under her breath. What she added, right out loud, perhaps because His Magnificence did not so much as peek sideways at the prettiest girl in the border country, was: "Hail, Sir Galahad!"

Andy scorned to reply. But the sarcasm struck deep, as no Force member worth his salt ration would boast, "My strength is as the strength of ten, because my heart is pure," much less, "I never felt the kiss of love or maiden's hand in mine." If it had been Lancelot, now, "the great knight, the darling of the court, loved by the loveliest" and "bruised and bronzed" or even Modred, "like a vermin in its hole." But Galahad! That sissy! So, though keeping mum, Andy flushed till his neck was ruddier than his vermilion hair.

Getting his own back did not take long. His first duty being to meet every one in town and establish himself on a friendly basis, he began a round of social calls that very evening. Not unnaturally, he started with the home of Jimmy Cavanagh (Flour and Feed, Insurance, Mortgages, Money to Loan), who just happened to be Betsy's dad. And not unnaturally, Betsy just happened to open the door.

Said Andy, very politely, "Are the grown-ups in, Betsy?"

Haughty as be-damned and Queen Guinevere (being three years out of high school) Betsy retorted, "Miss Cavanagh to you, sir—" then spoilt the whole thing by adding "Galahad!" and rushing upstairs. There, locked in her bedroom—the Lady of Shalott in her tower—she spent the next half hour making mental notes, for future guidance, on how Lynette brought Sir Gareth to heel by calling him names, while Andy discussed crop reports with Mr. Cavanagh and a Stonewall Jackson cigar.

Over Mustang hung tension, as at the approach of hail or summer frost.

Till, sure enough, remembering sauce-box Betsy, Joe came back.

He had a keen sense of the dramatic. Betsy, he felt, would be more impressed if he staged his next exhibition of gun-play without notice. Her absence—she was driving around with Dad in the buggy to look at those crops—marred the big moment. But still it had its points—the town again hushed in a summer afternoon, Flaming Andy and the flies dozing together in his temporary detachment and the Lone Wolf peacefully drinking and talking cattle prices as Joe burst into the saloon in a breeze of bullets.

"It's the bad man!" yelled the crowd, stampeding into cover.

Joe did not make them come out this time. Instead, to improve, as he thought, on his first performance, he began shooting at anything that took his fancy. He put a bullet through the portrait of the reigning Sovereign, another through the matching lithograph of the current President, for Joe was quite impartial. He shattered bottles on the tables. He blew taps off. And he regularly bawled, "Bring on your Mounted Police!"

The answer to his bawling proved worthy of Tennyson at his best. Joe was taking leisurely pot-shots at a match-box trembling on the shiny pate of Baldy Jones and, except for the crash of his revolvers and the chattering of Chick's dentures, the Lone Wolf was absolutely silent when Andy suddenly appeared through the swinging doors. Forty-Rod Milligan had slipped out to get him, unbeknownst. And he now came at the double, buckling on his .45 as he burned the trail. Looking like a big red barn, he coolly sized things up, then, speaking to Joe, through a lull in the firing, gently uttered two tremendous words:

"You're pinched!"

Joe, who had not seen him, spun round, quick as a cow-pony. He gaped, amazed to find a Mounted Policeman actually in Mustang. But, soon recovering, he grinned and shouted:

As the empty gun fell, Andy grabbed the other hand

"Come an' git me!"

True to the old tradition of never drawing a gun until he had to, Andy marched slowly towards him in silent acceptance of Joe's invitation. Shaken into panic, Joe lost his ugly head, opening up with the full weight of his artillery. In no time, the big red barn turned back into the buffalo bull—charged, head down, through a fury of fire—miraculously survived it—closed.

The bad man, now, had only four shots left and all in one revolver. As Andy reached him, he dropped the empty gun. Andy grabbed the hand holding the other and kicked the useless weapon out of reach. In a blizzard of curses from Joe—Andy never let out a peep—the warriors whirled three times around the room. Three times Joe fired but Andy's crushing grip spoilt his aim. Tables and chairs went flying, Mustangers scattered like steers before the rush of wolves.

Joe managed to beat the policeman to his knees. In half a jiffy, the bad man would get his gun free and his last shot would make Andy the centre of attraction at the next coroner's inquest. But somehow Andy recovered himself and the watchers roared as they saw that this second revolver was now in his hand, then pitched into a far corner, like the first. It was man to man now, unless the constable drew his gun. This Andy scorned to do. He wanted a straightforward trial of strength, nothing less. Appreciating his sportsmanship and on fire to see Canada's Glory pound the Pest of the Prairie into paste, his supporters gave another thunderous cheer.

Round and round again, arms spinning, like two threshing machines in fits. Andy staggered the bad man with a terrific drive. Joe regained control and charged. They clinched. Joe forced the policeman down on to a table. His long fingers were at Andy's throat. The table disintegrated. Andy got somehow to his feet and Joe to his. The bad man seized a chair. The crowd howled a warning. Andy dodged nimbly and the chair was shattered to bits.

Andy might now resort to similar weapons, under the laws of chivalry and of bar-room scraps. But he was more determined than ever to get this gorilla with his bare hands. Wild

To shouts of acclaim the gladiators burst throug

blood thoroughly up, he closed once more. Locked in a deadly embrace, the two men spun towards the door. To the left stood a tasteful Japanese screen, a veritable collector's piece. A sudden twist threw Andy off course and brought screen and wrestlers down together. Joe rose with his shirt in shreds. As for the screen, no collector—veritable or otherwise, except, perhaps, a junk man—would have looked at it.

They clinched again. But Andy evaded the issue with a wiggle worthy of Minnehaha in her favourite war-dance. Joe rushed him to the bar, pinning him against it with an intense bombardment. Though ruffled, Andy got Joe by the hair—in its mind's eye, the crowd heard the rasp of his scalping-knife. Joe screeched a high C quite as good as a coloratura soprano's and yelled red, white and blue murder as Andy swung him on to the bar for a brisk massage. Bottles and glasses cascaded,

or, and Andy lifted Joe with one terrific uppercut

crashing to the floor, then Joe and Andy cascaded into them.

Finding their feet, the punch-drunk pair exchanged hay-makers with awful deliberation, till Andy flung Joe into the wall with a slam that shook the building. This was too much for the reigning Sovereign. His picture leaped from its nail to the bad man's head, half stunning him and showering him with glass. Andy, glorious in raw manhood, waited for Joe to recover. But Joe, the caitiff, suddenly stooped and hurled a spittoon straight at him. Andy ducked and the thing rocketed through the Lone Wolf's last unbroken window.

That spittoon really riled Andy. Bottles, yes! Pickaxes, yes! Guns, undoubtedly! But spittoons weren't fair. So now he went for Joe in earnest. Rushing him to the piano, he banged out all the chords in Liszt's "Hungarian Rhapsodies" with the bad man's rump, though normally neither Joe nor Andy could play a note. Then, tossing him into the shrinking laps of Chick and Mozart Schmidt, Andy stood back.

"Had enough?" panted the pillar of law and order, rocking on its base but pulling out handcuffs.

No reply—the bad man tried to speak but could not. And the onlookers were similarly stricken dumb, so that a tomb-like hush held the wrecked and smoke-filled room.

"Had enough?" Andy gasped again.

But, no two ways about it, Joe was game. His clouding gaze roved here and there till it came to rest on the Milwaukee brewery's outsize colour print of "Custer's Last Stand". That turned the scale. Suddenly he tottered forward and, taking Andy off balance, collided with him so violently that the handcuffs sailed into the chandelier and the Redcoat Rider, and Joe in his own "last stand", burst through the swing-doors into Main Street.

Here 202 people—all Mustang's 300, less infants, invalids, the aged and those already packed into the Lone Wolf saloon—waited fearfully to find out who was murdering whom. They'd been waiting since Joe's first shot woke Granny Grimes, who'd come west in a Red River cart and bounced her back through many years to the time of the North-West Rebellion, yelling, "Git yer guns, boys! It's Big Bear!" Among them, now, as Andy hazily saw through nearly bunged-up eyes, was Betsy. Newly returned from crop inspection, she was standing on the seat of the buggy. And, in the uproar following the totally unexpected appearance of the gladiators, he realised not only that his own honour and the honour of the whole Force were just about lost but that she was hollering, as no lady ever should—though this was certainly no place for a lady:

"Go to it, Galahad; Rope 'im, ride 'im—" and much, much more.

Lifted to supreme heights by her support and that detested name, now publicly jammed around his vermilion crown, Andy in turn lifted Joe, with one terrific uppercut, into oblivion.

So it was over—the clash that made the battles of Waterloo and Gettysburg look like the balcony scene in *Romeo and*

Juliet. Compare the *Moonlight Sonata* with those *Hungarian Rhapsodies!* Or Boadicea in her chariot with Betsy in her buggy! Said Mustang, "Don't be goofy! No comparison—"

Anyhow, the last word lay with Andy. Having delivered Joe to the divisional guardroom and changed his uniform, he marched into Praed's office to follow up his written report on Joe's defeat.

The superintendent looked him over without speaking for almost a minute, eyes like big guns glaring from a turret to take in every detail—the bruises, the swollen lips, the left arm in a sling—and loosed a heartrending groan. Yet his anguish was eased a little by the cocky air, the gleaming buttons and boots. Then he read from the written report in a voice which echoed the snarl of a grindstone sharpening the headman's axe:

"Appendix A: Damage government and private property:

"1 jacket, regulation serge, destroyed

1 shirt, regulation (collar size 16), destroyed

1 cowboy outfit complete, ditto

1 antique Japanese screen, greatly prized, ditto

2 lithographs, ditto, ditto

27 glasses, ditto..."

And, breaking off, he roared;

"Ditto, ditto! I'll ditto you, by Judas! Roast and toast your utterly lost soul, I told you 'Take him very quietly!'"

"That's just what I did, sir. Forty-Rod—er—Mr. Milligan, the mayor, says I used admirable restraint!"

"Speak when you're spoken to! Then how about behaving 'without fear, favour or affection', as your oath requires? 'Without affection'! Pah! You were egged on by that confounded girl, that Betsy—I know, I know, the poor simp now wants to marry you—but if the Commissioner says okay, I'll eat my saddle, girths and all! Oh, well, never mind"—and Praed's face broke into a marvellous grin—"you did a first-class job! And I wish I'd seen that arrest!"

"Sir, your own deeds were my inspiration!" said Andy, meekly.

Monkey - Face

ARTHUR CATHERALL

MOST of the men aboard the big whale factory ship *Vaagso* had heard of Monkey-Face, but few of them had actually met him, for he was a deckhand on one of the little whale chasers. Those who had seen him said he was more like an ape than a man. He was big and strong, and so ugly of face that he defied description. Only one man had ever forgot himself and addressed him as Monkey-Face. No one was tempted to use the nickname again, for when they parted the fighters it was not Monkey-Face who was carried to the Sick Bay. The man was a good seaman, but he made no friends.

Dave Hawker had heard of him, but working as a radio operator on the factory ship he saw little enough of the whale chaser crews and did not meet Monkey-Face until the day he was called on deck and told he was to make a trip with the whale chaser, *Blue II*. The radio operator from that bustling little chaser had a dose of yellow jaundice and would be out of action for some time to come.

It was a frightening experience to be slung in a basket from

140

the factory ship down the salt scarred sides to the bobbing, dancing little chaser below. One moment the vessel was leaping upwards on a wave, the next it was dropping swiftly away into a deep trough. Then rough hands grabbed Dave and whisked him out of the swinging basket. He turned to say "Thanks" to the man who held him fast. He did not say "Thanks". The word stuck in his throat, for he was looking at Monkey-Face and the stark ugliness of that man robbed him of words.

Monkey-Face had been smiling, but the smile faded as he saw the look on Dave's face. He knew what this young Britisher was thinking, and he turned away, a scowl making his ugly features even more ugly.

"I ... I say, thanks very much," Dave had recovered, and was ashamed of himself. "It's pretty ghastly coming aboard. I've never been slung in a basket before like ..." and there his words tailed off into silence. The big man, with the receding brow and outjutting jaw—so like an ape—had glared at him, then turned away to do some essential piece of work.

In one way Dave was glad of this chance to see a whale chaser in action, and when the *Blue II* was steaming away from the factory ship, and he had a chance to speak to the bearded skipper, he told him how much he was looking forward to seeing whalechasing at close quarters.

The burly Norwegian laughed.

"I can't promise to let you shoot a whale," he said, "but I'll see you get a look face to face with the business. Just wait."

Dave had to wait until next day, for they steamed over a hundred miles before the look-out in their masthead crow's nest bellowed: "There she blows," and with an outflung arm indicated the direction.

The powerful engines which had been pushing the *Blue II* along at an economical ten knots, began to make the sturdy little vessel thrum and quiver. The gunner went out on to his little catwalk in the bows and loaded the explosive charge into the harpoon.

The days of driving a harpoon deep into a whale and then hanging on to it until it died were gone. A few seconds after

It was alarming to be slung overboard in a basket

the harpoon went home the explosive charge blew the life out of the whale, and that was that. It was quick, clean, and as painless as it could be.

Dave was almost holding his breath as they drew near the submarine-backed whale. Would it dive before they got near enough for the grizzle-haired gunner to squeeze his trigger? The whale seemed to be resting on the surface. Then its big fluked tail lifted, sign that it was going to plunge down. Perhaps it had felt the vibrations of the *Blue II*'s screws; on the other hand it might have got all the air it needed.

Bang! Dave jumped as the harpoon gun was fired. He did not see the barbed arrow streak out, but he did see the yellow coils of rope spin in the thin sunshine. He saw the whale thresh the water into foam and vanish. Then, from below the surface came a dull *boom-m-m*. That was it! The explosive head of the harpoon had done its work, and within half a minute the whale surfaced, dead!

It was as the *Blue II* slid alongside that her captain called for Dave. He was grinning as he indicated the whale.

"All right, Hawker," he said. "Get down on to her and pump her up. You said you wanted a close-up of whaling. Now's your chance."

Dave shot a quick glance at the members of the crew standing about. They were tough, bearded Norwegians, and they were all grinning. They obviously expected him to shrink back and shake his head. It was a challenge, and though Dave did not want to slide over the side on to the back of the whale, he somehow managed what he hoped was a jaunty grin, and climbed over the rail.

There were yells of appreciation from the *Blue II's* crew They liked a man with guts. A big man followed Dave, a long knife in his right hand. Somebody yelled to Dave to "Catch," and a few moments later a hose-pipe with a long slender nozzle was being handed down to him.

Dave's companion was Monkey-Face. He was smoking a huge pipe, and as Dave watched, Monkey-Face thrust the knife deep into the whale's back, making a slit into which the long thin nozzle had to be thrust.

To save time the whales are pumped full of air, so they will remain afloat until the catcher has a few to tow back to the factory ship. As Dave held the nozzle in the incision Monkey-Face had made, a motor aboard the catcher began to throb, and compressed air pulsed into the whale, pumping her up as a football is pumped up. When sufficient air had been pumped in, the nozzle would be withdrawn, a plug forced into the slit, and a flag would be stuck into the whale's back showing that it was a *Blue II* prize.

Suddenly there was an excited yell from the man still in the crow's nest, and within seconds there was a second *boom!* Another big whale had sounded just ahead of the whale catcher. The gunner had fitted his next harpoon and had been about to fill his pipe. He wasted no time, and the harpoon went home in one of the biggest bull blue whales he had ever seen.

One thing went wrong immediately. The bomb in the harpoon nose did not explode. Dave did not realise it, for he was suddenly horrified to see the *Blue II* beginning to edge away from the whale on which he was standing.

A man on the catcher yelled: "Pull the hose out... we'll come back for you."

The air hose was tightening rapidly, and would certainly have snapped if Monkey-Face had not whipped out the slender nozzle and allowed the hissing air hose to go free. It was hauled aboard the catcher as that vessel suddenly began to make speed. Her engines were churning up a wash of foam, and the mighty blue whale was helping her. He was a big bull stung to fighting rage by the harpoon in his back.

Dave jumped as the harpoon gun was fired

Dave turned to Monkey-Face, an expression of horror in his eyes. The big man took out his smelly pipe for a moment and then grunted: "They come back soon... do not worry, little boy."

Within five minutes he was proved wrong. The *Blue II* was never to return.

The chaser had tackled some hard-bitten bull whales before, but none like this. The big blue whale was a fighter, and he was close on ninety feet long, and may well have weighed as many tons. For just over a minute he went straight ahead then suddenly turned and came round in a quick half circle. Aboard the *Blue II* the captain yelled for the line to be cut. He could see the danger; but before the axe could fall on the taut rope, the damage was done. The catcher began to heel as the taut rope snagged under the rudder and the starboard screw. The trim little craft began to heel. It seemed impossible that she could turn over; but she did.

She heeled in one quick, steady movement. Dave saw the red painted plates normally below the waterline riser up and up. He could see her bilges, the grass and barnacles on her sides, then she turned completely over. There was a terrific crash, clouds of steam; a thumping explosion from below the surface as some heavy object tore loose, and then all that could be seen was a great mass of foam-flecked water, with huge wave rings spreading out and out, until they hit the whale on which Dave and Monkey-Face were standing in awe-struck silence.

Monkey-Face was a seaman from the toes up. He sensed what was coming and dropped to his knees. Dave wondered why he did that, but a moment later, he knew. As the first wave hit them the whale on which he was standing gave a sullen little roll, and Dave lost his balance. He tried desperately to save himself, but he never had a chance. Over the side he slid, and icy cold waters engulfed him.

It was Monkey-Face who hauled him back on to the whale, and it was Monkey-Face who slapped him across the side of the head and yelled: "Don't stand like big fool... dance...

The big whale had snagged the rope u

yump about ... or you freeze."

Dave did begin to *yump* about, for the disturbed water had quietened again. The foam which marked where the *Blue II* had gone down, taking every man with it, was calm as a mill pond once more. Only a few little floating objects told the tragic story. There was a lifebelt, a pipe, an upturned box, and one or two other bits of flotsam.

While Dave jumped and tried to keep himself from freezing, Monkey-Face was beginning to undress. He stripped to the waist, and Dave had never seen such a barrel-chested figure before. He was muscled like a Colossus and the red flannel vest he finally held out to Dave was long enough to come below his knees.

"Get it on ... boy," he grunted. "Get off your own wet

rudder and the catcher was turning over

t'ings... or you die purty quick," and he grinned, showing
teeth dyed brown from tobacco chewing and smoking.

Dave stripped, but before he put on the long vest Monkey-
Face rubbed him down. He had big hands. To Dave they felt like
files, for the palms were rough and calloused. They turned the
blue-ing skin of Dave's chest and back an angry red; but they
did start the blood circulating again. Ice was beginning to
crackle in them as he dropped his sodden clothes on the back
of their dead whale. He donned Monkey Face's long flannel
underpants, while that man was getting back into his thick
Fearnoughts, trousers which are almost like felt for thickness,
and guaranteed to withstand plenty of water before they get
really soaked.

They were both cold when they had finally divided Monkey-

Face's clothes, and they looked around in vain for signs of some other chaser. How long it would be before the factory ship's spotter plane took off to look for the vanished *Blue II* they did not know; but if it were too long there would be a dead whale and two dead humans.

"Do you hear... somet'ing?" Monkey-Face asked, cocking his head a little to one side.

Dave, sudden hope making his heart begin to thump, looked round as he asked: "Hear what? A ship?"

"No. A hissing. Listen... hard. You hear it?"

Dave knelt down because Monkey-Face forced him to kneel. There was no resisting the pressure of that big hand on his left shoulder. Kneeling there he heard it... a steady low whistle. It might have been a far distant train blowing off steam, except that there were no trains within a thousand or so miles.

"What is it?" he asked.

"You hear it?" and Monkey-Face seemed relieved. "I am glad. I t'eenk for a minute I go mad, since you do not hear. You know what it iss?"

Dave shook his head, and frowned as Monkey-Face pointed a gloved hand towards the slit he had made in the whale's back. The slit into which Dave had put the air pump nozzle. He stretched out a hand, held it over the slit, and his frown deepened. Air was whistling steadily out of the slit.

"I haf wondered why we go lower," Monkey-Face said soberly. "See... our whale sinks... soon all the air will be out. You remember, ve do not have time to plug the hole."

Dave's heart gave a sickening somersault as he realised what this man was telling him. When the last air had pumped out of the whale the big carcass would sink.

They tried to plug the hole with Dave's frozen vest, and did partially stop the air; but it was only a partial stoppage. All the time they were conscious of the low, ominous whistle of escaping air. All the time the whale was sinking lower and lower. Dave sat down. He did not feel quite so cold now, and was drifting off into a stupefied sleep, a sleep that would have had no awakening, when he was stung by a blow on the cheek, and opened his eyes to see Monkey-Face kneeling over him.

"You want to die, boy?" he bellowed. "Look... there is clothing only for one. If I take back my vest and long underpants... I can live. You understand? It is better for one to live... than for both to die, eh?"

Dave stared at him, but no words would come. If this great ape-like man did take back the clothing he had lent, Dave would die, and quickly. Nor could he refuse to give them back to the man.

"We take a chance, eh?" and Monkey-Face grinned. He took off a cheap ring he wore. It was of some silvery looking metal, aluminium, or some such alloy. In it was set a dark blue piece of glass. He held the ring in his right hand for a moment, then putting both hands behind his back he held them there for a few moments while Dave stared, too horror-stricken to even ask what Monkey-Face was doing.

"Now, choose," the two clenched fists were thrust before Dave's face. "I haf der ring in one hand. If you choose right...

Which hand held the ring? The choice meant life, or death

I gif you my clothes. If you choose wrong hand... without ring... then you gif me back my underclothes. Fair... eh?"

Dave nodded agreement. Yes, more than fair, for the underclothes did belong to Monkey-Face. He stared at the big fists, then jabbed at the left hand. Slowly the hand was opened... and there was no ring in the palm.

Dave wanted to swallow, and could not. There was a suffocating lump in his throat. Then Monkey-Face smiled. It was a queer smile, and it seemed to smooth away some of the ugliness.

"You vas frightened, eh? Look... take this ring, boy. Wear it always. You promise?"

Dave took the ring and nodded. Why he should promise anything he did not know.

"All my life, boy, I haf been laughed at," Monkey-Face said slowly. "Even my mother must have known how ugly I vass. No one makes friends with me. Now... I make friends with you. Wear my ring... *wear my clothes!*"

The factory ship's spotter plane saw them two hours later, and six hours afterwards a chaser came alongside and took them aboard. Monkey-Face was not dead, but he did not survive the trip home. They buried him at sea.

One hard-bitten whaler put the thoughts of everyone into a few words when he said: "You should never judge a sausage by its skin."

There were no medals; no blast of publicity for a man's self-sacrifice. Just that: *"Never judge a sausage..."*

The Loaded Dog

HENRY LAWSON

DAVE REGAN, Jim Bently, and Andy Page were sinking a shaft at Stony Creek in search of a rich gold quartz reef which was supposed to exist in the vicinity. There is always a rich reef supposed to exist in the vicinity; the only questions are whether it is ten feet or hundreds beneath the surface, and in which direction. They had struck some pretty solid rock, also water which kept them bailing. They used the old-fashioned blasting-powder and time-fuse. They'd make a sausage or cartridge of blasting-powder in a skin of strong calico or canvas, the mouth sewn and bound round the end of the fuse; they'd dip the cartridge in melted tallow to make it watertight, get the drill-hole as dry as possible, drop in the cartridge with some dry dust, and wad and ram with stiff clay and broken brick. Then they'd light the fuse and get out of the hole and wait. The result was usually an ugly pot-hole in the bottom of the shaft and half a barrow-load of broken rock.

There was plenty of fish in the creek, fresh-water bream,

cod, cat-fish, and tailers. The party were fond of fish, and Andy
and Dave of fishing. Andy would fish for three hours at a
stretch if encouraged by a "nibble" or a "bite" now and then—
say once in twenty minutes. The butcher was always willing
to give meat in exchange for fish when they caught more than
they could eat; but now it was winter, and these fish wouldn't
bite. However, the creek was low, just a chain of muddy water-
holes, from the hole with a few bucketsful in it to the sizable
pool with an average depth of six or seven feet, and they
could get fish by bailing out the smaller holes or muddying up
the water in the larger ones till the fish rose to the surface.
There was the cat-fish, with spikes growing out of the sides
of its head, and if you got pricked you'd know it, as Dave said.
Andy took off his boots, tucked up his trousers, and went into
a hole one day to stir up the mud with his feet, and he knew it.
Dave scooped one out with his hand and got pricked, and he
knew it too; his arm swelled, and the pain throbbed up into
his shoulder, and down into his stomach, too, he said, like a
toothache he had once, and kept him awake for two nights—
only the toothache pain had a "burred edge," Dave said.

Dave got an idea.

"Why not blow the fish up in the big waterhole with a
cartridge?" he said. "I'll try it."

He thought the thing out and Andy Page worked it out.
Andy usually put Dave's theories into practice if they were
practicable, or bore the blame for the failure and the chaffing
of his mates if they weren't.

He made a cartridge about three times the size of those they
used in the rock. Jim Bently said it was big enough to blow the
bottom out of the river. The inner skin was of stout calico;
Andy stuck the end of a six-foot piece of fuse well down in
the powder and bound the mouth of the bag firmly to it with
whipcord. The idea was to sink the cartridge in the water with
the open end of the fuse attached to a float on the surface,
ready for lighting. Andy dipped the cartridge in melted bees-
wax to make it watertight. "We'll have to leave it some time
before we light it," said Dave, "to give the fish time to get over
their scare when we put it in, and come nosing round again;

so we'll want it well watertight."

Round the cartridge, Andy, at Dave's suggestion, bound a strip of sail canvas—that they used for making water-bags —to increase the force of the explosion, and round that he pasted layers of stiff brown paper—on the plan of the sort of fireworks we called "gun-crackers". He let the paper dry in the sun, then he sewed a covering of two thicknesses of canvas over it, and bound the thing from end to end with stout fishing-line. Dave's schemes were elaborate, and he often worked his inventions out to nothing. The cartridge was rigid and solid enough now—a formidable bomb; but Andy and Dave wanted to be sure. Andy sewed on another layer of canvas, dipped the cartridge in melted tallow, twisted a length of fencing-wire round it as an afterthought, dipped it in tallow again, and stood it carefully against a tent-peg, where he'd know where to find it, and wound the fuse loosely round it. Then he went to the camp-fire to try some potatoes which were boiling in their jackets in a billy, and to see about frying some chops for dinner. Dave and Jim were at work in the claim that morning.

They had a big black young retriever dog—or rather an overgrown pup, a big, foolish, four-footed mate, who was always slobbering round them and lashing their legs with his heavy tail that swung round like a stock-whip. Most of his head was usually a red, idiotic slobbering grin of appreciation of his own silliness. He seemed to take life, the world, his two-legged mates, and his own instinct as a huge joke. He'd retrieve anything; he carted back most of the camp rubbish that Andy threw away. They had a cat that died in hot weather, and Andy threw it a good distance away in the scrub; and early one morning the dog found the cat, after it had been dead a week or so, and carried it back to camp, and laid it just inside the tent-flaps, where it could best make its presence known when the mates should rise and begin to sniff suspiciously in the sickly smothering atmosphere of the summer sunrise. He used to retrieve them when they went in swimming; he'd jump in after them, and take their hands in his mouth, and try to swim out with them, and scratch their naked bodies with his paws. They loved him for his good-heartedness and his foolishness, but when they wished to enjoy a swim they had to tie him up in camp.

He watched Andy with great interest all the morning making the cartridge, and hindered him considerably, trying to help; but about noon he went off to the claim to see how Dave and Jim were getting on, and to come home to dinner with them. Andy saw them coming, and put a panful of mutton-chops on the fire. Andy was cook today; Dave and Jim stood with their backs to the fire, as bushmen do in all weathers, waiting till dinner should be ready. The retriever went nosing round after something he seemed to have missed.

Andy's brain still worked on the cartridge; his eye was caught by the glare of an empty kerosene tin lying in the bushes, and it struck him that it wouldn't be a bad idea to sink the cartridge packed with clay, sand, or stones in the tin, to increase the force of the explosion. He may have been all out, from a scientific point of view, but the notion looked all right to him. Jim Bently, by the way, wasn't interested in their "damned silliness". Andy noticed an empty treacle tin—the sort with the little tin neck or spout soldered on the top for the convenience of pouring out the treacle—and it struck him that this would have made the best kind of cartridge-case: he would only have had to pour in the powder, stick the fuse in through the neck, and cork and seal it with bees-wax. He was turning to suggest this to Dave, when Dave glanced over his shoulder to see how the chops were doing— and bolted. He explained afterwards that he thought he heard the pan spluttering extra, and looked to see if the chops were burning. Jim Bently looked behind and bolted after Dave. Andy stood stock-still, staring after them.

"Run, Andy! Run!" they shouted back at him. "Run! Look behind you, you fool!" Andy turned slowly and looked, and there, close behind him, was the retriever with the cartridge in his mouth—wedged into his broadest and silliest grin. And that wasn't all. The dog had come round the fire to Andy, and the loose end of the fuse had trailed and waggled over the burning sticks into the blaze; Andy had slit and nicked the firing end of the fuse well, and now it was hissing and spitting.

Andy's legs started with a jolt; his legs started before his brain did, and he made after Dave and Jim. And the dog followed Andy.

Dave and Jim were good runners—Jim the best—for a short distance; Andy was slow and heavy, but he had the strength and the wind and could last. The dog capered round him, delighted as a dog could be to find his mates, as he thought, out for a frolic. Dave and Jim kept shouting back, "Don't foller us! Don't foller us, you coloured fool!" But Andy kept on, no matter how they dodged. They could never explain, any more than the dog, why they followed each other, but so they ran, Dave keeping in Jim's track in all its turnings, Andy after Dave, and the dog circling round Andy—the live fuse swishing in all directions and hissing and spluttering and stinking. Jim yelling to Dave not to follow him, Dave shouting to Andy to go in another direction—to "spread out", and Andy roaring at the dog to go home.

Then Andy's brain began to work, stimulated by the crisis: he tried to get a running kick at the dog, but the dog dodged; he snatched up sticks and stones and threw them at the dog and ran on again.

The retriever saw that he'd made a mistake about Andy, and left him and bounded after Dave. Dave, who had the presence of mind to think that the fuse's time wasn't up yet, made a dive and a grab for the dog, caught him by the tail, and as he swung round snatched the cartridge out of his mouth and flung it as far as he could; the dog immediately bounded after it and retrieved it. Dave roared and cursed at the dog, who, seeing that Dave was offended, left him and went after Jim, who was well ahead.

Jim swung to a sapling and went up it like a native bear; it was a young sapling, and Jim couldn't safely get more than ten or twelve feet from the ground. The dog laid the cartridge, as carefully as if it were a kitten, at the foot of the sapling, and capered and leaped and whooped joyously round under Jim. The big pup reckoned that this was part of the lark—he was all right now—it was Jim who was out for a spree. The fuse sounded as if it were going a mile a minute. Jim tried to climb

higher and the sapling bent and cracked. Jim fell on his feet
and ran. The dog swooped on the cartridge and followed. It all
took but a very few moments. Jim ran to a digger's hole,
about ten feet deep, and dropped down into it—landing on soft
mud—and was safe. The dog grinned sardonically down on

*No sooner had Jim shinned up the tree than the retriever laid
down the cartridge complete with fizzing fuse*

him, over the edge, for a moment, as if he thought it would be a good lark to drop the cartridge down on Jim.

"Go away, Tommy," said Jim feebly, "go away."

The dog bounded off after Dave, who was the only one in sight now; Andy had dropped behind a log, where he lay flat on his face, having suddenly remembered a picture of the Russo-Turkish war with a circle of Turks lying flat on their faces (as if they were ashamed) round a newly-arrived shell.

There was a small hotel or shanty on the creek, on the main road, not far from the claim. Dave was desperate, the time flew much faster in his stimulated imagination than it did in reality, so he made for the shanty. There were several casual bushmen on the verandah and in the bar; Dave rushed into the bar, banging the door to behind him. "My dog!" he gasped, in reply to the astonished stare of the publican, "the blanky retriever—he's got a live cartridge in his mouth—"

The retriever, finding the front door shut against him, had bounded round and in by the back way, and now stood smiling in the doorway leading from the passage, the cartridge still in his mouth and the fuse spluttering. They burst out of that bar. Tommy bounded first after one and then after another, for, being a young dog, he tried to make friends with everybody.

The bushmen ran round corners, and some shut themselves in the stable. There was a new weather-board and corrugated-iron kitchen and wash-house on piles in the backyard, with some women washing clothes inside. Dave and the publican bundled in there and shut the door—the publican cursing Dave and calling him a crimson fool, in hurried tones, and wanting to know what the hell he came here for.

The retriever went in under the kitchen, amongst the piles, but, luckily for those inside, there was a vicious yellow mongrel cattle-dog sulking and nursing his nastiness under there—a sneaking, fighting, thieving canine, whom neighbours had tried for years to shoot or poison. Tommy saw his danger—he'd had experience from this dog—and started out across the yard, still sticking to the cartridge. Halfway across the yard the yellow dog caught him and nipped him. Tommy dropped the cart-

ridge, gave one terrified yell, and took to the bush. The yellow
dog followed him to the fence and then ran back to see what
he had dropped. Nearly a dozen other dogs came from round
all the corners and under the buildings—spidery, thievish,
cold-blooded kangaroo dogs, mongrel sheep-and-cattle-dogs,
vicious black and yellow dogs—that slip after you in the dark,
nip your heels, and vanish without explaining—and yapping,
yelping small fry. They kept at a respectable distance round
the nasty yellow dog, for it was dangerous to go near him when
he thought he had found something which might be good for
a dog or cat. He sniffed at the cartridge twice, and was just
taking a third cautious sniff when—

It was very good blasting-powder—a new brand that Dave

The retriever stood in the doorway with the

had recently got up from Sydney; and the cartridge had been excellently well made. Andy was very patient and painstaking in all he did, and nearly as handy as the average sailor with needles, twine, canvas and rope.

Bushmen say that that kitchen jumped off its piles and on again. When the smoke and dust cleared away, the remains of the nasty yellow dog were lying against the paling fence of the yard looking as if he had been kicked into a fire by a horse and afterwards rolled in the dust under a barrow, and finally thrown against the fence from a distance. Several saddle-horses, which had been "hanging-up" round the verandah, were galloping wildly down the road in clouds of dust, with broken bridle-reins flying; and from a circle round the outskirts, from

idge and the bushmen burst out of the bar

The yellow dog caught him and nipped him

every point of the compass in the scrub, came the yelping of dogs. Two of them went home, to the place where they were born, thirty miles away, and reached it the same night and stayed there; it was not till towards evening that the rest came back cautiously to make inquiries. One was trying to walk on two legs, and most of 'em looked more or less singed; and a little, singed, stumpy-tailed dog, who had been in the habit of hopping the back half of him along on one leg, had reason to be glad that he'd saved up the other leg all those years, for he needed it now. There was one old one-eyed cattle-dog round that shanty for years afterwards, who couldn't stand the smell of a gun being cleaned. He it was who had taken an interest, only second to that of the yellow dog, in the cartridge. Bushmen said that it was amusing to slip up on his blind side and stick a dirty ramrod under his nose: he wouldn't wait to bring his solitary eye to bear—he'd take to the bush and stay out all night.

For half an hour or so after the explosion there were several bushmen round behind the stable who crouched, doubled up, against the wall, or rolled gently on the dust, trying to laugh without shrieking. There were two white women in hysterics at the house, and a half-caste rushing aimlessly round with a dipper of cold water. The publican was holding his wife tight and begging her between her squawks to "hold up for my sake, Mary, or I'll lam the life out of ye."

Dave decided to apologise later on, "when things had settled a bit," and went back to camp. And the dog that had done it all, Tommy, the great, idiotic mongrel retriever, came slobbering round Dave and lashing his legs with his tail, and trotted home after him, smiling his broadest, longest, and reddest smile of amiability, and apparently satisfied for one afternoon with the fun he'd had.

Andy chained the dog up securely, and cooked some more chops, while Dave went to help Jim out of the hole.

And most of this is why, for years afterwards, lanky, easy-going bushmen, riding lazily past Dave's camp, would cry, in a lazy drawl and with just a hint of the nasal twang:

"'Ello, Da-a-ve! How's the fishin' getting on, Da-a-ve?"

The Cure

FRANK KNIGHT

TAFF EVANS was Welsh, red-haired, five-feet-ten tall and the possessor of a romantic soul. Which means he fell for every pretty girl he met and most of them fell for him. But he was cured; and this is the tale of how it happened.

We were cadets together aboard the SS *Dorothea* during a rambling voyage around the Carribean and West Indies. I was just his senior by about three months, but neither of us took much notice of that. On the whole we were good friends, with occasional differences of opinion to add spice to what might otherwise have been a boring life.

We had a difference of opinion that evening in Puerto Margarita—which is on what our ancestors used to call the Spanish Main—when Taff spotted a girl singing in a shabby little café near the docks. He grabbed my arm. He was staring

with a light in his eyes that dimmed the wobbling neon sign.

"Just look at that!" he gasped. "Talk about a rose born to blush unseen!"

I had heard it all before. Besides, I was tired and had been thinking longingly of my bunk for the past half-hour.

"Come on," I urged, giving him a shove. "I want to get back to the ship."

I don't think he heard me. Certainly my shoving did not budge him an inch.

"And the voice of an angel!" he breathed ecstatically.

"Rot," I said, and he heard that and rounded on me like a stag at bay.

"You have no appreciation of beauty," he raved with his r's rolling and his voice going soprano on the top notes. "You are a mean-souled Saxon without a thought beyond eating and sleeping. Man, man, look at her eyes! Look at the shape of her mouth and the dimple in her chin! And she is singing beautiful songs, about freedom and the mountains and the stars at night..."

I had to take his word for that. He had lived in South America somewhere for a year or two before going to sea and had picked up a fairly fluent Spanish. That made him a useful companion to go ashore with in Spanish-speaking places and even the captain called him in to act as interpreter at times. But it did not alter the fact that at this moment he was making rather a scene on the pavement outside that café. So I groaned and let him drag me inside.

As I have said, it was a rough sort of place and the customers were rougher. Dockers, I guessed, with a sprinkling of local shopkeepers and so on. They had all been eating garlic. They were all drinking sour red wine from thick glasses. I ordered coffee and after a long while it came, black and strong and nearly cold. I loathed everything about the place, but Taff was seeing nothing but the girl.

Mind you, she was not bad. With a good wash and a hair-do and some decent clothes she might have been reasonably presentable. Quite pretty in a way, and those whacking great brown eyes, but ...

"I'll bet she's twenty-five," I said. "She's probably the proprietor's wife and has half-a-dozen scraggy kids in the background."

Taff ignored me.

"And if that's singing," I said, trying to sound scathing, "my grandmother's a prima donna."

He went on ignoring me. I scowled at my coffee and then the song ended and the girl came down among the customers.

Well, I was wrong about one thing. At closer range I could see she was not twenty-five, but no more than sixteen or seventeen—younger by a year or so than Taff or me. Moreover her face, now she was not singing, was several degrees better than I had thought, especially when she smiled. Quite good. Distinctly good. But that only made me worry more about Taff.

For one thing, she was obviously top-of-the-pops with those tough dockers. They were cheering and clapping and blowing her kisses like mad. And more than that—they were giving her money. She had an old cardboard box. They were tossing crumpled ten-peso notes into it till she had to pack them down to make room for more. Some of the more prosperous-looking chaps put in whole wads.

Then she came to our table. It was embarrassing because we were darned short of cash. That was why we were walking back to the ship instead of taking a taxi. So I raked out a twenty-cent piece and dropped it in on top of the paper money with a muttered apology. At the same time, privately, I wondered what the heck she was collecting for and where my hard-earned twenty cents were going. I felt annoyed and probably looked it.

Not so Taff. He just stared. Then she said something—in Spanish, of course—and he woke up and rattled back at her and she laughed and turned away and I heaved a sigh of relief thinking all was over between them and Taff had taken the brush-off.

But I was wrong. She turned back abruptly as though something had hit her. Her face had gone dead serious and her eyes seemed several shades darker. Then she fired a question at Taff, and another, and another and several more. And finally she flashed him a smile which had me squirming, let alone him, before diving among the customers once more and disappearing at the back of the shop. With her went my twenty-cent piece.

Out of it all I had picked up one notion, centred around the word *mañana*—tomorrow. It was one of my few Spanish words and I had heard it several times.

"Taff," I said accusingly when I at last had him outside, "you've dated her."

He grinned amiably. "Of course. And why not?"

"Because..." but I choked. There were so many reasons, ranging from the fact that she bit her nails, which I had noticed, to the more than suspicious glances aimed by various obviously jealous customers at Taff's back while she was at our table.

"You'll end up with a knife in your back," I said.

He grinned. "I'll take a chance. She's worth it."

He was hopeless, so I gave up. "What was she collecting

for?" I asked. "Herself?" Which was what I suspected.

"Orphans," he replied. "In the mountains somewhere. They don't believe in social services here."

I did not believe that story, either.

So we went back to the ship and I wondered what I could do to rescue Taff from what I was sure would lead to trouble. Tell the chief officer and perhaps get his leave stopped? But the mate would only laugh and Taff would hate me for evermore. Besides, he would do the same sort of thing in the very next port, and it might be worse. I comforted myself with

Taff's progress was such that I thought he risked getting a knife in his back

the reflection that it could not last long. We were due to sail in a couple of days.

Next evening I let Taff go ashore alone. I said I wanted to write a letter home before we sailed, which was true enough. I hinted that he might be better employed doing the same, but he merely grinned.

In fact my letter did not take long. I cut it short because the thought of Taff up there in that foul café was worrying me. After a good deal of hesitation I changed my clothes and went after him. Spying? Perhaps; but I can tell you I *was* worried.

I could not see him at first. The café was pretty crowded and hazy with cigarette smoke. Nor was the girl to be seen, singing or otherwise. I wondered whether Taff had taken her off somewhere. Was his Welsh charm as potent as all that?

But then I did see him, and her. They were half-hidden at a table in an alcove with a couple of dusty-looking palms in pots in the way. And to my surprise they were not alone. Two or three men were at the same table and they all seemed to be one happy party, heads together and hands gesticulating and generally discussing something of considerable interest. Only Taff seemed to be looking rather harassed, so far as I could see at that distance.

I sat down at one of the tables on the pavement just outside the doorway. They were practically deserted at this time of night and the bedraggled women who acted as waitresses did not seem to be bothering about them. That suited me because I did not want to have to buy a drink; still less did I want to put anything into a collecting box. I still felt sore about that twenty-cent piece.

Nothing happened for about half-an-hour. There was a biggish grey-haired man in a fairly respectable grey twill suit sitting at the next table, on the opposite side of the doorway, reading an evening paper. I passed the time trying to make sense out of what headlines I could see on the back page of his paper, without much success. Someday, I supposed, I had better learn Spanish. Also I felt rather an ass sitting there, and once or twice I saw the big man flick an inquisitive glance at me.

Why was I waiting? Why was he waiting, come to that? Or perhaps he was the proprietor.

And then I discovered that the alcove behind the palms was empty. Taff, the girl and their pals had vanished.

"Damn," I said aloud, and the big man lowered his paper and looked at me. Then he came across and sat down by me.

"Americano?" he asked.

"No, English," I said shortly, and I felt annoyed as I always do when an inhabitant of South America seems to assume that all foreigners come from North America. Haven't they heard of Europe?

"Ah, *Inglés*," he murmured, and seemed to be considering that fact carefully. Perhaps he was trying to discover in what way I differed from an American.

Then he waved his hand in the general direction of the docks and said, "You are *marinero*—of a sheep."

"Yes," I said, not caring to go into details because of the language difficulty. How did one say *cadet* in Spanish? Besides, if his *ship* sounded like sheep my *cadet*, or whatever the word was, might sound like goat or jackass to him.

But then he startled me. "And you are *broke*," he said, bringing out the last word clearly and with emphasis.

"Yes," I admitted, staring. "More or less, anyway. How did you guess?"

He shrugged and smiled, not unpleasantly. "You sit here," he said, "on the—the *pavé*? You do not drink. You say *damn*. It is *evidente*."

I had to laugh. I supposed it was fairly obvious. "But I did not say *damn* because..." I began, and then stopped. If I went on I should have to tell him about Taff and the girl. Better not. Who was he? He might even be her father! So I ended lamely, "Oh well, it doesn't matter. I am broke, and that's that."

I don't suppose he understood a word of that. He was too busy trying to work out his own next speech. And after a while he let me have it.

He leaned forward and tapped me on the knee. "It is not good," he said. And he jerked a thumb towards the doorway as he added, "The *casa*—house. Not good, not good, not

168

He gestured me away. "I say v a m o s—*go!"*

good." And he gave my knee a hearty thump each time he said it, to make sure I got the message, which I did.

I mean, I knew he was not referring just to the dirt and smells or the quality of the drinks; but I pretended to think he did mean that just to discover what else he would say.

"Oh," I said, shrugging as though I had caught the habit from him, "it isn't all that bad. I know the wine is pretty poisonous and the coffee I had last night was awful, but it is the nearest pub to the ship and..."

That was as far as I got. How much of it he had understood I don't know, but it seemed to annoy him, whatever it was. He uttered an oath in Spanish which I did not catch. He stood up, marched to the edge of the pavement and marched back. He glowered at me.

"It is not good!" he repeated in a kind of subdued shout, banging one fist into his other hand instead of against my knee, to my relief. "It is not good for Americanos, for *Inglésos*, for *extranjeros*. I say *vamos*—go." And he pointed in the direction of the docks with the dramatic effect of a Victorian father kicking his erring son out of doors. Then abruptly he sat down at his original table and unfolded his newspaper. The interview was ended.

So what was I to make of it? For a while longer I just sat there, not liking to be ordered about by strangers. Who the heck was he? And then I caught sight of one of those waitress women peeping round the door to see if he were still there, and nipping back and whispering that he was, and there was a sort of gloom over the whole café and men were shaking their heads over their wine.

And of course the answer came to me in a flash. He was a policeman! What or who he was waiting for I had no idea, but obviously he did not like that café and the customers did not like him. And he had warned me, a foreigner, to keep away from the place. Then I thought of Taff.

I stood up slowly and calmly—I hoped. I said with dignity and my best Spanish accent, *"Bueno noche, señor,"* which he acknowledged with the merest flick of his paper. Then I walked slowly away.

But I was not calm. I wanted to run—to run round the next corner and the next and get somehow at the back entrance to that café and find Taff and drag him away.

So I tried, and though I hurried once I was round the corner, I did not run. At least, I did not after I had splashed through a foot-deep puddle and tripped over an abandoned perambulator and collided with a couple of dustbins. For those back streets were as black as pitch and every back entrance looked the same as the next—a dark wasteland of stones, steps and clutter. And all the while I had a horrible prickly feeling at the thought of that policeman shadowing me.

I crept back to the main road, then walked smartly back to the ship. I got into bed and waited for Taff.

He came aboard at about eleven o'clock. "Oh," he said, "you're still awake." He sounded disappointed.

"Yes," I said. "Had a good time?"

"Very," he replied, not very convincingly, I thought.

"You sound a bit despondent," I said. "Didn't she sing for you?"

He scowled at me and for a moment I was almost sorry for him. My guess was that he had not been able to get her away from those male chaperones—her brothers, perhaps? I'd heard of the old Spanish custom of paying court to a girl in the presence of her family. It was not Taff's way at all. But it was not that. At least, he said it was not.

He flung himself down on his bunk. "That girl's in trouble," he said. "Big trouble."

"She seemed chirpy enough last night," I reminded him. "What kind of trouble?"

He took a long time about answering. Eventually he said, "I'm not supposed to tell anyone. It might land her in prison."

"Oh," I said, thinking of the man in the grey suit, "you mean trouble with the police. She's not a dope smuggler, is she?"

It was a logical thought. I'd heard of cafés like that where marijuana and worse could be bought in the backroom if one knew the password. I remembered how Taff had disappeared from that alcove into a backroom somewhere and a chilly trickle went down my spine. Supposing he had got himself involved?

But it was not that. Taff's red head gave an impatient shake and he demanded indignantly, "Does she look like a dope smuggler? Don't be daft. And it isn't anything she has done herself. At least, nothing wrong. It's her father."

"Oh," I said again. Then I kept quiet and waited, because I knew he was dying to tell me.

"It's politics," he said glumly. "Her father was on the wrong side in the last take-over and had to get out of the country. He's in Cuba now—at least she thinks he is. She wants to get out too, but they won't let her."

"Why?" I asked when he had relapsed into gloomy silence. "Why won't they let her?"

He shook his head. "They won't tell her. She thinks it's because they're waiting for her father to come back. She's the decoy. They expect him to come to her, and then they'll nab him. It's true enough. There was a detective watching the place tonight. There is every night. It's a heck of a situation."

"Must she stay at the café?" I asked.

He sighed. "She has to earn her living, singing and that. Besides, it's owned by her aunt, her only other relative." And he added from the depths of his romantic heart, "Poor kid."

I suppose I'm not romantic. It could be true, but was it? Certainly she was right about the detective—my man in grey. It was on the tip of my tongue to say so, but I swallowed the words instead. If I told Taff I had been spying on him he would be furious and I should not get anything else out of him.

"Well," I said, "you can't do anything about it. We've only one more day here."

He did not answer, but began to undress.

I wondered what was going on in his mind. I wondered what was going on in the girl's mind, if anything—anything concerning Taff, I mean. I remembered uncomfortably how on that first evening in the café she had quite clearly given him the brush-off and then had seemed to change her mind as though she had been smitten with a sudden idea. What idea? Was it what those men in the alcove had been discussing so eagerly?

And then a horrid thought struck me like a flick from a shark's tail. The girl wanted to leave the country. *We* should be leaving the country in precisely thirty hours' time. She wanted to go to Cuba. We were not going to Cuba, but to Kingston, Jamaica, which might be near enough.

I sat up. "Taff," I said urgently, "you aren't thinking you *can* do something about it, are you?"

He hitched his pyjama cord viciously about his middle, then switched out the light.

"Taff," I urged in the darkness, "for Pete's sake don't do anything crazy. Do you want to end up in gaol with her? You might get the ship arrested—and all of us! You'd get the sack, and it would be in all the papers, and..."

Taff's voice cut in before I could think of the next disaster. "Oh, shut up," it said. "Shut up and go to sleep."

Sleep! I lay piling one disastrous consequence on another until I had the entire world involved in nuclear war because of one daft act on the part of a red-haired Welsh cadet. But in the morning—oh yes, I did sleep eventually—the whole thing seemed somewhat ridiculous. Taff was going about his work quite normally—he was overhauling the gear in number three lifeboat, I was doing number four—looking rather sorrowful, but not like an arch-plotter. Should I say anything to any of the officers? I glanced at the chief officer's face as he passed by and it looked thunderous—possibly because the skipper had just been blaming him for letting a barge scrape along the ship's side during the night—so I decided to hold my peace. There are moments when it is not safe to tell a chief officer even that the ship is on fire. And somehow another moment never came.

But one thing I did decide. Whether Taff liked it or not, I would go ashore to that café in the evening to keep an eye on him.

And that, as it happened, was easier said than done. I went ashore as soon as Taff was out of the way. I went straight to the café and looked cautiously around in case my policeman was watching me. But he was not in evidence. So, armed with my last five-peso note I went inside, ordered a bottle of sticky-sweet mineral water and prepared to spend a riotous evening. My only trouble, apart from the heat and smell and flies, was that Taff was not there. Nor was the girl.

I waited. Nobody took much notice of me. The customers were smoking, talking, playing queer games with dice or tatty cards, sipping their sour wine.

I hailed one of the so-called waitresses and tried to get some sense out of her. Where was my friend? *Amigo,* I said. *Amigo,* she repeated, looking blank. The one with red hair, I said, patting the top of my head and saying *rojo.* She examined my head curiously, but only shook hers. So I tried asking about the girl. *La muchacha?* The one who sings—*comprenez?* And I warbled a note or two very *pianissimo* to convey what I meant.

That did it. She went off into peals of hysterical laughter and then weaved among the tables shouting to the customers,

Some policemen came out of the café and got into the van

apparently, that I was about to perform some sort of comic turn. At any rate all the customers stared at me as though I were mad or drunk or both. I stood up and stalked out, leaving the rest of my drink. I felt a fool and cursed Taff beneath my breath.

I went for a longish walk, keeping to the main road and bright lights and getting most of the way to town. Then I went into a respectable café and had a decent cup of coffee and felt somewhat better. I returned to the dockside joint, but this time surveyed it from a safe distance.

At first glance it looked the same. No sign of Taff, no singing damsel. Then I saw that it was not the same. A large policeman in uniform was standing in the doorway. The customers were sitting very still at their tables, doing nothing. Two more policemen seemed to be questioning them.

I walked past the place slowly and looked curiously in as any passer-by might. In fact half-a-dozen people were standing on the pavement doing just that, only more so. But as I passed a policeman came and shooed them away. They retired to the other side of the road and stared from there, so I did the same. And from there we could all see a big black police van parked just round the corner in the side street I had tried to explore the previous evening. From time to time other passers-by stopped to join us till we had quite a crowd. The policeman scowled at us from across the street. I scowled back, but I felt reasonably safe and anonymous in that crowd.

Mind you, my heart was thumping pretty fast. I was waiting to see poor old Taff dragged out from the back of that café— I guessed they were searching the back rooms then—and dumped into the van. And there was nothing I could do to help him, just nothing.

Then as time passed I began to wonder. Perhaps he was not there at all; or the girl; or anyone else the police wanted. Because nobody came out the front way except a policeman or two looking bored. And as far as I could see nobody had been carried out the back way. At any rate nobody had been dumped into the van.

Then, quite suddenly, the show was over. Half-a-dozen

policemen came out briskly and climbed into the van. Half-a-dozen more appeared from somewhere at the back and also climbed into the van. Someone barked an order and the van drove away. The crowd sighed with disappointment and melted away, though some of the men went over to the café to find out what had been happening.

I did not. It was beginning to rain. I gave the café a final scowl and went back to the ship.

I met the third mate on deck. He said, "You'd better turn in. We're calling all hands at five, sailing at six. Where's Taff?"

"I don't know," I replied. "I lost him ashore somewhere." Which was fairly true.

He grinned and asked, "Was there a girl with him?"

"Not when I last saw him," I said, which was also true. Then I went to the cabin to avoid further questions.

The odd thing is that I fell asleep as soon as I lay down. Maybe I'd been worrying too much. Maybe I'd given up worrying because it was obviously no use. Anyway I slept, solidly as a log, until a rough hand shook me and a rougher voice shouted in my ear, "Rise and shine! Rise and shine! All hands on deck and let go fore and aft!" Gosh, how I hate these boisterous waker-uppers!

Next moment, of course, I thought *Taff!* And my heart gave a bump of relief when I saw him in his bunk. I shook him, because he was still fast asleep in spite of the recent uproar, and when he opened his eyes I demanded, "When did you come aboard? Where were you last night? Did you see the police?"

That woke him. He sat up and blinked. "Eh? Police? Where?" He looked at the doorway as though he expected to see them waiting.

"At the café," I said. "Last night. I—er—happened to be passing. They seemed to be searching the place."

He stared at me. Then he reached for his trousers and mumbled, "At the café? No, I wasn't there."

"You weren't? Then where the heck were you?"

He was deliberately avoiding my eyes. I could see that. As

he pulled his shirt over his head he muttered, "Oh, various places. A friend's flat among others."

"But..." And then someone shouted that I was wanted on the bridge and I had to go. I didn't get a chance to speak to Taff again till breakfast time. By then we were clear of the port and heading north-west across the blue Carribean, with Jamaica two days' run ahead.

"Thank heaven that's over," I said with heartfelt relief. "I more than half expected we should leave you in gaol."

He looked at me. He did not grin or jeer or do any of the things I might have expected. Just looked—solemn as an owl

"When did you come aboard? Where were you last night?"

and kind of melancholy. And then he said quietly, "I've got her. She's in the forepeak."

Have you ever been dumbfounded—truly *dumb*founded? It's a horrible feeling, like paralysis. I'm fairly sure my jaw dropped, leaving my mouth open. But as to saying anything, I couldn't.

"She had a tip the police meant to raid the place," he said. "She thought they might take her away for questioning, and you know what that means. She was dead scared. But there was nowhere she could really hide, not for long, not without getting other people into trouble. So I hid her in the forepeak. She's there now."

This time I managed one word. "But..."

"I'm going to get her now and take her to the skipper," he said calmly. "He's a decent old stick at heart. And after all, she's seeking political asylum."

I had to admire his courage, or his optimism. From what I knew of the skipper he'd go clean through the roof with a blast-off powerful enough to take him to Venus. But it was a good idea to take the girl with him. Her big eyes might tone the explosion down just a little. I wondered how I could wangle a ringside position on the bridge to see the fireworks, but decided I had better stay out of it. Explosions sometimes hurt quite innocent bystanders.

"I'll be ready with soothing medicines," I said. "Go ahead—and good luck, you idiot."

So he went, and I went to a porthole from which I could see the 'tweendeck hatch through which presently poor Taff must emerge with his refugee damsel. But then as bad luck would have it the third mate on the bridge blew his whistle and I had to go up to see what he wanted.

I found the skipper there. Someone—Taff, probably— had not made a neat enough job of stowing the flags away after leaving port. The skipper had kicked them all over the place and demanded that I put them away—properly this time. That was the sort of mood he was in. I was sorry for Taff. And I should have my explosive side-seat after all.

Taff was a long while coming. I had just about finished the flags when he came up the ladder looking nervous and red in the face as well as in his hair. He refused to meet my eye. He was followed by a figure completely hidden by a kind of monk's cloak complete with a huge hood.

The skipper gaped. So did the third mate. Then Taff said hastily, forestalling the explosion he could see coming, "A stowaway, sir. I found him in the forepeak."

It was my turn to gape. *Him?* The figure swept off its hood and it was *him* right enough. A tough little chap in his early twenties with curly black hair and a cocky look as though he were rather pleased with himself.

Nobody else was pleased. As the storm broke I pushed the last flag into place and slid down the ladder to safety. The bridge rocked with the thunder of the skipper's voice.

Taff came down at last. He sat down, bowed his head on the table and groaned. And between groans he said, "Man, I'll never trust a woman again."

I suppose I had guessed the story by then. It wasn't the girl who wanted to leave the country at all. It wasn't the girl the police wanted. It was this man, Andreas Guevera, ex-guerilla leader and her boyfriend. She had fooled poor old Taff completely, right from the word go. The only consoling factor was that Guevera had a kind of chivalry or gratitude or something. It was he who had suggested he should be "discovered" as a stowaway. That let Taff out of trouble beautifully.

I never did learn for certain what happened to Andreas was a rumour later that he had joined Castro's army in Cuba. Guevera. We handed him over to the police in Jamaica. There It might be true. I wonder if the girl went there also?

What I do know is that Taff Evans was cured. He would not speak to a girl after that, if he could avoid it.

Duel in the Sea

JOHN KRUSE

I DIDN'T actually hear the frogs stop yawping, but when I jerked awake there wasn't a sound anywhere but for the sea. I eased up on one elbow and listened. Up-coast it would have meant leopard, but here outside Colombo in Ceylon it was more likely a pariah dog nosing around; or a couple from the hotel, maybe, taking a stroll along the sand.

I leaned back on the fishing nets which, but for the corks, would have made a good bed and waited for the frogs to begin again. The tide was out; through the open door of the hut I could see the black curve of it well out in the bay. On the headland beyond, the big hotel still had its lights on though it must have gone two o'clock.

I waited, but there was no one down on the beach, only

the hotel lights in the surf. I could hear the undertow plainly, like someone dragging a tarpaulin up a drive. But the frogs had stopped their croaking. I didn't much like it and I was just going to get up when I felt, more than heard, someone brush against the outside of the hut. I stayed where I was, listening with all the bones in my head.

The faint light coming in on to the floor from the night sky darkened slightly. I knew at once that someone was round the door from me, peering in. I thought of my sponging knife; but it was in my pack.

Very slowly a dark shape began to insert itself between me and the lights of the hotel, without any sound. From the darkness of it I could tell it was a native. I saw his sarong against the lighter sand, caught up and tucked into his belt to free his legs. In his hand something glinted—a knife.

I took him then, before he could see properly, jumping up and diving at him. He heard me move and stamped the ground like a jack-rabbit and ran. He made three steps down the beach before I hit his shoulders with my chest; then we were struggling in the loose sand.

He was small-boned and sinewy like all Singhalese. I caught a whiff of beetle-nut. He twisted about like a snake. I tried to get a grip on him, but he contorted, rolled sideways from under me, was up on his feet and away, dodging between the coconut palms. There were bungalows amongst the trees and a Buddhist temple and wire fences in the darkness. I let him go.

In the doorway of the hut I found his knife. It was an ordinary steel blade with hemp twisted round for a handle. I smelt it. Fish. So the fishermen were after me!

Up-coast in Puttalam I had had trouble with them. In Mullaittivu someone had dropped a cobra in on me while I slept; but that was after a hurricane had driven all the big fish out deep and put the prices up in the market. But at Batticaloa and Komariya and at Galle they hadn't bothered me any. They thought I was mad but I guess they respected a guy who hunted fish under the water, bringing in shark alone. But down here, where the demand always exceeded the supply and the reefs were ablaze with fish, trying to kill me didn't make sense.

I had been in Colombo four days and pulled in a hundred pounds of fish a day, which was as much as I could tow behind me swimming. It was a flea in a dog's ear to them. But I remembered then the scattering of red-shirted coolies I had seen loading the Maldivian schooners in the docks. Resentment against the whites was strong amongst the politically un-represented coolie class. It wasn't hard to see why they should pick on an Englishman—an Englishman who made his living by fishing, which was traditionally the occupation of the lowest caste.

It was a lot of eye-wash and it made me mad. I went into the hut and slung the knife down where Reuben would find it. Reuben was the old native who owned the shack. He hired out fishing gear and surf-boards and water skis to tourists. I rented the key off him for a rupee a night.

It was three hours to dawn, so I got back on to my pile of nets and pulled a slicker over me because it had changed to cool with the tide. Let 'em come, I thought.

But presently the frogs started their noise again. I relaxed a bit. We don't have these singing frogs at home, and I lay for a while listening to them and thinking how a man gets to some queer places trying to escape from things maybe that he wants most of all. It had started with—oh! a lot of things; I just didn't want any roots of my own, that was all. I didn't want to build something up and have it torn down.

Our trooper had put in at Colombo during the war and stayed there a fortnight to weld a bow-plate which was a certain captain's damn carelessness, and I had met a guy who speared fish. He said he was a Swede, but I guessed he was a Burgher, which is a half-native. I went fishing with him a couple of times and had never had such fun in my whole life.

After things had gone rotten at home it was the first thing I thought of—how I had envied that fisherman his life and how home had somehow got dirty. I tried Canada; bought an old Chevvy there and worked my way to Mexico. For what the old car fetched, a Dutch tanker captain let me ride on six thousand tons of petroleum from Tampico to Ceylon. And here I was and it was not like the place where you were a kid which never somehow looks the same; it was better—as green as a pool-table with a sea like blue mercury against gold.

I never found the Swede. I heard about him in different places, though. They said he had been drowned near where I was now, but no one knew for sure because he came and went with the fish. When a shoal he was working moved on he moved with it. He never drowned though, any more than an otter could.

I bought a spear-gun and started alone. In these days there were no books about under-water hunting, and there were things he hadn't told me. I lost the fore-finger of my left hand to a twelve-foot moray eel in the big coral reef off Trinco. Later I nearly drowned from a perfectly hellish stomach convulsion when hunting deep. That was before I stopped drinking *arak* and smoking. But I learned about shark before they learned about me. That was the prime thing.

I stretched out. The frogs still croaked. Where would it all end? I didn't know. It had got me; that was all. No man who has hunted under the sea and carried the spoils to market himself and held out over the price, going hungry when the seas were high and living like a king when the hot waters creamed over the summer reefs flashing with fish, can ever go back to being a garage mechanic or paint the front room of an evening or get up to the baby in the night.

I awoke to find the sun's red eye level with the sea. It made ribs of orange on the tide which was sliding in a flat curve up the beach.

I got up and went outside. The beach was deserted but for a few skeleton-like dogs hunting for stranded fish. Along by the hotel I could see the ochre sail of a single fishing outrigger, or *nau*, drawn up on the beach. There were no signs of life near it. The other outriggers had been out all night. I counted half a dozen sails lying about two miles out.

The scene looked peaceful and the sky promised to last the tide at least. I went down and took a plunge. When I got back

Reuben had arrived. He was leaning the surf-boards against the wall of the hut. They were the short kind and had written on them: "Club Beach". There was no club that I knew of, but it was Reuben's idea. He wore his hair in the traditional bun and from the back in his sarong he looked like a fat old woman.

"*Ibon*," I greeted him.

"*Ibon*, Mister Gardener," Reuben replied thickly, and I knew he'd been on the cocaine.

I told him what had happened. He listened dully. When I had finished he shrugged.

"They're all mad," he said. "They're mad with this new thing. Knowing this, you should not try to take their fish. They will kill you like they did the Swede."

"You think they killed him then?"

"I think what I think. They could have. What will you do?"

"Do? Nothing, I guess. I can handle it myself."

Reuben spat beetle-nut and showed his red-stained teeth. "So could the Swede."

He shrugged and went into the hut. Presently he came out trepanning two king coconuts clumsily with his machete.

We squatted down in silence and drank the oily milk and watched the sun creep up above the sea. Presently it got too strong for Reuben's eyes and he went back inside.

I stayed there with my thoughts until the sun got high enough to penetrate the water. Then I went in for my gear. Reuben was sitting on the nets, puffing at a reefer.

He avoided my eye.

"Going out?" he asked.

"Sure. Why not?"

He made the familiar gesture. "They'll kill you."

"And you'll kill yourself. Why don't you lay off those things?"

He grunted and pretended not to watch me cock the heavy spring of the gun. I checked the harpoon flopper head and thirty-foot steel line. As the gun was only accurate up to fifteen feet I kept the other fifteen in reserve with a checkline knotted round the muzzle. I tested the knot; then got out a two-foot

"They will kill you as they did the Swede."

spike from my pack and fitted it on to the muzzle of the gun.

Reuben's curiosity got the better of him. "What's that?" he wanted to know.

"A bayonet. For shark mostly. To stop them getting too close when you're playing them."

I coiled a length of strong cord round my waist, strapped on a knife, pulled the mask up on to my thigh garter-fashion and picked up my rubber fins.

"Coming?"

Reuben heaved himself unsmilingly to his feet and stood at the door and watched me go. Then he went back inside to wait for the tourists to come down from the hotel to swim.

The water was fresh but not cold—and I took it steady to

the reef which was about two miles out. I didn't put the mask on till I was nearly there, so as to keep a sharp look-out all round. The fishing outrigger by the hotel put to sea shortly after I started, but what breeze there was was blowing inshore and it was lying well back, not making much headway.

I unhooked the gun from the back of my belt and dived to get my position. The naked sunlight died to liquid green fire. I was in about five fathoms of water above a desert of yellow sand dunes, poised at the crest like waves perpetually about to break.

Moorish idols like wooden butterflies drifted about me, fluttering their thread-like fins. Near the bottom a slinky grouper was stalking a herd of gold, black and silver zebras. I couldn't have got near him in the open, so I kept going, nearly bumping into a poisonous lion-fish. He spread his scaly wings, confronting me with arched back and red, white and black fieriness. When I kept on into him he remembered that bit about discretion and swooped off.

I swam on towards the reef, watching the undulations of the desert beneath me. The sand was spangled with spiky and fingered conches, cowrie shells and tall-in-the-sand razor mussels. There were giant clams amongst the dunes, with their green and gold mantles spread invitingly, only the gape of their mouths giving them away.

Presently the sea-bed took on a covering of velvet-gold moss. A skate came off it like a big lunar moth and fluttered away. I went down after it, but it was too fast for me, melting into the blue distance like a shadow. I surfaced and dived again. Another skate came off the moss, then a ray, then another skate, another and another. They took off in flocks, like crows coming off grain, flapping and wheeling.

I threw my legs forward to get the gun up, but I was too slow. They had levelled off and with their flatness were too hard to hit. It wasn't worth the effort of reloading, so I came up and took a breather.

The sun was getting hot. This was the life! I could barely see the tops of the palm trees now. The outrigger was closer, I noticed—to the south of me. It seemed hardly to be moving.

I kept going for the reef, keeping a sharp lookout now for shark.

It was an underwater reef. From the top there was nothing; but coming on it from below was always a stupendous sight. It loomed up in the half-light, big as the whole world; no doubt the upthrust of some forgotten violence. It was split with black fissures and caverns which, without a lamp to check for moray eels and stonefish, would have been suicide to enter.

I dived and hunted deep amongst the ravines, the blood creaking in my ears like splitting ice. The place was brilliant with fish. Tangs, or surgeon, with their scalpel-like tails darted

They took off in flocks like crows, flapping and wheeling

about like flights of swallows. Squirrel-fish peered at me wide-eyed from their crevices. From every eave and shelf crayfish antennae sounded the water for danger. Octopuses, their tentacles hidden, lay tamped under rocks or shot about like jet-propelled missiles amongst the coral.

I remembered how on my first day here I had seen a fine sight. Suddenly out of nowhere, smashing the water with vast hovering wings, an eagle ray had appeared, paused and, gathering speed with beating pinions, vanished into the gloom. It was so quick and awful it had shocked me.

I had been shocked once before—in my learning days. I got caught with my gun unloaded in the open by a six-foot croco-dile—jawed pencil of silver which drew tense circles round me. It was a barracuda wondering just what the hell I was. When he was satisfied he sheared off; but big fish are good for reminding one that no matter how confident you may get, your pace underwater is still as slow as a snail's.

I chased some black mullet along the side of the escarpment, but they got away from me into a thicket of ribbon-weed. The thicket was deep. I tried to go down after them, but it hurt my ears; so I dislodged a boulder and watched it tumble down in slow motion, the weeds licking around it, finally wrapping it to a standstill. The mullet didn't come out, but a big thirty-pound *sier* did. It made for a ravine and I beat off after it with my fins, gaining height as I went so I could take in some more air.

The *sier*, or kingfish, is the most sought after of all Ceylon fish. It fetches two rupees a pound in the market, is rare and hard to find and harder to shoot. This one headed for the north end of the reef where the coral forests are.

I missed him several times, but picked him up again. He weaved in and out of the labyrinthine passages, round coral outcrops massive as hewn marble, through orchards of petrified cherry-blossom. In the creaking silence we twisted and floated through gloomy corridors, up towering urns of rust and verdigris, as though through the ruins of some decayed and festooned Versailles.

I forgot everything in the chase, breaking the surface like

a porpoise, gulping air and diving, staying down three and four minutes at a stretch. It was the greatest game on earth.

It lasted maybe half an hour. Where I got him it was like a stag's burial ground, with coral branches sprouting like antlers from what looked like thousands of white skulls. He turned too sharply to avoid a boulder, exposing himself, and I shot him just behind the gill.

I played him till he quit; then I unwound the cord from my waist and threaded it through one gill and his mouth and returned, trailing him, to the surface.

Re-springing the gun always took a lot of strength in the water and I did it bobbing up and down just below the surface. Then, tired from the effort of it and the chase, I floated up for a rest.

The next thing I knew there was a shout and something big and rough fell over my head, dragging me down. In the startled instant before I sank I saw an outrigger almost on top of me with two men standing in the bows. I was in a net!

The net must have been weighted at the corners with rock because it pulled me down fast. I had hardly any air in my lungs and I was tired. I tried to lift the net off me, but the weights closed in underneath me. In a last frantic struggle I got hold of the side of the net and clawed my way down and out of it. But something still held me, dragging me down; my towing line with the fish on it. I snatched out my knife and cut it and sprang, almost bursting, towards the surface.

I reached the air about thirty feet from the outrigger and lay back taking in great gulps of it. The fishermen shouted when they saw me and started paddling the *nau* towards me.

There were four of them. I had seen them before. They were from near the hotel. The captain was a sun-wizened old man. He shook his fist at me and with the other man standing in the bows began hauling in the net which was on a line.

I had a few moments before they reached me. I used them to get my breath back. With the harpoon I could hold them off at least far enough to stop them throwing the net again. But I hadn't got the harpoon. I had let go of it getting out of the net. I took a few more quick breaths and dived. But though I

There was a shout, and the weighted net was flung over me

dropped as straight as I could, I couldn't see the gun. I broke the surface as far from the outrigger as I could and got ready to go down again.

The paddlers headed towards me a second time. The net came up at that moment and the old man opened it across the bows. It was so heavy only the built-up gunwhale stopped them from shipping water.

I dived again. The gun was my only chance. Without it I was as good as dead. They could tire me out with the boat, then ride up close and drop the net over me and I would be too weak to get out.

In the back of my mind I was thinking that maybe that was what happened to the Swede. The strongest swimmer on earth couldn't survive against four men in a boat.

I swam steeply down the hulk of the reef and along, peering amongst the boulders at the bottom. I caught the gleam of the gun then, coming from amongst the soft coral flowers of a grotto. But it was deep. I nearly burst my ear-drums getting it. I got back to surface feeling that behind-the-ears sickness.

They came on again when they saw me. But when they got near enough I tilted the gun up so the harpoon broke the surface and shouted to them in Singhalese to keep away.

"The spear-thing!" one of them exclaimed. The back two stopped paddling. There was a lot of excited chatter.

"Without water it is no good," I heard the old man tell them.

"It is also a gun. Guns shoot well without water," said one of the paddlers. He was about the build of last night's intruder.

"The spear-thing is heavy," the old man explained. "It will not fly."

"How can we be sure?"

The old man started shouting at them, but the paddler cut him short.

"I have a better idea. It's quicker and better to watch."

While they were arguing I was trying to figure out how I was going to make the shore. They would be on top of me all the way, waiting for me to tire. I might manage it on my back, keeping the gun trained on them all the time. But they had to finish me, now they had started. Crouched down in the boat they could use the sail to overtake me and at the last moment throw out the net.

I thought about sinking them with the harpoon; but Ceylon outriggers are made from a single hollowed-out jack-tree log. The jack-tree is tough and they hollow it by fire, which makes it tougher, and even if I could hole it at short range they could plug it up again.

There wasn't a chance in hell of capsizing them. A *nau* can withstand any sea on earth. Two fly-away poles from the gunwhale are lashed to a heavy log float, making them impossible to turn over.

It was like one of those dreams where you can't escape. With a dead, hopeless feeling, I turned on my back and began kicking for shore.

The talkative paddler saw my action and shouted jeeringly in pidgin English:

"What's amatter, white man? White man wanna go home? Hey, George! Take a look at this!" He reached into the belly of the boat and fished out a scraggy-looking object. It was the carcass of a dog, which they had probably put in for bait. "Look, white man!" With a flick of his knife he disembowled it and flung it as far in my direction as he could. The others howled with laughter.

"Okay? Very good?" mimicked the paddler. They roared with laughter again.

If he had been in range I'd have let him have it then. They knew the smell of blood in the water would bring the sharks. They settled back to watch the fun.

The cold-bloodedness of it goaded me to such rage that I could only think of one thing: if I was going to die, so were they!

I dived and headed underwater straight for the boat. I passed the carcass of the dog twisting slowly downward through the water. When I saw the *nau* lying like a crab on the surface above me I came up gently on the far side of it, my nose just breaking the water behind the outrigger float. The natives were

I slashed at the cords that held the float

sitting on the gunwhale staring intently at the place where I had disappeared.

Hooking the gun on to the back of my belt, I got out my knife and began to cut the lashings which held the aft' cross-member to the float. I had slashed the cross-member completely loose before the Singhalese knew anything was up.

The after end of the float swung free and the *nau* began to list. It would have capsized eventually like that, but to make sure I swam to the forward cross-member and started on that.

From where I was I could see the old man waving his arms about. He was ordering the paddlers over the side to fix it; but they wouldn't budge. They were too scared of the sharks.

As I severed the last turn of the rope, the unsupported crossmembers plunged straight down into the water and the *nau* toppled over, pitching them into the sea.

I surfaced at once and struck out for the reef. If there were sharks in the neighbourhood I didn't want to be caught in the open. I heard the terror-stricken cries of the natives as they tried to clamber on to the side of the craft. But, being a log, I knew that it would slowly sink until it was just under the surface. No matter where they got to they wouldn't be safe from the sharks.

Watching down into the water as I swam, I suddenly saw a fifteen-foot grey shadow flick past about four fathoms below me. It was a tiger shark! That meant the worst kind of trouble. I watched him to see if he was going to double back, but he paid no attention to me at all. I guessed he was heading unerringly to where the carcass of the dog had come to rest. When he had snapped that up he would probably have a look at the boat.

I dived close in against the reef then, and held myself still against the rock and waited.

Almost instantly I felt the water crush against me and a great body smashed past just overhead. It was another tiger shark. I watched him diminish to a green wraith in the clear water, in the direction of the boat. In the dream-like virescence of the upper fathoms I saw him turn deliberately and circle twice. With an easy twist he nosed up to the surface and plucked at something.

Presently the first shark joined him, then another and another until there were five—cruising around close under the surface, from time to time nosing upwards then backing away, for all the world like trout in an aquarium.

When I surfaced for air the first thing I heard was the screaming. The old man had gone; so had the paddler. The remaining two were sitting astride the waterlogged boat beating the water frantically with their paddles and shrieking. Even as I watched one of them was dragged down into the water with a look of indescribable horror on his face.

But as I sank once more to the shelter of the reef I felt no pity for those who had tried to kill me. I felt nothing; only a sense of balance in the water, and a waiting calm. They were not of my world. My world was down here in the silence where the heart beat in the throat and dark blooms writhed on the undertide. With an emotion I can't describe I watched the great fish-shapes turn and turn again, reach up and dive. It was remorseless, like the cataracts of dark water draining and rushing through the reefs.

At last there was nothing more and they turned away, two of them heading inshore, the third out to sea, the last two nosing towards the reef.

One was about twelve feet, the other a good fifteen. I kept as still as a rock, but the small one spotted me.

Kicking the water with his caudal fin he shot straight at me. I stood on a rock shelf, held down by the weight of the gun, and let him come. I knew it was his experimental rush. Sure enough, when I didn't move he veered off and turned, circling in a wide arc.

The big one saw me then. He came right at me, turning so close that his displacement knocked me off the ledge. Before I could control my balance the other was back again. I tried to get the gun up, but I was twisting in the big one's backwash. He came in on his side with his mouth open. I opened my own mouth and yelled.

It sounded through the bones of my head like "Ulp!" but it jarred his hearing mechanism and he veered away sharply.

I had to get air. I started to rise, but the big one came round me again. He came slowly at first, finishing with a short savage rush. With what remaining breath I had I yelled again. The crescendic mouth missed me by a foot. The force of the water turned me over completely, tearing my mask off. I all but dropped the gun. With the water in my nose and eyes, somehow I groped my way to the surface and filled my lungs with air.

Without the mask I was practically blind. Terrified that he would come up under me, I went down again at once. But now everything was misty. I strained desperately to penetrate the green haze. A dark shape was moving below me. If that was one, where was the other? At any moment I expected to feel a shattering impact and the rending of jaws.

The shadow below me licked backwards and forwards several times. Then suddenly I knew it was tearing up towards me like an express locomotive. I swung the gun blindly in its direction, feeling for the trigger. The thing grew like an explosion—filling the whole ocean. I fired.

The shock of impact knocked me sideways. I clung on to the gun with both hands. There was a moment of floating, not knowing which way up I was, and then a jerk which nearly wrenched the gun from my hands. I had him!

The next moment I was being rushed through the water at

I was rushed through the water at a

a great rate, swung round like a cat by the tail, and rushed back. I tried to see, but the pressure on my eyes was too great. I knew if I couldn't get to the surface I should drown.

Then I felt the emergency knot on the muzzle of the gun snap with the strain. Fifteen feet of reserve line snaked out in the water instantly. It checked my progress; I floated; was jerked on again, but slower this time. With all my strength I fought my way to the surface; gasped for air; was dragged under; released again.

For half an hour I was jerked, ducked and towed round the reef. Once he dragged me down until my ears nearly split; then

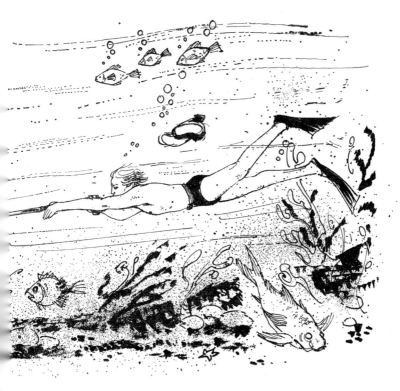

and swung round like a cat by the tail.

up again. Then he quit running and began to writhe and snap at everything in sight. He came at me again and again. I fought him off with the bayonet, till he snapped it off, then I used the gun. He bent up the end of the projector; then turned on himself and seized his own tail. That was what saved me. Once his teeth found flesh he never let go.

His contortions grew weaker and weaker until at last I peered through the green water and saw the great crescent of him twisting, drowned, on the line.

That was all there was to it, I guess. He was too heavy to tow home and I wasn't going to cut him adrift after all that. I detached the line from the gun and anchored him to an out-crop of rock. Then, hoping the other shark wouldn't find him, I swam back to shore.

I say swam; I floated most of the way. I was as weak as tonic water. A Swiss from the hotel helped me up on to the beach and took me in and bought me a Scotch. Then he paid for the hire of a rickety motor-boat because I hadn't any dough, and the two of us went back to the reef.

The big shark was still there, with his tail still clamped firmly in his mouth. I went down and untied him. Something had had a bite out of him, but most of him was okay. The Swiss watched me through a sponging-glass and when we were on our way back with the shark trailing behind he said that this was real adventure and that he had never had such fun in his whole life.

I got the thing to market in an ox-cart the next morning and sold it by auction. I made three hundred and seventy-five rupees out of it.

I didn't have any more trouble from the fishermen. After that they got the idea I was Buddha's uncle or something and kept away from me as though I had the plague. And when I went across to Trincomalee I didn't have any trouble there either. It was a good season at Trinco and I stayed there a month, during which period I caught thirty-six king fishes, about twelve groupers, and a Port Jackson shark which I couldn't understand being so far west.

The Conqueror Worm

GERALD KERSH

I MET Dempsey first in Stockholm. He was one of those pulpy personalities in which it is difficult to find anything definite. He was honest because he was afraid of the consequences of dishonesty; nobody quarrelled with him because he agreed with everything anybody said. His pale and insipid soul was dotted with silly little prejudices and principles, as feeble as the vestigial seeds of a banana. There was one particle which, hardened by pure fear, stuck in the middle of his brain—the fact that he had never done anything illegal. Other men base their pride on achievement or endurance: "I built a business," "I survived the war." Dempsey's self-respect centred round the thought: "I have never done anything like that." He stuck to me, like discarded chewing-gum to the sole of a boot, and would not be shaken off, until that memorable night when we found ourselves stranded in Nyevinossi-Novgorod.

Oh, that town, that miserable ice-bound town of Nyevinossi-Novgorod! There are no lamps in its streets. Why should there be, since nobody goes out after dark? And who wants to go out, since there is nowhere to go? It is a coal town, clinging to the mouths of the Nyevinossi Pits; bisected by the line of the Arctic Circle, it skulks, freezing, under the slate-coloured sky of the Kola Peninsula—black with smoke, grey with fog, rasped by the icy teeth of the bitter White Sea; redolent of dead fish, and utterly permeated with gritty coal-dust. The streets twist and turn, as if they had writhed with cold before being frozen stiff by the wind—the paralysing wind of the Arctic, which carries with it the unbearable desolation of the northern wastes and the heart-breaking melancholy of the Eastern tundras.

We were lost there. It was nearly midnight. Every window was dark, and the roads were treacherous.

"We can get the ferry to Izbaborg at six in the morning," I said.

"But what are we going to do till then?" asked Dempsey.

"Find lodging."

"But where?"

"Oh, I don't know. We'll have to ask somebody."

"But we can't speak a word of Russian —"

"Oh, shut up."

I knocked at the nearest door, but nobody answered. You would have thought that the town was dead. We walked on. Wind began to whistle through the narrow, deserted street.

"Somebody's coming!" said Dempsey.

A man was approaching, carrying a lantern. I called him: "Hoi!" He stopped, and we went up to him. As he held up the lantern to look at us, I caught a glimpse of his face. He was a Jew, very small, closely wrapped in a wolfskin coat, with a fur cap pulled down over his ears. His face was as narrow as if it had been pressed between two boards; marked with smallpox, and contorted in an anxious, mechanical grin, such as you see on the face of a man squinting against strong sunlight. I addressed him in German:

"Can you help us find a place to sleep?"

He replied in Yiddish: "Sleep? Can you pay?"

"Yes."

"Well, there's an hotel."

"Is there? Where?"

"Well, you go straight along until you come to Batko's; then turn to the left by the—"

"But how can we find our way in the dark? We're strangers here."

"Hum. All right. I'll show you. You come with me."

"I don't like the look of him," whispered Dempsey.

We followed the man with the lantern. The streets grew narrower, winding like snakes. We were lost in a maze of black tunnels, through which the rising wind rushed, roaring, flinging into our faces gritty fragments of ice. Dempsey took my arm, and clung to it. We came to the deep centre of the town, to a street so narrow that two men could not have walked abreast through it. Our guide stopped at an ancient and filthy wooden house which leaned over at an angle of sixty degrees on to three huge wooden props, which alone prevented it from falling down.

"Here you are, gentlemen. An hotel. Yak's. It's all right, I tell you!" The Jew knocked at the door.

"We can't go in here," said Dempsey.

"We've got to go somewhere," I said.

"I'd rather spend the night in the streets. I've got a funny feeling—"

"Ssh!"

The door swung open, and the entire opening was blocked by the immense bulk of a man. The light was behind him. We could see only his black silhouette. He stepped back.

"Come in," said our guide.

I pushed Dempsey in front of me, into the house. The man closed the door, and then, as he turned and faced us, I started back and put my hand on my revolver. I have never seen such a man. His bulk, alone, was terrifying: stripped, he must have weighed twenty-two stone. His colossal torso was muffled in a great bearskin coat—he seemed larger than an elephant; yet

"Here you are, gentlemen. An hotel. Yak's. It's all right."

even so, his head was too big for his body. His face appeared
to have been twisted out of shape by some fantastic disease,
until it bore a distinct resemblance to the head of a rhinoceros:
it had the same scalloped mouth, bestial forehead, and ponder-
ous jowl. His nose was smashed flat. An ancient scar, which
must have laid open the whole left side of his face, twitched up
a corner of his mouth in a perpetual snarl. His flat skull was
covered with coarse white bristles, and under his lower lip

hung a tuft like a shaving-brush. Our guide whispered to him: they both laughed. The anxious, grinning little face turned towards me, as he said:

"This is Yak. You'll be comfortable here. Such a bed! You'll never want to get up again. Goodnight! Sleep well!" The door closed on him. We were alone with Yak.

"Let's get out of here," whispered Dempsey, shaking like a leaf; but it seemed ridiculous, now, to go back into the streets. If I have one English trait, it is that I would face death rather than do something that seems ridiculous. Moreover, I had my revolver.

I said to Yak, in German: "We want a bed."

He shook his head. He did not understand; and all the time, he looked at us with one wicked little red eye.

"What's Russian for 'bed', Dempsey?"

"I don't know. Oh, please, please, let's get out of here!"

"And freeze to death?"

Yak moved, pushing us before him. He steered us upstairs, to the first floor, struck a match, and lit a lamp. The flame popped and spread. We were in a tiny bedroom containing a great old bed, and no other furniture. The windows, I noticed, had been firmly boarded up. I turned again to Yak, and said in a tone of authority:

"We must be called at five o'clock."

He shook his head.

I made gestures. I pointed to him; then to Dempsey and myself: indicated an imaginary clock; conveyed, in pantomime, sleeping and waking up, and spread out five fingers.

"What's Russian for 'five o'clock'?" I asked.

"Something like 'pyet chessov'," said Dempsey.

"Pyet chessov!" I said, very loudly.

Yak nodded, and then, with a grin that made my blood run cold, said: "Pyet chessov."

He went out. Something went *click*.

"He's locked the door!" cried Dempsey.

I tried the door. It was locked. I knocked. There was no answer.

"My God!" exclaimed Dempsey. "This is terrible. I didn't

want to come here. It's all your fault. You insisted. Now see what a mess we're in. I had a feeling that something was going to happen. Now we're caught, like rats in a trap. What are we going to do?"

"Perhaps it's only a custom here, in case a lodger runs away without paying his rent."

"He would have asked us to pay in advance," said Dempsey, "but he knows there's no need to. He'll get all we've got without asking. We'll never see daylight. We're finished."

"I've got a revolver."

"My God, my God!" whispered Dempsey.

"We can lie down, and keep warm," I said, "I'm freezing, and I'm dead beat. I'm going to lie down."

I did so, covering myself with the malodorous bedclothes—the greasy matting, and the mangy bearskin rug. Dempsey leapt into bed beside me, and sat bolt upright, tense with terror, and shivering so that the bed shook.

"Relax," I said.

"I can't."

"Take your boots off."

"I can't."

"Lie down."

"I can't. I've got a premonition. My premonitions are always right. I'm psychic. You might get out of this, I never shall. I tell you, I know I shan't get out of here alive. Listen. You've been my friend, my only friend. Take my papers and my—open your eyes, please, open your eyes and listen to me. I shall die here. Something tells me ... I *know*. There's death in this house—what's that?"

It was a shuffling noise. In the middle of the room looking at us with sickening curiosity, sat two large black rats. I waved a hand at them, to drive them away; they did not move.

"They're waiting for us," said Dempsey, "they *know*. Rats know."

A blast of wind struck the house. A piece of ice, dislodged from the roof, slid down with a grating noise and fell into the street. Dempsey's teeth were chattering like castanets. I laid my revolver between us, and propped myself up against the

Yak dropped a hand to his chest and fell against the wall

head-board of the bed. There seemed to be two weights pressing down upon my eyelids. I struggled against sleep, but vast waves of weariness were running through my body.

"What's that?" whispered Dempsey. Something was scratching at the door. I looked, with the big revolver poised for a snapshot. It was another rat.

"Keep quiet," I said, "let me get a few minutes' rest."

Nothing, nothing in the world could have kept me awake. Consciousness was slipping away from me ... down and down and down an infinite precipice of smooth black glass ...

Then I was asleep, and I remember that I was involved in a bizarre and meaningless dream ... I was being led out into a yard, and a voice was saying to me: "You are to impersonate the Emperor Napoleon ..." I saw the rings of a thousand rifle-muzzles. There was a terrific explosion. I was blown away, head over heels, roaring with laughter, over a tremendous black landscape, soaring like a bird. Then I looked up, and saw hovering over me a gigantic machine bristling with hooks. It descended, caught me. I struggled to free myself, and heard a voice whisper: "Wake up! For God's sake! Wake up!"

I opened my eyes with a groan, and saw the terrified face of Dempsey. "Look!" he said. "Oh, God, look!"

The door was opening. In the widening black oblong, I saw the revolting face of Yak, moving as silently as the ghost of an evil passion, indescribably hideous in the ghastly lamplight. He entered the room. Dempsey screamed, and then, drowning the scream, came the stunning bang of the heavy revolver, with the stinging smell of cordite. Yak dropped a vast hand to his chest, fell back against the wall, and sat down, his legs spread out in front of him. I leapt out of bed. Yak's right hand came slowly away from his breast, wet with blood, as he spread it out like a fan in front of us, stared, with utter astonishment, and said, in a fading whisper:

"Pyet ... chessov ..."

At that moment, the bell of a church boomed the first stroke of five.

"Idiot!" I said, as I snatched the revolver out of Dempsey's hand, "he was only coming to wake us up!"

We caught the first ferry-boat. Within a week, we had put five hundred miles between ourselves and Nyevinossi-Novgorod. Dempsey began to recover from the shock. At first, he said: "How was I to know? It was excusable." Then: "How do you know he was only coming to wake us up?" Then: "I'm not at all sure that I didn't save both our lives." And finally: "I'm absolutely certain that I caught him in the act. Thank God, I didn't lose my presence of mind!"

He grew quite aggressive. In Oslo, he reprimanded a barber. In Berlin, he swore at a waiter. I left him in Paris. That was in 1920. I hear that he is married since then. He treats his wife with extraordinary severity, and was heard calling her a "sickening idiot" in the presence of strangers. He still finds it difficult to stand a direct look, but he is a roaring lion with subordinates, and has cultivated a quite terrifying manner of handing his hat to cloakroom attendants.

He is acquiring something of the reputation of a man of iron.

Peril in the Camargue

BRIAN CLEEVE

I HEARD her calling me from a long way away. "Paul...
Paul..." Her voice very lonely in the wide silence of the
evening.

A small wind shook the reeds where I lay hidden, and far
out in the lagoon the flamingoes lifted their scythe-shaped,
serpent heads to listen. I lay flat, my chin pressed into the wet
sand, my body growing cold.

"Paul... Paul..."

I stared through the fringe of reeds at the shallow, steel-
bright water; at the sandbanks beyond, dark and glistening; at
the clumps and barriers of reeds, thickening towards the west
where the shallow sea lagoons and sandbars became marshland,

sea and land blending, melting into one another; channels of deeper water twisting and winding through the reeds; here and there an island of soil rising a few centimetres above the marsh, bound together by tough, salt-withered grass and the roots of a pine tree; quicksands, shining and trembling like wet, hungry mouths, waiting to suck down any foot that trod on them. Flat and desolate and lonely as my heart.

I felt so lonely I could have cried out like a bird. And yet I didn't want Léonie to find me. I didn't know what I wanted. Only to lie here, perhaps, and watch the flamingoes for ever; watch them sweeping their scythe beaks through the shallow water, feeding. Watch the sunset.

I didn't even know any more why we had quarrelled. We never used to. All the time in school we never quarrelled. And then we used to look forward to now, to the time when school was finished for ever, and all the length of the days was our own to do what we liked in.

To take the skiff far out beyond the last sandbank and fish in the sea. To lie like this all day and watch the wild duck and the flamingoes. To do nothing. To do everything. And yet now that we could, it wasn't the same. Nothing was the same.

"Paul, Paul." She was very near now. The first of the flamingoes opened his great black-and-scarlet wings in fright, and began to run. The others followed him, awkward and ungainly as if running on wooden stilts, their wings beating like great coloured sails.

"There you are," Léonie said.

I didn't look round at her. They were flying now, their long spider-legs trailing, skimming the silver water, the sandbank, the tops of the reeds.

"Why did you run away and hide?"

"I don't know."

She threw herself down, and began digging at the sand with her fingers.

"Do you want to know something?"

"I don't mind."

In the sunset her hair was red as well as gold, and her eyes were quite green. Like a cat's. I wanted desperately to be nice to her, but I couldn't. I looked back at the flamingoes, far away now, their legs folded, their bodies no more than cinders against the reddening sky.

"There are two strangers at your house."

I sat up at that. Strangers almost never came to the marshland. How long had it been since the last one, the man who had come to ring the wild duck? Two years? Three?

"What do they want?"

"Why don't you come home and find out?" she asked. She looked at me from under her eyelashes, a queer, sideways kind of look, her fingers still digging in the sand. The new way she had of looking. The one I didn't understand. It made me feel strange. As if I didn't know her any more.

"Why do you look at me in that stupid way?" I said. And quite suddenly she was furious, her face flaming, her eyes like green fire.

"Stupid yourself," she hissed, and flung a handful of sand in my face. But I saw it coming and closed my eyes in time. Then I was on to her, my hands gripping her shoulders, pushing her down on the sand.

"I'll teach you," I said. "Wait till I get you down. I'll fill your mouth with sand, you little pig."

She fought back in silence, twisting, punching at my face.

It was only in the last year that I had become stronger than she, and she could still hold me off for a time.

I began to laugh. It was like it had always been. "Just wait," I said.

She stopped fighting, rubbed her face against mine, whispered in my ear, "Oh, Paul, oh, Paul."

I lifted my head and looked at her, and I couldn't understand anything. My hands fell away from her as if they were afraid to touch her any more.

She smiled, tilting her head sideways, looking at me through her lashes. "Do you want to know about the strangers?"

I nodded, not knowing what else to do.

"They're staying in your house for the night. One of them is quite old, with a crutch. But the other one is young." She leaned forward and grinned in my face. "And handsome. Much handsomer than you, you silly old sourpuss."

She snapped her fingers under my nose and was up on her feet and away, waiting for me to chase her, her face a flame of devilment, bending down, ready to throw sand if I came for her.

"Sourpuss. Sourpuss."

Then she was gone among the reeds, and I heard her laughter fading as she ran...

I followed her slowly. She was always like that these days. What was wrong with her? It had never been that way before. We had been together like two hands. We'd understood each other without even talking, and if we fought it was only because we wanted to fight.

But now...

I splashed in a shallow pool with my feet, and felt better. And as the path twisted through the marsh, the reeds growing thicker and taller the nearer it came to the island, I began to wonder about the strangers.

Why had they come? Except for other fishermen and hunters like Léonie's father and mine, no one ever came. It was five kilometres to the island, rowing in the skiff across the lagoons and through the channels.

The reeds fell away from either side of the path, the ground became firmer under foot, lifted slightly on to our island, and I was home. Two cabins, a hundred metres from one another, separated by a stretch of rough, tussocky grass and reeds: Léonie's parents' cabin was at the far end of the island, ours at this end.

Pierre, my smallest brother, lay inside his little fence under the low, twisted, pine tree with its flat top like a green sunshade, and a black kitten played with him, hopping in and out of the shadows. The other children wouldn't be back from school till dark.

I went softly to the window of the cabin and looked in. And there they were, the two strangers, sitting one on either side of the black, iron stove, drinking soup out of our bowls. I could smell it through the open window, and it made me realise that I was hungry. But I was too interested to move for a little while.

One was old, all right, but not that old. Not as old as my father. The stubble of his beard was grey, and his moustache; but his eyebrows still had black in them. Thick, twisting eyebrows knotting over a hook of a nose.

I couldn't see if he was tall, but his shoulders were very big, hunched with muscle. You could see how strong they were, even under his thick, grey coat.

The other one wasn't handsome at all. A pointed chin and a small, thin mouth almost like a girl's. He had a scar at one side of it, so white I could see it even in the half darkness of the room. A long, white scar running from the corner of his mouth almost to his ear.

Beyond him my mother was cutting bread against her chest, and she must have seen the outline of my head in the window.

"Paul!"

"Yes, Maman." She rules the house, and when she calls like that it's best either to come or to go very quickly. I ran round to the front and made my entrance as best I could, ducking my knee to the strangers.

They looked up at my coming, and then the young one went on eating, not interested in me. But the older one lifted an eyebrow and beckoned me with his spoon.

"So you're the big son of the house?"

"Yes, monsieur."

My father looked up from where he was mending a bird-net in the corner, smiling his secret, faraway smile, as if he could hear what was being said. But he can only hear the birds crying and whistling. Those he can hear farther than I can.

"The two messieurs are staying for the night," said my mother. "They will sleep in here with you." She gave the two men bread, a thick slice to each on the point of the knife.

"Are you a clever boy?" said the older one, munching his bread after he had dipped it in his soup. I wondered if there was going to be enough soup for me.

"I said, 'Are you clever?'" And suddenly there was such a cold savagery in his voice that I felt it catch my throat.

"N-no, monsieur. Not very . . ."

My mother came forward and tapped the point of the black-handled breadknife against his chest. "He's clever enough for what you mean," she said.

She looked at me over her shoulder. "They're sleeping here, paying good money, and going at dawn. There'll be no need to say anything of them to anyone. Do you understand?"

"I understand."

"And you—" she turned back to the older man—"you can pay me now. One thousand francs each." I caught my breath at that; it was a fortune for just a bowl of soup and a space by the stove. The man smiled, putting down his spoon on his broad knee, sliding his fingers into some deep inside-pocket to pull out two mille notes.

"There you are," he said, still smiling down at the point of my mother's knife, as if he recognised in her a hardness the equal of his own. "No questions, eh? And no lies, and no memories?"

"That's right," said my mother. "We're poor folk here and don't hit money in the face. There's no call for me to ask you questions if you want a bed and soup."

I stared at her in astonishment. My mother had never done anything in her life simply for money. Sometimes in the market

"They're sleeping here, paying good money, and going at dawn."

she wouldn't sell at any price if she didn't like the look of the customer.

There was the time I was nursing the flamingo with the broken wing. Monsieur Doubs had heard about it and had come to offer us five thousand francs for the bird.

I still remembered the look in her face as she had said, "We don't sell living creatures here, monsieur." And strangely enough there was that same look on her face now. Under the hardness. As if she was sorry for them, and didn't want them to know it.

I would have liked to ask them if they were running away from prison, because Léonie and I had seen a film just like that, but I didn't dare. Instead I asked for my supper.

"There," said my mother. "And don't ask for more."

I took my bowl and sat on the fishbox in the corner beside

my father, watching his lean, brown fingers shape and pull and tap at the knots of the net. He glanced sideways at me, giving the slightest of nods towards the strangers, lifting one thin eyebrow, and pushing out his lower lip. His face said as clearly as words, "They're no good." Then he shrugged, as much as to say, "Your mother!"

I smiled, and he smiled, and we understood one another as if we had one heart...

I heard the skiff beaching behind the house, and a moment later my three school-going brothers tumbled into the room, to be struck dumb by the sight of the strangers. They sat down in a row on the bench by the door, their satchels between their dirty knees, their eyes like buttons. The two strangers looked at them, and at that moment Léonie came in.

She had changed out of her shorts and shirt into her Sunday dress. It was red and too small for her now, too tight everywhere. But she was very proud of it. And she came into the middle of the room and stood looking at the two men, and then at my mother, with a small, impudent lift of her head.

I could see my mother's right hand itching to smack her face for being so inquisitive as to come in at our supper-time, but she wouldn't in front of the strangers.

The one with the scar looked up at Léonie and smiled, putting his bowl down under the stool. A kitten came out from under the cupboard and began to lick it.

"What's your name?" said the stranger. It was the first time he'd spoken. He hadn't bothered to ask my name.

"Léonie. And what's yours?"

"Mind your own business," said my mother, but the stranger laughed, the scar puckering in his cheek. He had looked sullen and bored before, just eating his soup and saying nothing. But now he looked quite alive.

"They call me the Para," he said. "And they call him Ti-tic—" he pointed to the crutch beside the other man— "because when he walks he makes a noise. Ti-tic. Ti-tic." He laughed.

"I walk as fast as others," said Ti-tic. "Faster than some."

"And why do they call you the Para?" asked Léonie.

"Your mother will be wanting to give you supper," said my mother, handing out bowls to my brothers.

"I've eaten," said Léonie.

She sat on the floor near to the two strangers, coiling down very slowly because if she went too fast she'd burst her dress.

"Why do they call you the Para?"

"Because I was a Para," said the man, as if he was saying, I was a King. "A red beret. A paratrooper."

Ti-tic gave a short, harsh laugh, and wiped his moustache with his sleeve. "Some paratrooper!"

The Para's face went pale and ugly with anger. "Don't mind him. He's jealous, the old gimp. Ti-tic, Ti-tic," he sneered. "He doesn't like to hear me talk. I could tell you stories—" He looked round the room. "We're all friends here, eh?" He looked at my brothers as if he'd petrify them where they sat, and they stiffened into excited silence, their eyes wide and staring. Then the Para looked at Léonie, his mouth twisting as if with the wealth of stories pressing behind it to be told.

"Tell us!" breathed Léonie. She leaned towards him, teasing him, the way she does when she's making fun of me, pretending to be gasping to hear something, although she's never really much interested in any stories but her own. But, of course, the Para couldn't know that, and he leaned back and preened himself, thinking he was tantalising us.

My mother snorted, angry with everyone, and went out to feed the baby under the tree.

"Go on!" said Léonie. I expected her to look at me and wink, but she didn't.

"Well," said the Para, "there was a time south of Marrakesh. A band of rebels was making for the mountains, for a narrow pass, and we were to cut them off. They dropped us at night, fifty of us. Fifty! Against three hundred rebels! Six to one. But we didn't care. A para is equal to any ten other men. So we dropped into the pass at night, see . . ."

He made floating gestures with his hands and against my will I began to see the great, white, mushroom domes of the parachutes opening, floating down, like sleeping swans riding on the slow river of the stars.

"...burp guns and mortars. You should've heard them scream as the first blasts of fire hit them."

"Ooooh!" whispered Léonie, putting her knuckles to her mouth, widening her eyes, pretending terror. My brothers on the bench gasped in chorus.

"And there was a time when three of us were taken prisoner. They were going to torture us..."

My father was watching the Para's face. Although he can't hear, he can read lips. Now he looked at me, pursing his mouth and shaking his head very slightly, as if he didn't believe what the Para was saying. I was glad of that, because my father always knew, and I could tell Léonie afterwards. She might still only be pretending to be interested, but I wasn't quite sure any longer.

"And then another time..."

An hour must have gone by, and still he had stories. Wounds he had had, and escapes. How he had hunted down the rebel who slashed his face, and how he had won the Médaille Militaire.

The sun went down, and outside it was twilight, with darkness coming. For a long time Ti-tic had been slouched on his stool with his head sunk into his great shoulders and his eyes shut, breathing deeply and easily, as if he was asleep. Now he sat up and yawned.

"Still yapping?" he said. "Turn it off, little Para, and let everyone get to bed. We'll be moving before dawn."

"That's right," said my mother. "The children have to be in bed." She clapped her hands, and my brothers scattered off the bench like birds.

She looked at Léonie, and reluctantly Léonie uncoiled herself and stood up. "If I was a man I'd be a para," she sighed.

The Para nodded, smiling his twisted smile, tapping his chest. "You have to have it here," he said.

He watched her as she went out. And still he smiled, watching her go. I felt very glad that he would be gone by morning.

My father folded away his net, and began to spread out the palliasse that Ti-tic and the Para would be sleeping on. My mother took up the baby from his box in the corner, where she had laid him after his feed, and carried him with her into the other room, drawing across the curtain that separated it from us.

"Goodnight, messieurs," she said.

Ti-tic lay down, groaning softly as he settled his bad leg into place with his hands, his crutch on the earth floor beside him.

"I'm going out for a minute," said the Para, jerking his head at the pale oblong of the door. It was quite dark by now inside the room.

I lay down in my corner and heard my father padding across to the curtain. Then it was quiet. A cold draught whispered in from the open door, touching my face. But there was no point in shutting it until the Para came back.

I lay and waited, already half asleep. But for the draught I would have been quite asleep.

Five minutes. Ten. What could he be doing? Had he lost his way? It could be dangerous for him if he had gone far. But why should he go far?

I slid out of my blankets and went to the door. After the darkness of the room it seemed almost light outside. In the west there were still the red embers of the twilight, and in the east, a quarter of the moon. He couldn't lose his way in that.

"*Monsieur le Para,*" I called softly. There was no answer. I went round the side of the house to the back. He wasn't there.

In the distance I could just discern Léonie's house. The rough grass and reeds lay bare as silver under the moon. Léonie's house. Could he be there? Telling her more stories? But her parents would be going to bed, too, by now. And their house was dark. I began walking towards it, puzzled.

I must have been halfway there when I heard Léonie cry out. A sudden, thin cry of terror shut off as suddenly as it began, like a stream of water from a tap. I started to run.

It had come from beyond her house, a long way beyond. And there was only one path that way, leading for a few hundred metres into the marsh. Beyond it again there were quicksands.

I ran down the path like a hare, twisting along its turns and corners without so much as thinking of them, my feet finding them by old habit, my heart pounding. What could have happened? What could be happening to her?

"Run!" I shouted, and I threw more sand into the Para's face

And yet when I saw it, I seemed to have already known. They were on a wide patch of tufted grass, clear in the moon. And the Para was strangling her. She fought like a cat, not able to scream any more because her throat was choking, but clawing at his face, at his arms, baring her teeth, her face dark red with fury, the blood forced into it by his hands.

I ran at him, bending down to claw up sand in both my hands. As he turned I flung it into his eyes and his open mouth.

Léonie was out of his grip in a flash, and I heard the long, rasping sob of her breath as she dragged it into her lungs.

"Run," I shouted. "Run." He lunged for me, and I threw more sand before I dodged away. He went staggering past me, blinded, thrashing with his hands at the moonlight.

Then Léonie was beside me, sobbing with short, dry gasps of fury. "He's crazy!" she said. "We'll teach him."

She caught my arm, dragging me towards the path, turning not towards home, but away from it, towards the quicksands.

The Para had cleared his eyes now, and was coming again, has face twisted, his hands stretched out to grip us. He seemed enormous, towering over us like a tree. We ran. Not very fast, because of Léonie's dress. But it didn't matter because the Para didn't know the path, and half the time he was splashing knee deep in water. The path grew thin, and the water stood among the reeds in black, oily sheets. It became a series of grass hummocks that squelched under our feet, tilting and sinking as we jumped on them.

"Let him get close," whispered Léonie. But he was close already.

"Now!" she screamed, and we leapt sideways on to a small island of hard sand. But the Para went straight on. Knee deep. Waist deep. And the quicksand sucked and bubbled round him, hidden under its inch-deep camouflage of water.

We stood and watched him as he tried to get back to us, twisting in the grip of the sand. He seemed to make half a step, but his feet didn't move forward. Only his body leaned, dipping forward and down into the wet. I saw the shudder coming on his face as he realised he couldn't move. And he seemed quite small, not enormous the way he had looked just now.

"Get me out of this," he said.

Léonie laughed. "You're going to drown," she said. And I was shocked myself at the sound of hatred in her voice. The Para began to beat the water round him. Even then he didn't understand. "It's quicksand," said Léonie. "Do you know what that is, *Monsieur le Para? Monsieur le héros?*"

He looked at her, and all the colour sank out of his face. His mouth hung open, and he began to make a little rattling noise in his throat, like a baby beginning to cry.

"No," he whispered. "Not that..." And then he screamed. "Get me out, get me out, get me out!"

A flight of ducks rattled into the air from a creek beside us, frightened by the noise.

"I wanted it to be like the films," said Léonie, half to me, half to the Para. "Walking out with a boy."

He stared at her as if she was mad, but I understood. On the films you see girls going out with boys, and looking tenderly at each other, and whispering, and holding hands, and going to shooting galleries, until one day they get married. And inland they do those things in real life, too. But in the marshland there were only ourselves.

"He caught me up just before I went indoors," Léonie whispered. "And asked me if I'd go for a walk with him. I thought it would be just like the films and then he tried to strangle me."

"I didn't mean it," said the Para. His whole face was shaking, trembling. He reached out his hands to us, begging. "I was only kidding—just a joke—aaaah!" The water bubbled round his chest, and he sank a thumb's breadth deeper into the sand. "You can't let me die like this," he shouted. "You can't..."

"You're a hero," said Léonie. "You told us. Heroes don't cry."

"I'm not," he whimpered. "I was lying. I'm not a Para. I'm not a hero. Don't let me die." He didn't know what he was saying any more. "The flics are after me. I smashed a window and stole some rings. Goddam lousy rings not worth a mille each. And the flics have been after me ever since. Everyone's against me. You can't let me die..." He was blubbering now, twisting himself deeper and deeper into the sand.

I saw something happening to Léonie's face. As if she was going to be sick. "Get him out," she said.

She turned away as I lay down on the hard sand and stretched forward over the skim of water towards the Para.

"Grip my hands," I said.

"I can't move," he sobbed. "I can't reach."

"Don't be a baby," I said. "You can't drown in that. We were playing a trick on you. It's not much more than a metre deep. You must be touching firm bottom now."

Every moment he sank deeper into the quicksand

He let out his breath in a shuddering sigh, and closed his eyes. I could see he was exploring with his feet.

"Lie forward and relax," I said. "Go limp."

I got my fingers round his wrists, began to draw him towards me, digging my toes into the sand to give me purchase.

It wasn't very hard. He could have got himself out if he'd known how. The quicksand sucked and shuddered. Bubbles wallowed greasily up round his body, bursting in the moonlight like flowers opening. He lay almost on the surface now, his hands, his elbows, his shoulders on firm sand. At last he was out, climbing shakily to his knees, his chest heaving with great, shuddering gasps as the fear went out of him.

I turned away, not wanting to look at him any more than Léonie had. And as I turned he grabbed my wrist and twisted, yanking it behind my back and up, lifting me on to my toes with a streak of fire burning and darting in my shoulder.

"So it was a trick, was it?" he said. "No, don't try any more sand," he called to Léonie, "or I'll break his arm." He twisted his hand and I felt the tears come into my eyes with the pain.

Léonie let the sand she had snatched up dribble between her fingers. "Now come here." She looked at him uncertainly. "Come here!" He twisted more and I couldn't stop from crying out. She came a slow step towards us, looking from my face to his, her eyes frightened, her mouth trembling.

"You can't," she said. "Not when we pulled you out..."

"I'm not a kid," he said. "You can't... you can't," he mimicked her viciously. "Give me your arm, or I'll break his."

"Don't," I shouted. "Don't. Run for it. Get my father—"

His fist took me in the small of the back, and I arched like a hooked fish, the breath of my voice gone out of me with the agony.

"Now will you give me your arm?" he said. "I'll teach two kids to play tricks on a man like me. When I walk down the road in Marseilles even the flics get out of my way."

Very slowly Léonie held out her wrist towards him.

"No!" I screamed. "No!" Twisting until I thought my arm was broken.

"That's it," said the Para. "You're beginning to learn, eh?"

He lifted his own free hand quite slowly to take her wrist.

And then it came. Like a hawk striking. Not a sound. Just a shadow. And then a crack like a stick snapping. The grip on my wrist slackened, vanished. And the Para was down on his knees, one arm hanging loose, broken, touching it with his other hand, and keening deep in his throat with the pain.

I looked up and there was Ti-tic, adjusting his crutch under his shoulder again. The crutch with which he had just broken the Para's arm.

Léonie and I backed away, side by side.

"Don't be afraid," said Ti-tic. "We'll be going now. This trash isn't fit to mix with decent folk." He stirred the Para with the point of his crutch. "Get up, you poor rat."

The Para stood up, nursing his broken arm against his chest now, not looking at us. Against the great, slope-shouldered bulk of Ti-tic he looked small, nothing. A shrunken rat.

"Shall I tell them the truth about you?" said Ti-tic. The Para only shuddered, his back to us, his head bent. "That you're my son?" Ti-tic lifted his face up to the sky as if he was cursing it. "My only son."

He looked at us suddenly and harshly under his great, twisting black eyebrows. "A Para! He was never a Para. He attacked somebody in Arles. And went to gaol for it. And came out and attacked someone else. I said I'd hide him, take him through the marshes. Why? God knows why."

We stood trembling, barely understanding Ti-tic's words, the terrible pain of his eyes. The Para said nothing. Never even raised his head. And I turned away because it was horrible to see.

"Go on. March," said Ti-tic. I heard a grunt as if he had pushed the Para with the point of his crutch.

Then at last the Para spoke, his voice broken and pleading, all the fear of hell in it. "You won't leave me?"

"No, you poor rat," said Ti-tic. "I won't leave you." They began to move up the path, the Para first, Ti-tic following, swinging on his great crutch like a gorilla. "Tell your mother we moved on," he said. Beside me Léonie was crying.

"It's all right now," I said. "They've gone." But she went

on crying; and not knowing what else to do I put my arms round her, the way my father used to put his arms round me a long time ago. And suddenly it was very warm like that, and we fitted together like two hands clasped. Like the two wings of one bird, folded.

"Why are you crying?" I whispered.

"Because life is terrible," she said. "Not like the films."

"It could be like the films," I said. "I mean—you and me ..."

The Crevasse

ALAN HEMUS

PER awoke to the ringing of the alarm and with sunlight on his face. He knew before he glanced through the window that today there would be neither fog nor storm on the icecap. Per had lived all his life in the shadow of the great white dome and he knew the moods it had. He washed and quickly dressed, pulling the thick-soled boot on his deformed left foot, and went down to his early morning's work.

The hotel was quiet.

Per helped the hired girl clean up the kitchen, washing dishes and glasses left over from the night before. Then he picked up the box containing his brushes and went out into the corridors. There were seventy guest rooms in the hotel and Per had the task of cleaning the shoes and climbing-boots left outside each door. There was much coming and going of guests before he had finished and breakfast was almost over in the dining-room. Per ate quickly in the kitchen and then made his way to the manager's office. His father was seated at his desk and squatting on the floor by him was the other son of the family. Nils, a boy younger by five years than Per, who was fourteen.

Per wished them good morning and went on, "There will be no more work for me until after lunch and I have finished my school papers. I am going out for a walk."

"Do you good," replied his father, smiling. His eyes travelled down to Per's heavy boot. "Keep to the paths, boy, and don't go far."

Per pulled a sweater over his shirt and left the hotel. He followed the path round the lake towards the broken ground and confusion of boulders that marked one side of the moraine which edged the downwards course of the glacier from the ice-cap. The river of ice had a golden gleam in the warm sun. In winter it was coated with several feet of snow and people came to ski on it.

Walking was a painful effort to Per. Even on level ground like the path, where others could stride smoothly, Per was forced to move with uneven shambling steps, his left leg dragging. Sometimes, hearing unhurried footsteps overtaking him, he would drive himself frenziedly forward, his face white and strained with determination. There were times when he won, when the footfalls faded behind him and then, a distance further on, he would breathlessly sit down and rest, ignoring in his triumph the ache in his leg.

Today the footsteps rapidly approached. Per began to hasten, but the steps, without an increase in the tempo, were soon close. Per glanced over his shoulder and saw a tall man, lean and slightly stooped, who moved with the easy slack-kneed action of the practised mountain-walker. Per recognised him as Mr. Wood, a guest at the hotel.

"Nice morning, lad," said Mr. Wood, slowing his pace to suit Per's. Mr. Wood had clenched between his teeth a briar pipe that spilled out trailing tendrils of aromatic smoke. He was a schoolmaster in England and a regular visitor at the hotel, coming to Norway once or twice a year.

"It will be fine all day, sir," said Per politely.

They walked along in silence, and reached the moraine. Mr. Wood tapped his pipe on the heel of his boot. "I'll be leaving you here, lad," he said. "I've set myself a long route to cover today."

"It will be nice," said Per wistfully, "to sit in the sun high in the mountains and eat a pack lunch."

"Not bad," agreed Mr. Wood. "See you later, son." He began to move along a track that followed the outer edge of the moraine. It was a steep and narrow path. Mr. Wood went along it with an easy stride.

Per sighed and turned away. He crawled into a crevice at the foot of two boulders and when he came back he was dragging a bundle.

"So this is what you're up to," said a voice, unexpectedly, and his brother was standing over him. Per frowned at him.

"Dad would scrag you if he found out you were climbing."

"Hello, pest," he said ungraciously. "What are you doing here?"

"Spying on you," said Nils cheerfully. "It's made me wonder, the way you've been slipping away every chance you have."

"A man is entitled to a little privacy," said Per with dignity. "Even from his own family."

Nils was enrapturedly examining the trove that Per had unearthed from between the boulders. There was a twenty-foot coil of half-inch nylon rope, flexible and strong, and a haversack containing odds and ends of climbing gear, including a couple of pitons and a tin water-bottle. There was also an ice-axe, which Nils handled lovingly.

"Whew," he breathed. "Where did you get all this?"

"The English party last year," said Per. "They gave it to me when they were sorting out their stuff before going home. The rope was included because it had broken on one of their climbs. I whipped the frayed end myself."

"Why do you hide it here?"

"I occasionally go for a climb," said Per, exploding his bombshell blandly. He motioned to the high and far-off dome of the ice-cap. "There are one or two good faces at the top of the moraine."

"You are a one," said Nils admiringly. "Dad would scrag you if he found out."

Per nodded glumly, this was quite true. Per was convinced that he could do athletic things much better if he were allowed to practise them, and when he was much younger his father had encouraged him. Then, at the age of eight, Per had broken his leg whilst doing small ski jumps with other boys of the village, there being little control or delicacy of balance in a club foot. Since which time Mr. Hange had sternly forbidden him to take any part in the winter ski-ing or summer mountain-walking.

"Anyway, I won't tell him," said Nils, and grinned impishly. "Providing..."

"Providing what?" asked Per.

"That you let me come with you."

"This is blackmail," grumbled Per, but secretly he was pleased at creating such respect. He swung the rope to his shoulder and said, "All right, but make yourself useful. Carry the haversack, and don't forget to fill the bottle in the lake."

"Yes, sir," chuckled Nils.

They started up the moraine. Nils was bubbling with enthusiasm and in the mood to go skipping ahead up the steeply-rising path, but Per placed himself in front and doggedly stayed there, holding down the pace to his own slow limp. He halted a few times and made much display of admiring the scenery. Nils, in no way deceived, stood with him.

An hour later they came up against a blank face of rock and began to detour along the base of the cliffs buttressing the cap. Below them the ground fell away in a series of terraces and as it descended the patches of earth became more frequent amid the slabs of rock, the clumps of birch thicker, until finally the way to the lake led through gently-shelving stretches of woodland and grassy slopes.

Per and Nils turned back to the cliffs and began to climb a grassy defile that eventually emerged on a small plateau. About them were boulders and tumbled rock walls with planes at all angles. To one side a short drop led to the face of the glacier.

"This is a waistband," said Per, taking a long length of stout cord from the haversack. "You wrap it round your waist, knotting it like this."

Nils interrupted. "Over there, Per. Who is it?"

Four hundred yards away a figure was slowly moving across the crinkled surface of the glacier, a familiar figure, lean and slightly stooped. Per frowned. He said, "It's Mr. Wood. He should know better than to be out alone on the ice."

"I expect he knows what he's doing," Nils shrugged. "He's used to the mountains."

"I suppose you're right," said Per, and turned his attention to the waistbands. "This metal clip is a karabiner and it clips to your waist and is then fastened to the rope."

He deftly bent a loop into both ends of the rope, then clipped the loops to the karabiners each now wore on their waistbands. Nils watched in a respectful silence. Per began to explain the use of a rope, that it is merely a support and not for hauling people about. In the middle of an earnest discourse, he broke off and began to stare fixedly across the glacier.

"How do you use the pitons?" Nils asked.

Per ignored the question. "Mr. Wood," he said, and his face had turned pale. "He's disappeared."

"He must be there," said Nils. "He's had no time to reach the other side."

Per was scanning the ice, frowning. His eyes suddenly became still. He said, "Close your eyes for a moment to rest them. Then follow the direction of my finger and tell me what you see."

"There's a sort of dark patch."

"A crevasse," Per said quietly.

"A man could spend all day falling down one of those cracks," Per's father had once said, and Per was thinking of this as he stared at the place where Mr. Wood had been. He said urgently, "You move faster than I can. Go straight down to the hotel and turn out a rescue team."

"And you," said Nils, questioningly.

Per had made up his mind. "I'll find a route out there. I can prod my way with the axe."

Nils unclipped the rope. "Don't take any chances," he warned his brother, and took off down the defile, racing with the sureness of a goat. Per hung the haversack on his back, pushed an arm through the coil of rope, and worked his way down the side of the moraine to the ice. He began to move across it, holding the axe reversed in his hand and testing with the steel tip before each step.

Ice-caps, or snowfields, in Europe are relics of the last ice age, when most of the land was thickly carpeted with ice. When the earth began to appear again, these were left in a few mountain regions, great masses of frozen snow imprisoned by a surround of high peaks. There, in the wild regions of the Scandinavias and the Alps, they have lasted for hundreds of years, any summer thaw more than made up by the winter snowfall.

A glacier is a form of drainage from such a snowfield, a

seepage over a low place in the guarding cliffs, a torrent of ice creeping relentlessly, yet almost imperceptibly down the mountainside to the lower valleys, forced on by the tremendous pressure behind it. Within a glacier there is movement of another kind, the internal shifting of great masses that shows at times with the appearance of a rent that seems to lead into the depths of the earth: the crevasse.

It took Per nearly twenty minutes to fumble a cautious way across the four hundred yards of ice. In winter the glacier was covered with several feet of snow and then it was safe and good for ski-ing. In summer the bare ice showed, the snow a brittle or slushy crust where it had not completely thawed, with just a thin film covering the mouth of a crevasse and a plunge to eternity.

Per found a long slot in the ice, ten feet in length by a yard across. He tested completely round the edge with his axe and found it firm. Then he lay at one side and peered into the depths. The sun was shining brightly but just a few feet below the lip lay impenetrable darkness. Per vainly strained his eyes. He was crawling back from the edge when his ears gave him the answer. The sound was faint and at first he had confused it with the trickle of thaw water.

"Mr. Wood," Per called. "Can you hear me?"

There was no reply. Per stopped up one ear with his hand and hung head-down over the lip. The sound was unmistakeably a man's heavy breathing. Per moved back and pondered what he should do. It seemed unfair that he, of all people, should have such a problem. There was an obvious action to take, but the thought of it made Per shiver. He tried to dismiss it from his mind, but it kept coming back and he began to feel ashamed of himself.

He took off the haversack and began to fumble inside. "And you a mountaineer," he jeered aloud, his voice echoing across the white plain.

The ice was pitted with small fissures. He used the small mallet and drove the pitons in hard within a few feet of one another and about a yard from the edge. The next thing was to

To Per's horror the man lay on a wedge of ice that might slip
into the abyss at any moment

drive in the ice-axe and moor it to the pitons with a spare waistband. The last to clip one end of the rope to the karabiner at his waist and fasten the other end to the axe.

He ran the rope between his legs and over his right shoulder and went slowly backwards over the edge, paying out the rope the way he had practised so often. His final action was to push the haversack under the rope where it ran over the lip, and then he was in the void, spiralling gently downwards.

Per's main worry was the shortness of his rope. Three feet of it lay outside the crevasse and he had used at least two feet in his knots—which meant, supposing he were to disregard his sling and descend to the full reach of the rope, that he was limited to going down about fifteen feet.

The breathing seemed louder.

Ten feet down his right foot touched something yielding, slid off and came on a solid surface. There was nothing under his left foot. Per swung to his right, paying out more rope, and then the strain was taken off him, his feet secure on what felt like a ledge, his back hard against the opposite wall. The breathing was very close now and his groping hand touched hair, then a face.

Mr. Wood was unconscious. Per had a sudden memory of him walking springily up the moraine. There was something significant about the recollection and suddenly Per realized what it was and he began to fumble hastily in the pockets of Mr. Wood's anorak jacket. He found first the pipe, then the tobacco pouch, and then what he sought.

Per's reaction on lighting the match was to freeze with shock. The crevasse went down a long way. It was shaped like a bottle and Per and Mr. Wood were at the place where the neck ended. Mr. Wood must have brought down a block of ice in his fall. It was now wedged precariously across this narrow part of the cleft and Mr. Wood lay upon it, his legs trailing over the depths. As the match flickered, Mr. Wood groaned and stirred, and the block shifted in its uncertain bedding.

This was the moment when Per could have chosen to take himself to safety. No one would have blamed him and Per knew it. A strong and healthy youth might well have given way to the temptation. Per did not. Per had been forced to fight pain and weakness all his life, and this was just his familiar enemy in another form. He fastened his own waistband to Mr. Wood, then the karabiner and the rope, working on that shifting block above the black void.

There was no time to rest or even to pause. There remained the long climb, hand over hand, to the top of the crevasse, and then the struggle over the lip. He would be using the rope, but no longer would it be tied about his waist to support him. Even

He was supporting the full weight of the unconscious man

when he reached the open the job would not be finished.

Per turned to the rope . . .

The rescue team found him a yard from the edge of the crevasse. He was seated on the ice, firmly planted, his crippled foot hard against the ice-axe. His face was bloodless, his eyes closed and he did not hear them approach. The rope was belayed over his shoulder and stretched from him into the crevasse. It was as taut as a bar of steel. At the other end, still unconscious, swinging gently, was the figure of Mr. Wood.

The block had fallen.

The Englishman went back to the hotel on leaving hospital a month later. It was a short visit before he returned to England. He saw Per in private and both felt exceedingly embarrassed. Mr. Wood said, "I've been wondering about that foot of yours. There is an operation to fix that kind of thing."

Per nodded. "So I have been told. My father has seen the doctors and I am to have it. It will not be a complete cure, but it will do a lot for me."

Mr. Wood suddenly smiled and the embarrassment passed away. "You'll get by, lad," said Mr. Wood. "A lot of men could have two heads and still not make proper use of them."

"Sir," said Per, not quite understanding.

"Come to the lounge," said Mr. Wood, and suddenly shivered. "I'll buy you an ice-cream."

"Just orangeade, please," said Per, also shivering.

The Singing Saucers

ANGUS MACVICAR

MY name is Jeremy Grant. I am seventeen years old, and my uncle is Dr. Lachlan McKinnon, Head of the Scientific Institute for Peace at Uhlanbad in Germany.

"Jerry," said my uncle one day, "you must write your own personal account of the adventure we shared."

So here it is—the terrifying business of the Singing Saucers.

Last September curious reports began to appear in the newspapers.

In South America a circular object flew down the valley of the Paranama, "glowing like fire" and emitting musical sounds. In Australia a similar object passed over a village in the wilds of Queensland, and its "shout", according to the aboriginal inhabitants, destroyed many of their corrugated iron shacks.

Other stories of this kind came from China and India; but at first, busy with our research into space travel at the Institute, we were inclined to dismiss them as "flying saucer stuff".

Then one evening, on a television newsreel, we saw the picture of a steel bridge across the Rhône, not far from Avignon in the South of France. It was twisted and broken, its girders splintered as if by artillery fire.

I clearly remember the words of the newsreader: "At three o'clock this morning the inhabitants of Pont d'Esprit were awakened by strange sounds. Rushing from their homes they saw a huge object hovering above the bridge. Shaped like a humming-top, it glowed with internal light and gave out sonorous musical notes, like an organ. A French Army unit, stationed in the village, decided to open fire; but as the crackle of automatic weapons died away the musical sounds appeared to concentrate in one discordant note, and the bridge collapsed. Finally the object vanished, flying upwards at incredible speed."

That night, in the research laboratory, Professor Hermanoff was carrying out an experiment with long-distance radar equipment. All at once he called to Uncle Lachlan and me. We saw the screen of his instrument filled with tiny flashes and heard a faint rattle of sound like raindrops on a roof.

"A concentration of relatively small objects, Dr. McKinnon. A thousand miles directly above us."

"How many?"

"Nearly a hundred."

"They seem to be stationary," I said.

He nodded, slowly. "Like hawks, perhaps, ready to pounce."

Next morning we had a visitor, a small, quiet man with a furrowed forehead, who introduced himself as Sir Archibald Temple, scientific advisor to the Secretary of the United Nations Organisation. He sat in an armchair by the library fire, facing us.

"What I am about to tell you," he said, with prim authority, "is strictly confidential—for the moment. Understand?"

We nodded.

He went on: "I imagine you have read various accounts of

A French army unit decided to open fire

a new type of flying saucer?"

Uncle Lachlan acknowledged this. "To begin with we were rather sceptical," he said.

"Until last night, when the news broke about Pont d'Esprit?"

"Exactly."

Sir Archibald's tired eyes narrowed. "Unfortunately," he said, "the reports were only too true. We have attempted to play them down in the newspapers, to forestall panic, but bluntly the facts are these. For the past few months clusters of "flying saucers" have been observed in space, about a thousand miles above the earth. Occasionally one detaches itself and approaches the surface, as if to make a closer inspection. It gives out a series of pleasant sounds, the cause of which is unknown to us. But we are aware that these sounds can come together in one piercing, discordant scream—a scream which is able to shatter a steel bridge in much the same way as a high-pitched note on a violin shatters a wine glass."

Outside a blackbird trilled in the Institute garden. A shiver crawled along my back, like the onset of a nightmare.

"Do the 'saucers' contain life?" inquired Professor Hermanoff, in a flat voice.

"That we do not know. But obviously they contain a form of intelligence. Last week, on their own initiative, the American Government sent up one of their new atomic rockets to investigate. It was unmanned, guided by radar, and fitted with a film-camera. Inadvisedly, the ground-controller made the rocket approach too near the cluster of 'saucers'. It was immediately destroyed, and the sound have which caused its destruction was picked up and recorded by some of our instruments."

"The strangers may have imagined it was going to attack?" suggested Uncle Lachlan.

"That is what we think. But it remains vital that by some means we should discover more about them. The materials of which their 'saucers' are made, for example. Most important of all, their origins and intentions." Sir Archibald paused. "That," he said, finally, "is where you come in. We are appealing to you for help."

"How could we help?"

"You and your colleagues, Dr. McKinnon, are the most experienced space travellers in the world. You have a new ship, which can be controlled and manoeuvred in space. Above all, you are men of peace and goodwill and have already made contact with animate beings from another world."

"Specifically," said Professor Hermanoff, "what do you want us to do?"

"We want you to fly as close as possible to the mysterious 'saucers', observing and photographing. At the same time we

"We want you to fly as close as possible to the mysterious saucers, observing and photographing," said Sir Archibald

should like you to try to communicate, either physically or mentally, with whoever or whatever is inside. It is a great risk we are asking you to take," said Sir Archibald, "but it may prove vital for the safety and comfort of mankind."

In the circumstances we could not refuse.

Two days later Professor Hermanoff, Uncle Lachlan and I took up our positions in the ship, closing the steel hatch against the resinous scent of the pine woods. It was a ship of revolutionary design; a flattened sphere which spun upwards like a corkscrew, giving artificial gravity inside. Powered by a dozen jets, emitting atomically charged droplets of water, it could be propelled in any direction with equal facility; and it rotated down to Earth again like a falling leaf.

We rose into the clear autumn afternoon at moderate speed. The telescanner showed the woods and rivers of Germany diminishing below us to picture-postcard size. On the radar-screen we saw the flashes and heard the intricate pattering sound which recorded the cluster of strange ships a thousand miles above. It would take us exactly half-an-hour to reach their position.

I was afraid; no good denying it. But my job was to plot our course, and I stuck to it dourly, trying to ignore the terrifying possibilities.

The Earth fell away beneath us like a patterned ball. The bright blue sky darkened into indigo, and the stars shone like fairy lights on a Christmas tree. The hum of the motors and the soft hiss of the air-pressure valves tended to soothe my troubled nerves. Once or twice I glanced at the others. Uncle Lachlan's craggy face was drawn and pale. Professor Hermanoff, delicately fingering the controls, hid his thoughts behind a Slavonic inscrutability.

Suddenly, we heard it—a soft, insistent clangour. It was like the distant sound of church bells and organ music on a summer evening.

I went and stood beside Uncle Lachlan at the telescanner. On the screen was a picture I shall never forget—a hundred bowl-shaped objects bobbing and weaving like solemn dancers in a ballet, with light sparkling around them. Through the sound-receiver came their music, swelling up in an irregular pattern.

Closer we flew, watching and listening, until at last we were only a hundred miles from the cluster.

"Space-suits," said Uncle Lachlan, quietly, as a ship's captain might order his crew into life-jackets.

We put on the tough, pressurised clothing, keeping the transparent helmets handy beside us. Our leaden boots made clanging noises on the deck. The radar was now of no practical use, so I switched it off, and Uncle Lachlan navigated by sight alone, while the cabin echoed with unearthly music.

When we were about a mile distant from the strange space-craft Uncle Lachlan brought our ship to a standstill. We hovered there like a lonely, inquisitive child on the outskirts of a mob of giants.

Fitting a powerful telescopic lens, Professor Hermanoff brought the film-camera into action, shooting his pictures through a circular window of toughened glass. At the same time Uncle Lachlan attempted to signal by means of the radio-transmitter and a strong searchlight.

For a time nothing happened. I was desperately uneasy, expecting every moment that the "saucers" would begin to move towards us, their music changing into a scream which might blast us out of existence.

Then the mass of bobbing, spinning machines slowly divided, and a larger ship came into view, even more brightly lit than the rest. Simultaneously a compelling voice spoke in my mind: "Send the boy to us. Send the boy."

I looked at Uncle Lachlan and Professor Hermanoff. There had been no sound, simply a thought-message; but I knew at once that it had come to them, too.

Uncle Lachlan called out: "Not Jeremy! I will come."

But insistently the thought returned: "Send the boy."

The big ship moved closer, swaying and turning. My lips were dry; there was a salty taste on my tongue.

"Let me go," I said, at last. "It's our only chance to find out the truth."

"It could be a trick," said Professor Hermanoff. "You may

A compelling voice spoke in our minds. "Send the boy."

be kept as a hostage."

I knew this was true, and felt far from happy; but I said: "They may be quite friendly. They are more intelligent than we are, with more power and knowledge. Don't let's assume that they wish us harm."

Uncle Lachlan's face was craggier than ever. I knew he was remembering the shattered bridge across the Rhône and the broken shanty-town in Australia. But his sense of duty was stronger than his fears for me.

"Jeremy's right," he said. "His mind is fresh and innocent. They may distrust adult intelligence."

I put on my helmet and went down into the vacuum chamber

in the lower part of the hull. At the touch of a switch the space door opened, and I stepped out into nothingness. To begin with the gravity in the mass of the ship kept me suspended close to it; but strapped to my back were cylinders of compressed air, and when I manipulated the valve I was propelled gently in the direction of the big, bright "saucer".

That short flight was a nerve-racking experience. Several times before, of course, we had practised leaving the ship and doing a space-walk. Such was part of the necessary drill in case of emergency. But we had scarcely imagined an emergency of this kind.

Thoughts whirled in my head like Catherine-wheels. Would the strangers allow me to return to Uncle Lachlan and Professor Hermanoff? What kind of creatures were they? Did love

The space door opened and I stepped out into nothingness

or hate inspire their actions? Were they creatures at all, or disembodied spirits?

The ship around which all the others were circling towered above me like an enormous building, and as I came within its gravitational pull, I was able to switch off the compressed air jet. Its hull appeared to be constructed of faintly luminous metal. Oddly enough, the musical sounds died away as I approached, but they continued to whisper in my ears like ghostly silver voices on the radio.

And then my fear left me. One moment I was tautly scared. A split second later I was relaxed and confident, floating in through a dark opening in the big ship. A door closed behind me. A voice in my mind directed me along an upward sloping tunnel, and I entered a cabin lined with queerly-shaped instruments. There was a slow purring sound, probably from an unseen motor. Round the curved walls were transparent tubes of glowing light.

But what interested me most, in my unexpected mood of calmness, was the sight of a human being seated by a control panel in the centre of the deck. He was an old man, and bearded, clad in rich white garments. His eyes gave me an impression of kindness and infinite wisdom.

"My son," he said, in a musical voice which belied his appearance, "I am glad you have come."

"But—but you're just like us," I stammered. "An ordinary man, speaking ordinary English."

He smiled and shook his head. "It is an illusion. My actual appearance would be incomprehensible to your Earth-bound mind, so I have projected an idea of physical shape. Similarly my thoughts take on the sound of English speech only as they touch your brain."

The vision was so clear and solid-looking that I could only stare at him in amazement.

"Are you the only person in the ship?" I said.

He gestured towards a door behind him. "There are others. But they need not concern you. I invited you here so that I might ask you questions."

"What kind of questions?"

I could only stare at him in amazement

"About the Earth. Lately our instruments have recorded explosions on its surface and the departure of rocket-ships to one of the smaller planets. We became alarmed, lest you should be planning a warlike invasion on outer space. I was given command of this expedition, therefore, and instructed to discover the truth. Several times I have approached Earth, but the only thoughts I have picked up from your people have been those of fear and hatred. When attacked we showed our strength but took care not to destroy life, which we have learned to reverence and preserve. We have come in a friendly

247

way, simply to acquire knowledge, and yours is the first fresh and innocent mind we have discovered."

"I was afraid," I admitted.

He smiled. "Fear is an emotion which can be overcome. But tell me, do you hate us? Are you determined to make war?"

"No," I said. "We only hate each other. We only make war on each other."

There was a long silence, interrupted by the murmur of hidden machinery and by the occasional click of an instrument. Then the old man shook his head.

"You have relieved our anxieties. At the same time your answer makes me sad."

"Who are you?" I asked. "Where do you come from?"

"We are the inhabitants of Mars. We live in the deep valleys where the atmosphere which once covered our planet still tenuously survives. For thousands of years we have been studying our sister-planets. More than once we have repelled attacks from Venus, which lives under a mantle of cloud, artificially created to make it hard for other worlds to study its people and their intentions. But our instruments, based on the principle of infra-red rays, broke through the barrier at last—and just in time. The Venusians were planning war against us. But we shattered their reconnaissance 'saucers' with our sound waves, and now they have turned their attention to the Earth."

"You mean, those ordinary silent 'saucers' that we sometimes see are reconnaissance ships from Venus?"

"Yes, my son."

"How soon will they attack us?"

"When their plans are complete. That may be in ten years, a hundred years, or ten hundred years. I do not know."

"May I go back to the ship now?"

"As you wish. I am sorry for the people of the Earth, but you may yet be in time to bury your differences and prepare to meet the threat."

I remembered one question which Uncle Lachlan would certainly want me to ask. "Before I go, what causes the musical sounds given out by your ships?"

He touched several studs on the panel before him, and I heard a series of bell-like notes. "They are sound-waves coming from the impact of small pieces of hollow metal, waves magnified a hundredfold by an amplifier. Each ship is supplied with a score of individual sounds. Played separately they are harmless and mark the position of the ship in space for the benefit of its neighbours. But when they are played together they cause a dissonance which can destroy any type of metal known in the universe."

"Even the ships from Venus?"

He nodded, and a thought struck me. "If—if we are attacked," I said, "would you come to our assistance?"

For a moment he looked at me, smiling. "You have supreme faith in our goodness," he said, at last. "Such faith will not go unrewarded."

I said goodbye. At the entrance to the tunnel leading down to the space door I turned to wave. Beyond the control panel I had a glimpse of something strange. It was long and spindley, with a hint of waving tentacles. Next moment it was no longer there.

Neither was the old man.

When I got back to the ship Uncle Lachlan and Professor Hermanoff fussed over me in relief. I answered their questions as best I could.

Presently the music in the telescanner sound-receiver began to grow faint. We looked at the screen. The strange ships were moving away from us, seeming to curtsey in farewell. Our mission had ended in success; but I was unhappy. The Martians had discovered the state of our civilisation on Earth, and it made me feel ashamed.

We spun there in space, watching the "singing saucers" grow tinier and tinier. It was time for us to return home; but Uncle Lachlan seemed loath to give the order, and I understood why. We had caught a glimpse of something so wise and kind, something so much superior to our own intelligence, that it was difficult to face earthly realities again.

Suddenly, long after the Martian ships had vanished in the dark blue distance, we turned from the telescanner to find that the radar had picked up a new and rapidly approaching object. Professor Hermanoff calculated that it was about three hundred miles away and coming directly towards us at a speed of over two thousand miles per hour.

Uncle Lachlan brought the telescanner into line with the radar-beam, then adjusted the telescopic adaptor which would give us vision up to two hundred miles.

We waited. A minute passed. Two minutes. Three minutes.

And finally we saw it, hurtling through the sky. Another "saucer". But this time one of the usual variety glimpsed by watchers on the Earth; a shallow circular lid, with a trail of sparks. The thought occurred to me: *"Inside are men of Venus,*

The "saucer" interposed itself between us and Earth

the enemy race which has been watching the Earth, waiting for a suitable moment to attack."

Hurriedly I told the others what the Martian had said. Uncle Lachlan rubbed his chin. "Better get out of it!" he snapped, and Professor Hermanoff switched on the power for a quick descent to Earth.

The ship vibrated slightly as we went into a spiral, though of course, owing to the artificial gravity created by our spin, the fall was not otherwise apparent to us inside. Watching the telescanner, I noticed at once that the "saucer" too, had altered course, keeping us directly in its angle of advance.

Second by second it grew larger on the screen, until at last the telescopic adaptor could be dispensed with. I suspected a definite threat in its approach, and though neither of them said a word I know now that both my uncle and Professor Hermanoff had the same instinct of danger.

It came to within a mile of our position. Then it stopped in its tracks and began to sink earthwards alongside us.

A light flickered from one of its portholes.

Uncle Lachlan caught my arm. "It's Morse!" he exclaimed.

As he jotted down the message a problem worried me: *"How do they know Morse, those visitors from Venus?"* But almost immediately I hit upon the answer. For years they had been observing the Earth, noting every detail of its life. The constant stream of Morse pouring out from ships and radio stations must have been gradually deciphered and understood by them. " *'Follow us, or you will be destroyed.'* That's their ultimatum," said Uncle Lachlan, grimly.

Professor Hermanoff gripped the edge of the telescanner, his knuckles gleaming in the light.

The "saucer" darted down and sideways, interposing itself between us and the distant Earth. As it did so, I saw that its perimeter bristled with small cylindrical objects, like guns. These were pointing in our direction.

Again the Morse light flickered.

Uncle Lachlan said: "They're giving us thirty seconds to make up our minds."

Beneath us, five hundred miles away, the Earth hung

The ship from Venus broke up into a million fragments

suspended, a gigantic pock-marked sphere. I could make out the oceans and the continents, America in shadow, Europe gleaming in the sun. The rugged west coast of Britain was concealed under a wisp of cloud.

I felt in my throat a lump of self-pity. Why should we have been singled out as the first victims of Venusian enmity? But then, were we really the first? What of all the high-flying aircraft that had disappeared without trace? What of the thousands of people who had vanished from their homes, never to be seen again?

"Fifteen seconds," said Uncle Lachlan.

I shivered. Were we to be taken to Venus as experimental guinea-pigs? Or were we to die, here in the emptiness of space?

Then I remembered. "Uncle Lachlan," I said, abruptly, "the Martian promised to help if we were attacked. I'll try to send him a message."

No one spoke. I concentrated my thoughts on the old man with the wise and kindly smile. *Help us!* I called to him through space.

Five seconds. Three seconds.

"Help us! Help us!"

And suddenly I knew that my plea was to be granted. Peace and comfort came to me, and I smiled to the others. They looked at me oddly, and I remember the little beads of perspiration which glistened on Professor Hermanoff's forehead.

"They're coming," I said.

Almost as I spoke we heard their bell-like notes on the sound-receiver, distant at first then approaching in a great sweep of sound.

They came out of the dark sky like avenging angels, whirling across the screen in flashing spirals. Their music was everywhere. We saw them below us, between us and the Venusian ship. I could almost feel sorry for the enemy, caught like a lonely rat in a circle of leaping dogs.

The music welled up in a crescendo. And then it changed. It became a single scream, high-pitched and terrible. But the Martians had directed it downwards, screening us from its effects by their own mass. They had directed it against the enemy; and while we watched, fascinated and silent, we saw a vivid flash as the ship from Venus broke up into a million fragments.

Then the sky was clear, and the friendly ships were bobbing away from us. Into my mind came a thought-message: *"Return to Earth in peace. Remember, we are on your side."*

Professor Hermanoff pushed over a lever to accelerate our descent. Down and down we went, like a falling leaf, until the purple woods of Germany filled the screen and we released the braking parachutes.

ACKNOWLEDGEMENTS

Thanks are due to the authors, their literary agents and publishers with whom arrangements have been made to include certain stories in this book:

To Angus and Robertson, Ltd. for "The Loaded Dog" from *Joe Wilson's Mates* by Henry Lawson.

To Curtis Brown, Ltd. and *Argosy* for "The Heidelberg Affair" by Lionel Davidson.

To the author for "Skin of the Crocodile" by Norah Burke.

To the *Elizabethan* for "The Crevasse" by Alan Hemus.

To John Farquharson, Ltd. and *Argosy* for "Peril in the Camargue" (originally "The Long White Scar") by Brian Cleeve.

To the author for "Duel in the Sea" by John Kruse.

To C.W. Martyr, Esq. and Rupert Hart-Davis, Ltd. for "Smith *versus* Lichtensteiger" (slightly abridged) from *The £200 Millionaire* by Weston Martyr.

To Hughes Massie, Ltd. for "Black Water Creek" by Robert Craig.

To A.D. Peters and Co., and Eyre and Spottiswoode for "Charley's Tiger" (originally "A Possible Candidate for the Presidency") from *I Love Galesburg in the Springtime* by Jack Finney, and to The Harold Matson Company, Inc. for the Canadian rights of this story.

To The Ryerson Press, Toronto, for "Sir Galahad and the Bad Man" from *The Red Serge* by Harwood Steele.

To A.P. Watt and Son and William Heinemann, Ltd. for "The Conqueror Worm" from *Neither Man nor Dog* by Gerald Kersh.

© 1968 The Hamlyn Publishing Group Limited.
Published for Odhams Books by The Hamlyn Publishing Group
Limited, Hamlyn House, The Centre, Feltham, Middlesex
Made and Printed in Germany